Mynderse Library

Seneca Falls, New York

BAKER & TAYLOR

◀ The ▶
Story Teller

Berkley Prime Crime Books by Margaret Coel

‹ The ›
Story Teller

Margaret Coel

BERKLEY PRIME CRIME, NEW YORK

THE STORY TELLER

A Berkley Prime Crime Book
Published by The Berkley Publishing Group
A Member of Penguin Putnam Inc.
200 Madison Avenue, New York, NY 10016
The Penguin Putnam Inc. World Wide Web site address is
http://www.penguinputnam.com

First Edition: October 1998

Library of Congress Cataloging-in-Publication Data
    Coel, Margaret, 1937-
        The story teller / Margaret Coel. — 1st ed.
            p.   cm.
        ISBN 0-425-16538-8
            1. Indians of North America—Wyoming—Fiction.   2.
    Wind River Indian Reservation (Wyo.)—Fiction.   3. Arapaho
    Indians—Fiction.   I. Title.
    PS3553.O347S76   1998
    813'.54—dc21   98-13765
                                                          CIP

Printed in the United States of America

10   9   8   7

For Aileen Marie Harrison

ACKNOWLEDGMENTS

The author wishes to thank the many people who lent their expertise and advice to this novel. Among them are:

Dr. Tom Noel, professor of history, University of Colorado at Denver; Michael L. Fiori, detective, Homicide/Investigations, Denver Police Department; Jennifer C. Rowe, officer, Denver Police Department; Ginger Jones, coroner's investigator, City and County of Denver; Dr. David F. Halaas, chief historian, Colorado Historical Society; Dr. Virginia Sutter, member of the Arapaho tribe; Anthony Short, S.J.; Karen Gilleland, Ann and Tony Ripley, Sybil Downing, Beverly Carrigan, George Coel, and Kristin Coel.

Special thanks to David F. Halaas, Andrew E. Masich, Richard N. Ellis and Jean Afton for their book, *Cheyenne Dog Soldiers: A Ledgerbook History of Coups and Combat.*

◄ The ►
Story Teller

Prologue

Professor Mary Ellen Pearson adhered to a carefully constructed routine every Monday evening. This evening was no different. At ten minutes before nine o'clock, she checked her briefcase to make certain all of her papers were in place. Discreetly, of course. It would never do for one of the students in her Culture of the Plains Indians seminar to suspect she was eager for the class to end. At the first pealing of the bells from St. Elizabeth's across the campus, she hoisted the briefcase, bid her students good night, and departed the classroom.

She hurried down the wide corridor paved with caramel-colored tiles, in and out of shafts of light streaming from the fluorescent bulbs overhead, and swung through a doorway into a small office much like her own. She froze in disbelief. The office was empty. Mavis Stanley had left without her. How could Mavis have done so? They always left together on Monday evenings, two female professors at the edge of retirement, hurrying along the shadowy campus paths, a formidable phalanx to deter waiting muggers.

Not that the University of Colorado campus in Denver was unsafe, as their male colleagues often reminded them. Nevertheless it was an urban campus sprawled against the southern curve of downtown Denver, and the leafy trees and grassy knolls could not conceal the noise and energy of the city lurking beyond. One could not be too careful.

With clenched jaw, Professor Pearson retraced her steps along the corridor. The overhead lights seemed dimmer, the building silent as a vault. Her footsteps clacked into the emptiness. Other classes had let out; students had already fled. She was alone.

Avoiding the elevator, which was often unpredictable, she made her way down two flights of stairs, skimming past the shadows on the landings, and exited the building through the glass-paned door on the west. The Rocky Mountains rose in the distance, a jagged darkness against the last milky band of light in the sky. Skyscrapers looming on the north, windows ablaze, cast eerie patterns of light and shadow across the dark campus.

Professor Pearson gripped her briefcase under one arm as she plunged down the walkway to the parking lot on the other side of Speer Boulevard. Several students—even one of her own colleagues—hurried by. How silly, her fearfulness, she told herself. Other people were still about. She was perfectly safe. She was becoming an addled old woman.

She crossed Speer Boulevard on the green light, passing through the yellow columns of headlights from waiting vehicles, and started up the gentle rise of earth that surrounded the parking lot. Traffic belched into the darkness behind her, but ahead the parking lot sat in a well of light shining down from the metal poles around the periphery.

A few cars were scattered around the lot; she could see her Impala at the far end. Relaxed now, she started down the rise, her feet groping for solid underpinnings in the soft dirt, when, out of the corner of her eye, she saw a figure darting along the rise across the lot.

She stopped, eyes glued to the figure—it looked like a man—lurching in and out of the shadows, hesitating, watching. Suddenly he ran down the little slope and across the asphalt. Ran toward her! She stumbled backward, pivoting, trying to get a purchase on the uphill slope. The squeal of tires, the screech of brakes burst through the night as she caught herself against the hard coldness of a metal light pole. Sheltering behind it, she stared down at the white 4x4 rocking to a stop.

In an instant, two men were running toward the shadowy figure zigzagging between the parked cars, dodging the grasping arms. Then she saw the raised arm, the glint of metal, the thrust toward the crouching figure, and heard the whack of metal on bone. The figure staggered, dissolved before her, and the others scooped him up, lifting arms and shoulders and legs, pushing him into the back of the 4x4, a bag of rocks now, something not human, crowded and folded onto the floor as the tailgate slammed shut. The others jumped into the front seat; there was the sharp, hollow sound of doors slamming.

The scream welled inside her, an enormous flood rising in her throat, stoppered by her own fear. *They've killed him!*—her mind shouted the words—and she had done nothing, had allowed her legs to turn into numb and formless objects over which she had no control. The shame of her inaction fixed her in space, the metal pole a shaft of ice in her hands, the briefcase at her feet.

The 4X4 was gathering speed, racing across the lot, banking into a sharp right onto the street and heading north into the maze of skyscrapers. The sound of squealing tires faded into the darkness, overridden now by the piercing sounds that rose around her, surprising her as she anchored herself to the pole and screamed and screamed.

❮ 1 ❯

A white-yellow haze hung over Highway 287 as Vicky Holden drove north along the foothills of the Wind River Mountains. To the east, the plains ran into the distance, parched and cracked under a sky bleached pale blue by the sun. A dry breeze scuttled across the clumps of wild grasses and bent the sunflower stalks. It was the first Tuesday in June, the Moon When the Hot Weather Begins, but it was already the kind of heat the elders told about in stories of the Old Time, when her people had lived free on the plains—the kind of heat that melted the hooves of the buffalo into the ground and pulled the shaggy hides over their bones, like gunnysacks. The kind of heat, she knew, that could take her breath away.

She had the highway to herself. Since crossing the southern boundary of the Wind River Reservation a good thirty minutes ago, she'd passed only a couple of pickups. She held the Bronco steady at sixty-five, trying to ignore the irritation that nipped at her like a yapping dog she couldn't shake off. If the cultural director of the Arapaho tribe had wanted an appointment, he could have driven to her law office on Main Street in Lander. Instead she was driving to his office in Ethete, at least thirty minutes each way, when her desk was piled with other matters demanding her attention.

"We want to avail ourselves of your services," Dennis Eagle Cloud had said on the phone this morning.

"Best you come to the reservation." There had been
something hard to define in his tone—a hint that whatever he wished to discuss should be taken out and ex-
amined only on the reservation, not in a white town. Or
had she imagined it? She wished now she had asked for
some explanation, pleaded her own busy schedule.

But she hadn't. Hadn't suggested a meeting at her office because she didn't want him to call another attorney. It had been almost four years since she'd come
home and opened a one-woman law practice in the
naive and idealistic hope she might help her people. But
so far her list of clients included as many whites as Arapahos. She was the lawyer for divorces, adoptions, wills,
and real-estate leases, while matters such as tribal lands,
and oil and gas and water—important tribal matters—
went to a law firm in Casper. The tribal officials had
never sought her services.

Until this morning. Which, she knew, was the reason
she'd agreed to the two o'clock meeting in Ethete. She'd
put down the phone feeling elated and discouraged at
the same time. The call had finally come, yet Dennis
Eagle Cloud was not a member of the tribal council—
the business council, as the Arapahos called the six
elected members who handled Arapaho affairs on the
reservation. He was a tribal employee, a low-level official. How important could the matter be?

Then it hit her. As the cultural director, Dennis had
been working with the Native American Graves Protection and Repatriation Act, the federal law that allowed
tribes to reclaim some of their artifacts from museums.
The Arapahos had already taken back numerous sacred
objects. Maybe he had run into some kind of snag and
needed legal advice. Her irritation began to subside.
This could be a very important matter indeed, and Dennis had called her, not the Casper firm.

For a moment she allowed herself to wonder if the
cultural director was also involved in efforts to claim

some of the old lands in Colorado—lands promised to the people who'd been attacked in the Sand Creek Massacre more than a hundred years ago, but never given to them. She shrugged off the idea. That was a matter for the business council, which meant the Casper firm was undoubtedly doing the legal work. But if Dennis was about to hand her the chance to work on something involving NAGPRA—well, it could be an opportunity to prove herself worthy of other important matters.

She slowed for an easy right into Ethete and parked in the shade washing down the front of the red-brick building that housed the tribal offices. Grabbing her briefcase and black shoulder bag, she slid out into the heat, trying not to bang her door against an old pickup, although the pickup sported so many dents and scrapes and rust patches that another one of the world's hard knocks hardly seemed to matter.

It was cool inside the tribal building, a startling, man-made coolness. She nodded at the receptionist behind the desk across the lobby and hurried down the corridor on the right. Dennis Eagle Cloud stood outside a door at the far end, as if he'd seen her drive up and had been waiting while she negotiated the parking lot and lobby. He was about her age—early forties—with dark skin and dark eyes and black hair that curled over the opened collar of a white cowboy shirt. "We been waiting for you," he said, waving her forward, an impatient gesture.

"We?" she said, stopping in front of him.

He took her hand and shook it loosely, as though he might be afraid of crushing it. Then he ushered her through the doorway into a small office almost completely taken up by a wide-topped desk. Beyond the desk, occupying a straight-backed chair against the wall, was one of the tribal elders, Charlie Redman, the storyteller.

Vicky felt a stab of shame. This was the reason for her drive to Ethete. Dennis had wanted to spare the elder the long drive to Lander. She stepped around the desk toward the old man, who was starting to get to his feet—blue jeans, electric-blue cowboy shirt, tan Stetson moving toward her.

"Please don't get up, Grandfather," she said, using the term of respect for Arapaho elders. The old man reached out and took her hand, holding it a long moment. His eyes had a dreamy look—he might have been looking beyond her, she thought, to some other place more real than the small office tucked at the end of a corridor. The silver bracelets on his wrists made a small clanking noise as he returned her hand. "You are good, Granddaughter," he said, as if he'd inquired about her health and had reached his own conclusion.

"Grandfather wants you in on this." Dennis Eagle Cloud motioned her to the vacant chair next to the elder. As soon as she'd sat down, the cultural director bent over the desk, picked up a thin blue folder, and handed it to her. Large black letters marched across the top: DENVER MUSEUM OF THE WEST. In the center was the logo of a cowboy on a bucking bronco, lasso swirling overhead. Below the logo, in small type: *Inventory of Arapaho Funeral Objects and Other Sacred Objects in Compliance with the Native American Graves Protection and Repatriation Act.*

So, it was about NAGPRA. Vicky tried to keep her face unreadable, tried to conceal her excitement. Almost four years, waiting for her people to trust her with something important. "What seems to be the problem?" she asked.

Dennis sat back against the edge of the desk, arms crossed over his middle. "NAGPRA requires museums to provide each tribe with a complete inventory of objects belonging to that tribe. Soon as we sign off on the inventory"—a nod toward the folder in her hand—"we can claim our things from the Denver Museum of the West."

Vicky flipped through the pages. A running list of artifacts and descriptions: *Spear—leather thongs, eagle feathers. Rattle—fur pieces, lightning design. Warrior shirt—tanned hide, decorative designs.* Dozens of other objects.

She looked up, aware that both the director and the elder were watching her. The matter seemed clear. The museum had supplied the inventory; the Arapahos could acknowledge it and take the next step to claim the items. Not every item could be claimed under NAGPRA, she knew. Only sacred and burial objects, and cultural objects belonging to specific families. There was room for negotiation, however. A task for the cultural director.

"Why do you need my services?" she asked, handing back the folder.

"It ain't there." This from the elder, who shifted sideways in his chair. The legs made a little scratching noise against the floor.

The cultural director spoke up. "We assumed all the Arapaho artifacts in the museum were on the list." He was tapping the edge of the desk with one hand, a steady rhythm of impatience. "But when I asked Grandfather Redman to look over the list, he said the museum left something off."

Vicky turned toward the old man. "You're saying the inventory isn't complete, Grandfather?" She struggled for a tone of respect, although the old man's concern was hard to imagine. Surely the museum would comply with federal law. The consequences of not complying were serious: loss of federal funds, even felony indictments.

The elder said, "My ancestor's book ain't on the list. I seen it in the museum."

Vicky drew in a long breath. Her own assumptions collided against the truth in the old man's voice. "Please tell me what you saw," she said, leaning toward him, feeling the familiar anticipation she had felt as a child when the elders began to tell a story of the Old Time— a grandfather story—and she was about to learn something she hadn't known before.

Charlie Redman cleared his throat, a low, gravelly sound. Eyes ahead, on that other place where he dwelled, he began: "My ancestor was No-Ta-Nee. He rode with Chief Niwot in the Old Time down in Colorado. No-Ta-Nee had the job to keep the stories, you know." A quick glance sideways, as if to confirm that she did know. Then, at a leisurely pace, he said, "No-Ta-Nee kept the stories about the people, everything we believe and everything that happened, and he told the younger generation so they would know. One day he found one of them ledger books the government agents used, so he wrote down the story about the last days the people lived in Colorado. Wrote it all down in pictures, exactly right.

"Many years later"—he made a movement with his hand, as if to wave away the passage of time—"No-Ta-Nee's ledger book come to the museum. He was in a lot of battles with the soldiers, so maybe the book got lost on the battlefield and somebody picked it up and give it to the museum. I don't know how it come there. But when I was this high," he explained as he raised his hand to his shoulder, "one of the Jesuit priests that was here at St. Francis Mission seen the book in the museum. So he took my grandfather and me down to Denver. It was in the summer of 1920. We went on the train. And we rode one of them trolley cars down a street with tall buildings on both sides and got off at a building with white columns in front. Inside was a small glass case, and the only thing in the case was No-Ta-Nee's book. It was beautiful."

A ledger book! The idea that an intact ledger book written by an Arapaho warrior might still exist sent a thrill coursing through Vicky like an electric current. She had heard the elders tell about the ledger books drawn by the Plains Indian warriors—the story of actual events recorded in detailed pictographs. She had seen pages from ledger books in museums. She had even seen framed pages for sale once in a gallery in Denver. But she had never seen an Arapaho ledger book.

Vicky glanced at the cultural director. His expression reflected her own excitement. He said, "Almost every warrior had a ledger book that he drew in. It was his own personal journal where he kept a record of all his deeds and honors. Some of the warriors, like No-Ta-Nee, were chosen by the elders to write about tribal events. Used to be hundreds of ledger books on the plains."

Vicky smiled at the thought. Hundreds of books drawn and prized by people the whites had considered illiterate and uncivilized.

The cultural director shifted against the desk. "Unfortunately most of the ledger books were destroyed. There's only a handful of intact books that survived, and they're in museums. Point is, Vicky, we wouldn't know about No-Ta-Nee's book if grandfather hadn't seen it. How many other valuable artifacts are the museum people holding back, hoping we don't know about them?"

Vicky was quiet. The elder had seen the ledger book in 1920. *1920!* NAGPRA required museums to account for artifacts in their posession only as far back as 1991. In her courtroom tone, she said, "There is no legal basis upon which we can ask the museum to account for something it may have owned eighty years ago."

Dennis shrugged. "We're fully aware of that, Vicky."

Quiet filled the small room. Vicky sensed the warmth of the elder's gaze on her. This was not about following the letter of the law. This was about trust. The elder had seen the ledger book. He wanted to know where it was. She said, "I can inquire about the ledger book, but it may be difficult to get an explanation. Museums prune out collections all the time." She was grasping, but she plunged on: "Some curator might have decided the museum had enough objects decorated with Indian art. Maybe the museum sold the ledger book to another museum."

"Oh, sure," Dennis said, tapping a pencil against the edge of the desk. "Museums sell history books by Plains Indians every day."

"Maybe they didn't know the pictographs told of actual events," Vicky persisted.

The cultural director stared at her fixedly, as if he were trying to see into her mind. "You've become like them," he said. "You believe whatever they tell you."

Vicky flinched. It was true. She had been away from the reservation for ten years. Had become an attorney, *ho:xu'wu:ne'n,* like a white woman. Maybe she had even learned to think like white people, but she was still Arapaho. "Come on, Dennis," she said, making an effort to ignore the insult. "It took a while for scholars to recognize that the drawings on tipis and shields had deeply religious symbolic meanings and that a lot of other Indian objects were more than decorative art."

"And as soon as they figured it out, they wouldn't let any objects with pictographs out of their hands," Dennis said. "No way would they sell a ledger book."

"Maybe it was too late. Maybe the book had already been sold."

The cultural director thumbed through the inventory pages, peering at each one, as though the spaces between the lines might tell him what else was missing. "If the museum sold the book, we got the right to know who bought it so we can get it back."

Vicky interrupted. "NAGPRA doesn't give us that right, Dennis."

"If the museum people won't tell us what happened to the ledger book, we'll know they're holding out on us. They can't be trusted." Dennis lifted the folder and slapped it onto the desk.

The old man thrust out both hands, a sign of silence. Turning to Vicky, he said, "You must take care of this, Granddaughter. Your ancestor—the grandfather of your father—was a baby still on his mother's back when the people left Colorado. It was a hard time. My ancestor wrote it all down so that the younger generations would know, young people like you. You must get our story for us."

Vicky could hear the sound of her own breathing in the quiet seeping through the small office. Outside somewhere a car door slammed—a muffled sound, enveloped in the heat. There was no evidence the museum had ever owned the ledger book—only the story of an old man. But Charlie Redman was the storyteller, trained as a boy, just like his father and grandfathers back to the oldest of times, to be a living archive of the people's history. She had heard him tell the stories many times at tribal gatherings. He could speak for hours, hardly drawing a breath. His memory was prodigious. Prodigious and accurate.

But an old man's story in the white world? About what he had seen as a boy? The museum curator would laugh her out of the office. She glanced up at the cultural director still perched at the end of the desk, a look of satisfaction crossing his face. He knew she would have turned him down had he come to her office with such a request. So he had brought her here. How could she refuse the elder?

A sense of frustration roiled inside her: what they expected was impossible, a waste of time to ask the museum to account for an artifact outside the requirements of NAGPRA. Yet her frustration was tempered by an odd sense of pride. Maybe the very impossibility of the task was a measure of what her people thought of her. She got to her feet and faced the old man. "I can't promise anything, Grandfather."

Charlie Redman held her eyes a moment. "You must do your best for your people," he said.

◄ 2 ►

The man in the black suit paused in the doorway of the old school building—a giant black beetle caught in the rectangular frame. He stepped inside and swung around, scrunching his bulbous nose. "Musty odor," he said.

Father John Aloysius O'Malley, pastor of St. Francis Mission on the Wind River Reservation, followed his visitor, Father James Stanton, through the doorway. The other priest stood gazing down the wide corridor to the right. Then he turned his face upward, as if he were studying the high ceiling, the glass fixtures dangling from thick, black cords, the sunlight slanting across the stairway that climbed the far wall.

"The school's more than a hundred years old," Father John said. "It has the right to smell a little musty."

The other priest emitted a sound that registered somewhere between a *hrmmp* and a snort. A hard man to convince, Father John thought. He'd felt a stab of disappointment an hour before when the blue Buick had pulled into St. Francis Mission and the bulky, gray-haired priest in black clericals had emerged from behind the wheel.

He had been expecting the provincial, who had promised to stop by on his visit to the Indian missions in the Wisconsin Province. Instead, he had sent his assistant—a man with a reputation as a financial genius.

The provincial had been detained in Denver on important matters. What was it Father John had wanted to see him about?

So instead of convincing his boss that it made sense to convert the old school building into a museum devoted to the history and culture of the Arapahos, Father John had found himself trying to convince the man in charge of keeping the purse strings tightly knotted.

"The building's in excellent condition. Strong foundation, thick walls." Father John wished Charlie Redman or one of the other elders were here to tell his visitor how the old building was sacred; how it had once held the fragile dreams of children; how such a place should hold their history.

Father John led the way down the corridor, stopped at the first doorway and waited as the other priest followed. "The director's office would be here," he said.

"Takes money to hire a director."

"Yes, of course." Father John had spent the last month, while he was on retreat in Boston, going over the obstacles. There were many. But the easiest to overcome was the matter of the director. "There's a young man," he said, "an Arapaho by the name of Todd Harris, just finishing a master's degree in ethnohistory. He's willing to take a small salary for the experience of starting a museum." He hoped that was still true. His assistant, Father Geoff Schneider, had said Todd came to the mission last Saturday. He'd seemed upset about something, disappointed Father John wasn't around. He didn't get back from his retreat in Boston until Sunday.

The other priest made a circuit of the empty room— a classroom where Jesuits a century ago had taught Arapaho children how to read and write, how to add and subtract and divide—necessary skills for their new life on the white man's road. "Museums need a lot of staff," he said.

"We have volunteers," Father John said. That was a

fact. St. Francis Mission depended upon volunteers to teach the religious-education classes, the adult high-school classes, to visit the sick and the shut in, to help maintain the grounds, clean the church, and launder the altar cloths. The jobs were many, but Arapahos were generous.

The other priest let out a guffaw. "Volunteers! Unreliable, in my view."

Father John said nothing. This was a political game, and after almost eight years at an Indian mission in the middle of Wyoming, he no longer knew the rules. Although he did know the first rule was probably to wear clericals when meeting a superior. He'd worn blue jeans, plaid shirt, and cowboy hat—what he usually wore. A serious mistake, he saw by the disapproving look in the other priest's eyes as he'd lifted his bulky, black-clad frame out of the Buick. Undoubtedly another was not to antagonize the opponent by challenging his views. That rule Father John resolved to follow.

"The archives and library will be on the first floor," he said, leading the other priest down the corridor to another classroom that had once rung with the voices of children. "Scholars and students can use our materials for research." He was thinking of the cartons of old records and documents crammed into the closet-sized archives next to his office in the administration building. It was time they were sorted, made available to the public.

Father Stanton glanced through the doorway, then slowly turned and started down the corridor. Father John followed. "Exhibit halls will be upstairs," he went on, sensing the lack of interest, the made-up mind. Finally he stepped around the other priest, forcing him to a stop. "The Arapahos need the museum," he said. "They're starting to reclaim some of their sacred and cultural artifacts from museums around the country.

The elders are anxious to have the school turned into a museum."

"I'm sorry, Father O'Malley." The other priest shook his head. "What you suggest would require a large outlay of funds."

Another obstacle, Father John realized, but one he had been turning over in his mind the last few weeks. He said, "We'll need start-up money. But then we'll obtain grant money. And there will be donations." He stopped himself from adding, "And unexpected miracles." Hardly the kind of financial plan to impress a number cruncher.

"I see," Father Stanton said. "You have no operating funds. Yet you expect the province to risk a considerable amount of start-up money. Even if we put up the money, Father, how long could the museum operate without funds? Two weeks?" He gave his head a hard shake and walked toward the door.

"You're wrong," Father John said, breaking the rule he had resolved to follow. "Once the museum is operating, once people know about it . . ."

The other priest stepped out onto the porch. "Another matter," he said when Father John joined him. "I didn't want to bring it up."

Here it comes, Father John thought. The biggest obstacle, the hardest to overcome. He said, "I haven't had a drink since I left Grace House almost eight years ago."

"Yes, yes." The other priest shrugged. "But an undertaking of this magnitude. The financial risk and worry. So much pressure, Father O'Malley. And isn't it true? A recovering alcoholic is never far from the next drink."

Father John walked past the other priest and set both hands on the porch railing, staring out at the mission grounds: the white stucco church with the belfry jabbing into the sky, the two-story brick residence, the yellow stucco administration building. Sunlight sparkled on the wild grasses and danced through the branches of the cottonwoods that shaded the buildings. It was quiet, except for the shush of the wind in the trees. Eight years, he was thinking, and he had begun each day with a prayer that it would not be the day he took the next drink.

Facing his visitor, he said, "The mission doesn't depend upon me. Neither would the museum."

"It's impossible," Father Stanton said. He started down the steps—a stiff-legged maneuver—and headed toward the Buick parked in Circle Drive.

Father John caught up and walked alongside him. "I want to know what the provincial thinks," he said. Was this one of the rules? Pulling rank? After all, he and the provincial went back a long way—to their days in the seminary—although he hadn't seen Father William Rutherford in years. The gamesmanship left a sour taste in his mouth, like the aftermath of bad coffee. The museum would help the Arapahos preserve their history and culture. Why couldn't this other priest see that?

"The provincial hears a hundred so-called good ideas from Jesuits every week," Father Stanton began. His breath came in short jabs. "Everything from running preschools and day-care programs to operating soup kitchens. And now a museum! What are we? Some kind of social-welfare or civic organization? We are educators, let me remind you."

"There are many ways to educate. The museum—"

"The decision is final." Father Stanton yanked open the car door and, gripping the wheel, pulled his bulky frame into the seat, the front of his black suit coat bunching over his fleshy stomach.

Leaning against the open door, Father John said, "How long will the provincial be in Denver?"

"The provincial relies upon my decision in these matters." Father Stanton gave the ignition a quick turn. The engine burst into life.

"How long?"

"I'm not his secretary." A tug at the door handle.

"Tomorrow?" Father John persisted. "The next day? When does he leave?"

Father Stanton shot him a look filled with exasperation and contempt. "The provincial will be tied up in meetings at Regis for the next few days."

Slamming the door, Father John stepped back as the rear wheels dug into the gravel and the car lurched forward. A few days, he thought. If he drove to Denver tomorrow, there was a chance he could see the provincial. But that meant the mail, the messages, and the work piled up on his desk would have to wait. And his assistant would have to postpone the backpacking trip he had planned and handle things at the mission awhile longer.

Father John watched the Buick weave through the shade of the cottonwoods lining Circle Drive and plunge down the straightaway that led out of the mission onto Seventeen-Mile Road. "I'll see you in Denver," he said under his breath.

‹ 3 ›

Vicky set the file folders into her briefcase and closed the flap. She had everything she needed. Everything she'd copied yesterday in the library at Benner and Hanson, the largest firm in Lander, concerning the Native American Graves Protection and Repatriation Act. Enough, she was confident, for this afternoon's meeting with the curator at the Denver Museum of the West.

The only meeting, she hoped. With luck, she would find a perfectly logical explanation for the fact that the ledger book was not on the inventory list and would fly home first thing tomorrow. She would convince Dennis Eagle Cloud and Charlie Redman that the museum could be trusted, and her people could reclaim what belonged to them. Her carry-on, which was all she needed, was in the Bronco. She was dressed for the trip in an attorney uniform: tailored gray dress and heels. An uncomfortable uniform, she knew. It would be as hot in Denver as it was here.

She was not looking forward to another trip to Denver where she had spent ten years as an undergrad, a law student, and, finally, a lawyer in a downtown firm. Every day of those years she had longed to be back on the reservation, surrounded by the vast spaces of earth and sky. Since she'd come home, she had approached any trip—even the shortest—with a heavy heart.

She glanced at the little silver watch on her wrist. Less than an hour to get to the Riverton airport. Even with the usual light mid-morning traffic and no delays for highway construction, she would have to hurry.

Swinging her briefcase off the desk, she started across the office, aware for the first time of voices behind the closed door. She had instructed Laola White Plume, her new secretary, to cancel appointments for today and tomorrow, yet one of her clients must have come in. The uneasy feeling Vicky had been trying to ignore rose inside her like the bitter aftertaste of a bad meal. She was leaving the office in the hands of an eighteen-year-old girl, still giddy from having walked across a stage and picked up a high-school diploma. Still giddy from having landed her first job. And not just some job swabbing out motel rooms or clerking in a discount store, but the beginning of a career.

An ambitious girl, her new secretary, with plans to attend night school at Central Wyoming College in the fall. Vicky had seen something of herself in the girl, she supposed, which was why she had hired her. But the on-the-job training had been wearing. Laola had a lot to learn about dealing with the public, which was obvious from the rising tone of anger in the voices in the outer office.

For an instant Vicky thought about fleeing out the back door and down the stairs to the parking lot. She could call Laola from the airport and explain her abrupt departure. But the voices were louder, more insistent, and Vicky flung open the door.

"You don't understand!" a young woman in her early twenties shouted at Laola, who had planted herself a few feet from the doorway, as if to block the visitor's entry.

Laola swung around. "I told her you ain't seein' any clients today."

Vicky winced. Grammar was part of the on-the-job

training. She would mention it again when she returned, not in front of the other young woman in blue jeans and yellow blouse, who was making a wide track around the secretary.

"You're Vicky Holden?" There was a quickness and desperation in her voice, as if she expected Laola to interrupt.

Vicky didn't recognize the woman, but she was Arapaho: the sharp angles of the cheekbones, the small hump in the nose, the long black hair parted in the middle and swept behind her ears.

"And you are . . . ?" Vicky said, pushing aside the thought of an airplane waiting on the tarmac.

"Annemarie Jemson." The woman waved one hand, a dismissal of unnecessary preliminaries, of the usual dance of politeness. "Todd Harris's fiancée."

Vicky remembered. One of the Jemson girls. They had been little kids thirteen years ago when she'd left the reservation, and she hadn't seen them since.

"I tol' her to come on Friday after you get back from Denver," Laola said. "You got an opening at two o'clock."

"I'm on my way to catch an airplane," Vicky said.

"I know," the girl interrupted. "I saw Dennis Eagle Cloud this morning. He told me you were going to Denver, so I drove over here hoping to catch you before you left."

It occurred to Vicky that something might have happened on the reservation, and this young woman had been sent to fetch her. "Is there an emergency?" she asked.

"Emergency!" The young woman seemed to grab at the idea, as if an unexpected lifeline had floated toward her. "Yes, that's it! Todd's got some kind of emergency."

"Can't you come back on Friday?" This from Laola. "Vicky's got to catch her plane."

Annemarie ignored the secretary. "I've got to talk to you."

"Walk out to the car with me," Vicky said.

Their footsteps made a rhythmic slapping noise in the outside corridor that ran along the second floor of the small office building. "What makes you think Todd has some kind of emergency?" Vicky asked.

They hurried down the stairs in tandem. "He's not around," Annemarie said. "I've been calling his apartment for three days."

"Three days?" Vicky turned and stared at her. Heat rose from the sidewalk and bounced off the brick building. "You're worried because he doesn't answer his phone?" A picture was forming in her mind: a handsome young Arapaho man in the big city, where the temptations were mighty. Todd may have a fiancée on the reservation, but other young women, beautiful and available, were in Denver.

"It's not what you think," Annemarie said, fear and impatience in her expression. "We're getting married in September. This isn't about us. When he was here last Saturday—"

"He was here last Saturday?" Vicky heard the sharpness in her tone. Turning abruptly, she walked to the Bronco parked at the curb. She was losing precious time. She'd probably get a speeding ticket on the way to the airport, might even miss her plane, all because she had given Annemarie her attention, when she should have backed up Laola, whose instincts, on this occasion, were better than her own. She flung open the door and slid onto the burning seat.

Annemarie held the door and leaned down. "Todd was stressed-out. I mean, he's supposed to be finishing up his thesis, but he drives up here. Didn't call or anything. Just shows up Saturday night." She stopped, drew in a shuddering breath. "He said he couldn't stay, that he had to get back to Denver, that something was going on."

"Did he say what it was?" Vicky jammed the key into the ignition and gave it a quick turn. The engine growled into life.

"He wouldn't tell me." Her voice was a whine. "He said I didn't want to know, and if anybody asked, I was to say I didn't know anything. He said it could be dangerous."

Drawing in a long breath, Vicky shifted in the seat and gave the young woman her full attention. "You haven't talked to him since?" It was a statement, not a question.

Annemarie ran her fingers under her eyes and looked away. Bringing her eyes back, she said, "I don't know if he got back to Denver okay."

"If he was in some kind of trouble, why did he come here?" Vicky asked.

"To see Father John over at the mission," Annemarie said, as if it were obvious.

Vicky heard the catch in her breath at the mention of the pastor at St. Francis Mission. She glanced away: the wide stretch of Main Street, the cars and trucks lumbering by. How many cases she and John O'Malley had worked on together: getting some kid out of jail, helping somebody through a divorce, a funeral. She was the lawyer; he, the counselor. A good team. She had never met a man like him—sure and strong. In the last three years she had grown to care about him more than she had wanted, more than she could acknowledge, more than was possible. He was a priest. He had obligations and vows, which he meant to honor. A month ago he had left St. Francis Mission.

The news had flashed across the moccasin telegraph in tones of abandonment—as if he had abandoned the people. And the search for an explanation had begun. The emergency calls from dying parishioners, the constant stream of troubles. Who called a priest except someone in trouble? The chronic lack of funds, the worry, the sadness. It was too much for one man. And through all the explanations, guilt had nagged at her, a constant companion; she knew why he had left. She had allowed her feelings to drive him away.

She tried to concentrate on what the young woman was saying, something about Father John not being back from Boston yet. Yet. The word jolted her and made her acutely aware of the space she was occupying, the heat enveloping the car, the sun slanting through the windshield. She had never expected to see him again.

Trying to ignore the jumble of feelings, she glanced up at the young woman. Tears were welling in Annemarie's eyes. "Did you call Todd's grandparents?" Vicky asked. Doyal and Mary Harris had lived in Denver as long as she could remember.

Annemarie shook her head. "They're old. I didn't want to worry them."

Vicky understood. It was a sign of respect not to worry old people. She pulled a small pad and pen out of her bag and handed them to the young woman. "Give me Todd's address and telephone number," she instructed. "I'll try to talk to him while I'm in Denver. And give me his grandparents' number."

"Oh, Vicky, thank you." Relief and gratitude mingled in the young woman's expression as she scribbled on the pad. "Call me as soon as you find him," she said, handing back the pen and notepad. The girl had also written down her own phone number.

Vicky pulled the door shut, pushed the gear into forward, and wheeled onto the street. In the rearview mirror she caught a glimpse of Annemarie walking toward a brown pickup, head bowed, arms tucked at her sides. A right turn at the corner, and the girl was gone. Vicky felt a small shiver run along her spine, like some unbidden and inexplicable premonition.

She pressed hard on the accelerator. A quick look at her watch confirmed what she feared. She would have to race the clock all the way to the Riverton airport.

◀ 4 ▶

Vicky couldn't get Annemarie's story out of her mind. Settling back into her seat as the plane rose above Riverton, she went over what the girl had said: Todd suddenly appearing, unannounced, agitated about something, wanting to talk to Father John. Why would he make the long drive to the reservation unless he was in some sort of trouble? That's when people always turned to Father John—when they were in trouble.

And then Todd had disappeared into Denver. Disappeared? Annemarie hadn't been able to reach him for three days. That hardly constituted a disappearance. There had to be an explanation. Another girlfriend, most likely. In any case, after the meeting at the museum, she would find the young man, make sure he was okay, and explain how worried Annemarie was. Whatever was bothering Todd Harris, it wasn't fair to keep his fiancée in the dark.

Feeling more relaxed, Vicky set her forehead against the rounded frame of the window and watched the great expanse of earth below, streaked in sunshine and shadow, melting into the rim of the sky. Wild grasses were the faintest of green now, but she knew they would soon turn brown in the summer's heat. There was the occasional farm, the clump of reddish-brown buildings, the emerald circles of cultivated fields, but most of the land was open, the way it had been when her people lived here in the Old Time.

She imagined another June, the time to move the village from the lee of the mountains onto the plains, where the great herds of buffalo could be found. The chiefs riding in the lead, women behind, with infants in cradle boards strapped to their backs, dogs in the rear, pulling travois piled high with clothing and household items, the warriors galloping back and forth, guarding the line. Somewhere below, among the cottonwood trees along the banks of the shimmering streams, the long line halted. The men tethered the ponies, the women scurried about setting up the tipis. They would think the shadow passing overhead was an eagle.

The squawk of static, the pilot's voice droning through the cabin called her back to the present. Ten more minutes, and they would land in Denver. In the distance now, Vicky could see the skyscrapers gleaming silver in the sun, the tentacles of the city reaching onto the plains, the miniature cars and trucks rolling along ribbons of highways. To the west rose the massive white peaks of the Rocky Mountains. Then the airport came into view, its white Teflon roof peaked like the mountains, like the tipis in the villages of her people.

Forty minutes later Vicky gripped the steering wheel of the rented Taurus, heading west on I-70, a highway she had driven often in the years she had spent in Denver. It seemed different now. More automobiles, new exit and entrance-ramps, or had she just forgotten the rush of a city, the steady *brrr* of traffic, the smell of exhaust fumes? She banked through a series of turns that locals called the "mousetrap" and joined the stream of cars flowing south on I-25, past the warehouses and industrial buildings, past the run-down motels and country-western bars. The highway had once been a trail her people had followed as they moved along the front range of the mountains.

At Speer Boulevard, she swung south and headed across the South Platte River, then turned into downtown Denver. Locked in traffic now, she inched along sidewalks crowded with business people, briefcases in hand. Another turn, and she passed the small white building with marble columns marching across the entrance. She left the Taurus in a parking lot a block away.

The sun burrowed into her bare arms and the asphalt burned through the soles of her pumps as she strode through the intersection, the din of the city—horns and sirens, the growl of engines—rising around her. She looked just like the throngs of lawyers and secretaries and bankers, she thought: tailored linen dress, hair pulled back and clipped at the nape of her neck. But she was not one of them. Not because her skin was brown—she passed others with brown skin—but because she belonged to this place. This was where the villages of the *Hinono eino* had stood, where her people had traded with whites coming onto the land, where her people had died, their blood soaking the earth that lay buried under asphalt and piles of brick.

She passed the small shops with designer clothes draped in the windows, the glass-walled entrance to a hotel, the revolving doors into a skyscraper. Huddled next door, like a survivor of another age, reluctant to announce its presence, was the Denver Museum of the West.

The gray-haired woman behind the doughnut-shaped desk in the lobby seemed intent on shuffling a stack of brochures. After snapping the last of them into place, she raised her eyes. "Yes?" she said, a prolonged drawl.

"Vicky Holden. I'm here to see Rachel Foster."

The woman swiveled toward the phone on the right curve of the desk. There was the tapping of keys, a few muffled words into the receiver, and she swiveled back. "Ms. Foster's expecting you. Third floor. You can take the elevator." She tilted her head toward the alcove behind the desk.

Thanking her, Vicky started toward the alcove, her heels clicking on the marble floor. An archway yawned on the right, and in the gallery beyond stood a large canvas tipi, white as snow. She walked through the archway and slowly circled the tipi, studying the geometric designs painted in blues and reds and yellows on the sides: lines and circles, pyramids and diamonds symbolizing the earth and mountains, the villages, the paths individuals must follow. She tried to read the story the symbols told, but it was difficult. Circles inside squares, diamonds and crosses juxtaposed, vertical and horizontal lines interlocked—all shading the meaning. Mostly women wrote in symbols laden with meaning, whereas men wrote in realistic, detailed pictographs. She wondered about the woman who, more than a hundred years earlier, had painstakingly drawn the prayer symbols for her family.

Beyond the tipi was another archway with a sign at the entrance: THE STORY OF THE CHEYENNE MASSACRE AT SAND CREEK. Vicky flinched. Her people had also been killed at Sand Creek. Slowly she walked into the large room with polished wood floors and glass-fronted display cases. In the case on her left stood a miniature village: circles of white tipis, tiny figures of women tending kettles over glowing fires, men wrapped in buffalo robes, hunched down, cleaning rifles and stringing bows, boys herding ponies into a corral. Traces of snow littered the ground; ice crusted the creek winding through the village. It was winter when the massacre occurred, November 29, 1864, a day burned into the memory of her people.

Vicky moved toward the next display, drawn and repelled at the same time. The painted horizon depicted a gray dawn, a hazy sun lifting out of the east, and the Colorado Cavalry, Third Regiment massed on the bluff overlooking the sleeping village. She instinctively stepped back, wanting to flee the malevolent force about to hurtle toward her. Pivoting around, she walked out of the galleries toward the elevator.

On the third floor, she stopped at the door with the small sign that read RACHEL FOSTER, CURATOR. She rapped once before letting herself into an office about the size of her own, but much neater: books perfectly aligned in bookcases, two leather-slung wood chairs in front of a desk, its polished surface clear except for a computer. A woman in her late forties, Vicky guessed, leaned toward the monitor, red-tipped fingers tapping the keyboard. Stylishly cut blond hair brushed the shoulders of her red suit jacket. There was a slash of red at her lips. "I've been waiting for you," Rachel Foster said, lifting her eyes slowly from the monitor.

Vicky approached the desk, feeling like a kid called into the principal's office. "I'm afraid I was caught by your exhibit on the Sand Creek Massacre," she said, a kind of apology, although she felt little inclination to apologize.

The curator waved her toward one of the leather chairs. "Quite an exceptional exhibit," she said. But not a valid excuse for keeping her waiting, the tone implied.

"We were there, too," Vicky said, taking the seat and setting her handbag at her feet, the briefcase in her lap.

"I beg your pardon?" Rachel Foster lowered her chin, eyes squinting in coldness. For an instant Vicky recalled the look that used to come into the eyes of her ex-husband, Ben, as he leaned against the fence of a corral and assessed a wild mare: how much trouble to break her?

She blinked back the memory. "Cheyennes weren't the only people massacred at Sand Creek," she said. "Many of my people died there."

A mixture of exasperation and impatience came into

the curator's eyes. "A highly contested theory," she said. "Professor Bernard Good Elk consulted with us on the exhibit. He's head of Native American studies at Regis University. Surely you know him?" She gave a little wave as if it weren't important, and hurried on: "He has devoted many years to studying the massacre. His research supports the theory that only Cheyennes were there. About five hundred, I believe he told me. One hundred and sixty-three were killed."

Vicky swallowed hard. Almost one third of the dead—fifty men, women, and children—were Arapaho. Was everything to be taken from her people, even their history? She saw the implications: if only Cheyennes were at Sand Creek, then only Cheyennes would have a right to the Colorado lands promised by Congress to the tribes that were there. She said, "Perhaps Professor Good Elk should come to the Wind River Reservation and interview the descendants of the Arapaho survivors."

The curator gave her a wan, forced smile. "I'm sure he would have done so, had he thought it productive." Clasping her hands on the desk in front of her, she said, "You mentioned on the phone there was some sort of problem."

Vicky extracted the blue folder from her briefcase, then let the briefcase slide to her feet. It made a muffled thud against the carpet. "We have reason to believe the inventory of Arapaho artifacts may be incomplete," she said, locking eyes with the woman on the other side of the desk.

Gripping the arms of her chair, as if to steady herself in a sudden gust of wind, Rachel Foster blurted, "Incomplete? You can't be serious. I personally oversaw the compilation of the inventory myself. We furnished inventories to numerous tribes, and I can assure you they are all complete. Our consultant was another highly respected expert—Professor Emil Coughlin. You must know him."

Vicky shook her head. She had never heard of any of these so-called experts.

The curator went on, eyes narrowing in impatience. "Don't know him? A highly regarded ethnohistorian? Why, he is known around the world for his expertise on the artifacts of the Plains Indians."

"That may be true," Vicky said in her courtroom tone, calm and firm. "But the inventory does not include the Arapaho ledger book."

"A ledger book? In our collections?" The curator's voice rose in incredulity. "Why would you suppose that, Ms. Holden? Indeed, I've never heard that an Arapaho ledger book even exists."

Vicky drew in a long breath, her hands gripping the folder. This was the difficult part: a ninety-three-year-old man, a story—all the evidence she had. She said, "One of our elders saw the ledger book on display in the museum in 1920."

"Nineteen-twenty?" The other woman threw back her head and laughed. The sound was dry and strained. "Is this some kind of joke? Some old man says he saw a ledger book here almost eighty years ago?"

"Exactly."

"It could have been another museum."

"He believes it was this museum," Vicky said.

The curator set her elbows on the desk and brought her red-tipped fingers together in a tent below her chin. "Please, Ms. Holden," she began, amusement in her eyes, "you can't expect me to take this seriously. This is beyond what NAGPRA requires."

Vicky held the other woman's gaze. "We have a right to know the whereabouts of our ledger book."

Rachel Foster said nothing for a moment. The amused expression faded into grimness. "I take your inference that we are hiding something quite personally," she said finally. "My job is to know every item in the museum's collection, and I do my job very well." Suddenly she was on her feet. "Come with me." She swung around the desk and started toward the door.

Vicky picked up her briefcase and handbag and followed the curator down the short hallway to the elevator. They rode in silence to the lower level: a steady pull downward. The doors opened onto a carpeted corridor that ran along a glass-enclosed wall. Beyond the wall, Vicky could see shelves stacked with books and gray cardboard cartons. She followed the curator through a door with LIBRARY printed on the clear glass panel. The room was square, with dark-wood tables lined up in rows, polished tops gleaming under the fluorescent ceiling lights. Several researchers sat hunched over papers and books. A young woman with a wedge of brown hair over her forehead and tiny half-glasses looked up from the desk on the left. A small sign on the desk said REFERENCE LIBRARIAN.

Rachel Foster sailed past, and Vicky followed. The muffled sound of their footsteps, the occasional turning of a page, broke the library quiet. A right turn, and they were in the stacks, slipping sideways around the cartons and books, the piles of newspapers jutting beyond the metal shelves.

"Every item is briefly identified," Rachel Foster said. Her red nails trailed along the plastic labels at the edge of one shelf as she walked on. "Complete identifications are in the files."

Vicky stopped, her eyes on the labels: *Gorsuch collections, 1913; Black and Riddle Papers, 1902–1910.* And beneath a shelf of old books: *Colorado History, 1858–1888.*

The curator had disappeared, and Vicky hurried along the stacks. She found the other woman punching in security numbers next to a metal door on the far wall. "What you see here," she said with a wave toward the stacks, "are library materials, a small part of our collection."

The door slid open, as if some invisible arm had pulled it back, and Vicky followed the curator into a cavernlike space as large as a football field and at least two stories high. The air felt cool—the controlled, even coolness of a morgue. There was an odd musty odor, like that of old spices and decaying fabrics. Rows of large metal shelves resembling scaffolding stretched into the far shadows. At a glance, she saw the items on nearby shelves had been gathered through the last century: Victorian chairs and tables, feather boas, flapper dresses, poodle skirts, saddles, firearms.

She hurried to stay abreast of Rachel Foster, who, with single-minded intensity, was marching down an aisle with shelves looming on both sides. The shelves were crowded with Native American artifacts. Abruptly the curator stopped and swept out one hand. "The Arapaho collection," she announced. "You will find everything listed on the inventory."

Vicky moved slowly along the aisle, allowing her eyes to roam over the items: beaded moccasins and gloves, breastplates strung with eagle bones, pipes decorated with feathers and beaded thongs, eagle-feathered warbonnets that, she knew, had once been worn by chiefs. From somewhere came a faint rumble of traffic, and she realized the storeroom reached far under the city streets. For an instant she felt as if she'd stepped into another time, surrounded by objects waiting with mute patience for owners to return and take them up again, while the city pulsed overhead in the distant future.

She reached the end of the aisle and turned, slowly retracing her steps, eyes combing the shelves. Nothing resembled a ledger book.

Rachel Foster waited, arms folded across her waist,

red nails tapping her elbows. "I hope you have satisfied yourself," she said.

"Perhaps the ledger book is lost somewhere." Vicky swung the briefcase toward the shelves extending around them. "It could be wedged between cartons, or hidden behind some other artifact."

"Impossible," the curator said. "We know the precise location of everything in the collections. I can assure you if we owned a ledger book worth one-point-three million dollars, we would know where it was."

Wheeling about, Rachel Foster started back along the aisle. Vicky stayed in step. When they reached the cool hush of the library, she said, "We'd like an explanation as to what became of the ledger book. You must have records dating back to 1920."

The curator turned and faced her. "Of course we have records." There was a note of scarcely disguised contempt in the woman's voice. Nodding toward the filing cabinets against the wall at the end of the stacks, she said, "The old records are in the files. We have records for each item acquired from the day the museum opened in 1896 until 1975. After that date our records are in the database." She drew in a long breath, turned, and started back through the library.

"Then you must have a record of the ledger book," Vicky said, staying in step.

The curator stopped again and turned—a deliberate movement. "Are you suggesting we search every file cabinet?"

"If necessary, yes," Vicky said.

"Impossible!" The curator took in a gulp of air. "Records prior to 1920 are nothing more than notations jotted on slips of papers." Another gulp, and she went on: The overburdened staff. A wild-goose chase. Beyond the requirements of NAGPRA.

Vicky gripped the handle of her briefcase, struggling to control her growing impatience. "The law requires you to furnish my tribe with a complete and accurate inventory of Arapaho artifacts. We know the ledger book was once in the museum. We want to know what became of it. I must ask you to check your records."

The curator glanced about, as if to beckon assistance from the tables, the researchers, the young woman behind the desk. Then: "You are making this very difficult." Little dots of spittle peppered her chin.

Vicky said nothing, watching the other woman's eyes travel again over the room. After a moment the curator brought her eyes back. "It will take some time," she said.

"I'd like a copy of the ledger book record by Friday," Vicky said. She'd been hoping to settle matters and fly home tomorrow. Now she would be lucky to get home for the weekend.

"Friday! Two days! Impossible."

"I'll be back on Friday," Vicky said.

❮ 5 ❯

It was almost noon before Father John drove out of St. Francis Mission. He'd spent the morning returning phone calls and tending to the most urgent messages on his desk. The rest he'd stacked into piles—less urgent, important, not important—that he would handle as soon as he got back.

He caught Highway 135 and headed south. Not far beyond the southern outskirts of Riverton, the ranch houses and clusters of barns began to fall away, leaving the open land running into an azure sky and the two lanes of asphalt ahead shimmering in the sun. Hot air rushed past the half-opened windows and mingled with the sounds of *Rigoletto* blaring from the tape player on the seat beside him. Except for an occasional semi roaring past and the small herds of antelope racing along the highway, he was alone.

"Another trip?" Father Geoff had said, when he'd told his assistant he was going to Denver. As if the pastor of St. Francis Mission was always casting about for some reason to leave, when the truth was he hated having to leave again. He'd only returned from Boston three days ago. He was glad to be home. Yet Boston had been home for almost thirty years—the throb of traffic and rush of people once as familiar as the rhythms of his own life. How strange and jarring they had seemed on this last trip. He'd felt only a sense of relief as the plane had lifted into the clouds, leaving the city far behind, like the life he had once led there.

He had spent two weeks at the Jesuit retreat house in Boston, praying over the direction of his life and, in the privacy of the chapel, renewing vows he had made to God seventeen years before. Made of his own free will, gladly. Knowing that he would not be like other men, would not marry, would never have children, that his life would take a different direction.

After the retreat, he'd spent another two weeks visiting old friends, taking in the museums and a couple of concerts. He'd set aside an afternoon to spend with his brother, Mike, and his wife, Eileen. Nothing had changed with Mike. He still made it clear—the reserved manner, the forced camaraderie—that he wished Father John would go away and not return, as if he feared he might still be in love with Eileen. How silly, Father John thought. After all these years.

There was a time he *had* loved Eileen. He still remembered the stab of pain when, three months after he'd entered the seminary, she had run off and married his brother. But that was years ago—a lifetime ago. He hardly recognized the woman—the faded red hair, the wide hips and large, rounded breasts. What had become of the lithe, slim colleen with red-gold hair and flashing green eyes he'd guided across the dance floors at Boston College?

These were not thoughts he wanted. Father John snapped down the visor against the sun glinting off the hood. He had chosen a different direction, had been called to a different life—a life he'd found difficult at times and filled with temptations. He hadn't stood the test well. He'd let everybody down when he'd started drinking—his superiors, his students at the Jesuit prep school where he used to teach American history, himself. He thought of that time as his Great Fall, when he had fallen from what everyone had expected.

He'd spent almost a year in recovery at Grace House and, afterward, old Father Peter had agreed to let him work at St. Francis Mission, a place he'd never heard of, among people—the Arapahos—he knew little about. He'd arrived in the emptiness of the plains, feeling both grateful and depressed. Grateful to the old priest for taking a chance on him, depressed at the distance between an Indian reservation and a university history department, where he had hoped to be.

But the more he'd gotten to know the Arapahos, the more he had felt at home, as if his life had been pointed in the direction of St. Francis Mission all along. Still the temptations persisted, the thirst that came over him at unexpected moments, especially in the evenings, when he was alone. And then the day, nearly four years ago, when he'd looked up from his desk and seen the woman dressed in a blue suit, carrying a briefcase, a small fist about to rap against the opened door.

"Excuse me, Father," she'd said. He'd known who she was even before she introduced herself—the dark skin, the black hair pulled tightly back, the black eyes shining with intelligence. The grandmothers had been clucking for weeks over how Vicky Holden had gone away and become *ho:xu'wu:ne'n*, a lawyer, like a white woman. And now she had come back. As if she could ever come back, the grandmothers said, as if things could ever be the same. From that first day he'd known he must not spend much time with this woman.

His instincts had been right, he thought, stomping down on the accelerator and passing a truck. The Toyota vibrated around him as he pulled back into his lane, the stretch of asphalt empty ahead. Last month, when he'd thought Vicky had lost her life to a deranged killer, he'd wondered how he would stand it. And when he'd found she was okay, he'd known he had to step back, get his own bearings. He had fled to Boston.

He'd returned with a sense of peace and determination about the things he wanted to accomplish at the mission: the new classes and programs and, especially, the museum in the old school. He felt a twinge of guilt at leaving his assistant in charge of the mission again, especially since Father Geoff had to cancel his plans for a backpacking trip into the Wind River mountains this weekend. But it could be another year before the provincial returned to Regis, another year before he could meet with him. The Arapahos needed the museum now. They had already started to reclaim funeral and cultural artifacts from museums around the country. Just yesterday, the cultural director, Dennis Eagle Cloud, had called to say he was expecting a shipment of artifacts from the Smithsonian. He'd wanted to know if the mission had any storage space, until he could find a permanent location. Father John had offered the empty storerooms on the second floor of the administration building. Storerooms were hardly a substitute for a museum.

"How are the plans for turning the old school into a museum?" the director had wanted to know.

"Coming along," Father John had told him, a forced tone of optimism. He refused to take Father Stanton's word as final.

An hour with the provincial, Father John was certain, and he could convince him. Start-up funds were all he needed. Enough to renovate the school building, purchase display cases and other equipment, and pay the director's salary the first few months. After the museum was established and had proved itself, there would be foundation money. And benefactors were generous. He'd spent almost eight years running St. Francis Mission on the generosity of strangers. If he could run the mission that way, well . . .

It was the weak link in his argument, he realized. It was going to be tough to convince the provincial of his financial plan, but he and Father Rutherford went back a long time, and he was counting on discussing the matter face-to-face with an old friend, without interference from bureaucrats like Father Stanton. Part of an hour was all he needed, and then he'd be back in the Toyota driving home to the reservation.

Before he left Denver, he intended to call Todd Harris and make sure the young man was still interested in taking on the job of director. He'd tried to call him yesterday, but there was no answer. Father Geoff had said Todd had stopped by St. Francis last Saturday. He seemed agitated, unlike himself. Seemed disappointed Father John hadn't gotten back from Boston.

Father John hadn't thought much about it at first, but he'd begun wondering what was so important that Todd had driven all the way to the reservation when he could have called. Maybe Todd had accepted another job, now that he was close to finishing his master's. It wouldn't surprise him. The young man had talent and insight, qualities that would make him a welcome addition to any museum. If he had a better opportunity, Father John intended to advise him to take it, even though, he hoped, Todd would think the best opportunity would be a museum on the history and culture of his own people.

Ahead, Rawlins glimmered on the plains like a white, sun-splashed pool. A few miles, and Father John was driving down the main street, past the sand-colored, flat-roofed shops and boxlike stores that looked as if they had erupted out of the flat, dry land. The wind whipped across the concrete apron of the gas station. He filled up the Toyota, paid the bill, and bought a Styrofoam cup of coffee. He'd sipped the coffee in front of the station, then walked up and down a few moments, grateful to stretch his legs. He'd been driving several hours. It was still a long way to Denver.

❮ 6 ❯

Vicky's hands trembled against the hot steering wheel as she pulled into the rush-hour traffic. What had she accomplished at the Denver Museum of the West? Nothing, except to alienate the curator who had made no promises when she'd left her in the lobby. There was every possibility the curator would have the same excuses on Friday. Overworked staff, too little time. And then what? Perhaps she could file a federal lawsuit under NAGPRA, claiming the museum hadn't been forthcoming, or file a lawsuit under Colorado's open-records law, asking permission to search the records herself.

She drummed her fingers on the rim of the wheel as she waited for a green light. Neither option was good. She had no proof the ledger book was still in the museum. She had only an old man's story. And even if she could convince a judge to grant a hearing, Charlie Redman might not live long enough to tell his story in court. In the meantime the tribe's claim to other objects in the museum would be stalled. Anything could happen while a lawsuit dragged on. Other artifacts might also disappear, and in the end, Arapahos would recover even fewer of the sacred and cultural items that belonged to them.

She had a sinking feeling that she'd made a mess of things. Certainly the museum's collection seemed well organized, everything labeled and in place. Why did she insist upon locating a ledger book that might no longer exist? What if it had been sold? What if it had fallen into the hands of a dealer? The pages could be cut out and framed in the homes of collectors around the world, the story lost forever. Why couldn't she just return to the reservation and advise Dennis Eagle Cloud to sign off on the inventory, claim as many items as the law allowed, and forget about the ledger book?

The light switched to green, and she pressed down on the gas pedal, heading south with three lanes of cars racing for home, her mind trying to sort out what it was that pulled her on, like an iron fist clamped to her shoulder. Her own stubbornness? Her determination to prove to her people she was a good lawyer—she could handle the tough, important cases? Or was it Rachel Foster's arrogance, her cool insistence the museum had never owned an Arapaho ledger book? And yet . . . and yet, the curator had said the book was worth $1.3 million. How did she know the exact value of a book she claimed she knew nothing about?

The sun splashed against the windshield as Vicky wove through the traffic. The ledger book was somewhere. It was real, and it belonged to the *Hinono eino;* it was their story. She had to find it, no matter how many lawsuits, no matter what it took.

She shot through an intersection just as the light turned red. The digital clock on the dashboard blinked 4:30. Marcy Aker, the old friend she'd arranged to stay with, had said she'd be home by four-thirty from the downtown law firm where she and Vicky had once occupied adjoining cubicles. But Marcy could be delayed. Vicky remembered the late nights she had pulled when something unexpected had come up at the firm. She decided to see if Todd Harris was home.

Abruptly she switched into the turn lane and wheeled east onto Speer Boulevard, heading in the opposite direction from Marcy's house. Another left turn, and she was curving past the Neoclassical buildings surrounded by the wide swaths of lawn and beds of flowers in the Civic Center. Ahead, the golden dome of the State Capitol glistened in the sun. Another few blocks, and she was driving down apartment-lined streets where cars stood bumper-to-bumper at the curbs, reminding her of how impossible it usually was to find a parking place in Capitol Hill. So different from the open spaces on the reservation. At home she could park in the middle of the road if she wished.

Just ahead a woman left a parking spot, and Vicky rolled slowly forward, past the brick apartment building with the address above the entrance that Todd's fiancée had given her. She maneuvered into the vacant space, slid her bag off the seat, and hurried through the mottled shade of elm trees lining the sidewalk, the accumulation of the day's heat pressing around her like a heavy buffalo robe. Above the roofs of the apartment buildings, the ridge of mountains rose into a cloudless blue sky. Strips of snow clung to the high peaks, sparkling in the sun like rivers of gold. It was the gold, Vicky knew, that had lured white people to the land of the Arapaho. Gold that had brought the soldiers who had driven her people from Colorado.

A small entry, no more than a brick-enclosed stoop, jutted from Todd's building. She let herself through the outer door and tried the main door. Locked, as she expected. A panel of mailboxes filled the right wall, and Vicky began scanning the names below each box. Third row down was T. HARRIS.

She pressed the button below the box and waited. A long shot that Todd would be here. There were a thousand places in the city where a young graduate student might go after classes. She should have called first, she thought, giving the button another hard push. The air inside the small space was hot and smelled of burned coals, like the smoke from an outdoor barbecue.

She was about to give up when she noticed that Todd's box was jammed with brown and white envelopes, various colored flyers. Her eyes scanned the cardboard carton on the concrete floor, the folded newspapers and magazines stuffed inside. Stooping down, she began shuffling through. The newspapers belonged to Todd—a collection of the *Rocky Mountain News* for most of a week.

She stood up and surveyed the names on the mailboxes until she found the one labeled *MGR*. She held down the button a long moment. No answer. Outside an engine backfired—a reverberating boom in the heavy heat. She gave the button another push and waited. Then she began pushing the other buttons—top, middle, bottom.

A voice burst into the heat-filled entry. "Who is it?" It sounded like an elderly woman. The name next to the last button was M. EVANS.

Vicky leaned toward the speaker, gave her name, and said she was a friend of Todd Harris. "Do you know him?" She stopped herself from addressing the woman as grandmother. Grandmother was not a term of respect in the white culture.

"Todd?" A hesitation in the voice. "Ah, yes. A very nice boy. He's okay, isn't he?"

The question hit Vicky like a cold blast of wind, like a confirmation of her own misgivings. "I don't know," she said. "I'm trying to find him."

"Well, I'm very glad," the woman said. "I haven't seen him in a while. Not since—oh, my, it must have been last Sunday. Yes, I was on my way to church, and he was just coming in. He looked, well . . ."

"How did he look?" Vicky prodded.

"Very tired, I would say. Yes. Very tired indeed."

Sunday, Vicky was thinking. Annemarie had said Todd was on the reservation the day before. He must've just gotten back to Denver.

"Could I come up?" Vicky asked.

"Oh, my." The fear in the voice was so strong, Vicky could almost feel it. "I always make it a rule never to open the door for anyone I don't know. It's a very sensible rule, don't you believe?"

"Yes, of course," Vicky said, struggling to hide her own frustration. "Would you give Todd a message when you see him?"

"Well, I'll try." The voice seemed faint and far away, as if the old woman had grown tired and sought a chair somewhere.

"Ask him to call me at this number." Vicky fumbled through her bag for her Day Timer. Finally she had it. Slowly she read off Marcy's number, hoping the old woman was jotting it down.

The rush-hour traffic seemed heavier as Vicky drove back across the city. She couldn't shake a nagging sense that Annemarie was right, that Todd was in some kind of trouble, even though her rational mind—the lawyer part—insisted there was nothing to worry about. Last Saturday he was fine. Upset and stressed perhaps, but what graduate student finishing a thesis wasn't upset and stressed? True, his fiancée hadn't talked to him since, and the old woman—*Miss* Evans, she suspected—hadn't seen him since Sunday. At least he had gotten back to Denver safely and hadn't flipped his car into a ditch somewhere along the empty roads of Wyoming. More than likely her first instincts were correct. Todd had met someone new. He'd driven to the reservation to tell Annemarie and had lost his nerve. So he'd gone to St. Francis to see Father John. It could even explain the young man's absence. He was probably staying with his new girlfriend. A plausible story.

Why, then, didn't she believe it? Vicky wondered as she caught Speer Boulevard and drove to old North Denver, a section of Victorian homes climbing over gentle hills. The sun rode above the mountains ahead, shooting blinding rays across the hood of the Taurus. The windshield refracted a thousand colored lights that spun in front of her like a kaleidoscope. She drove with the visor down, one hand cupped above her eyes. Still, there were half seconds as the boulevard curved into the sun when she was blinded in the moving traffic.

She parked in front of a red-bricked bungalow sheltering among giant oaks and elms, like the other bungalows lining the street. The front door flew open before she could set down her carry-on bag and ring the doorbell. Marcy stood in front of her, about forty pounds heavier than Vicky remembered, in a flowing, blue-splashed kimono with wide, cubelike sleeves. So different from the tailored, conservative suits Vicky remembered. Her hair was blond, not the chestnut of several years ago, and piled on top of her head, curls corkscrewing in different directions. But her eyes were the same, dark blue and speckled with lights.

"My dear." Two fleshy arms came out of the kimono and pulled Vicky toward her. "It's good to see you." Then, stepping back, her hands on Vicky's shoulders, she added, "You haven't changed at all. Not at all! You are absolutely the same."

Vicky bit back the impulse to protest. Of course she had changed. She felt older, sadder perhaps at the realization that not everything she had hoped for would be included in her life. But in a strange way, the realization had brought her a calmness she'd never felt in the years in Denver. She said, "How are you, Marcy?"

"At peace. At peace." The other woman moved backward, holding the door open, and Vicky stepped into a large room of white walls and polished wood floors, like a modern sculpture enclosed in brick. Sunshine streamed through the bare windows and played across the white sofas and glass coffee table, the abstract oil paintings, the Indian rugs scattered about. In the far corner, an array of copper pans dangled above a kitchen island.

"Welcome to my space." Marcy allowed one arm to flow toward the room, like the movement in a ballet.

"Where does Mike keep his easy chair?" Vicky asked. A mistake, she knew instantly by the startled look in her friend's eyes.

"In his living room," Marcy said, a lighthearted falseness in the tone.

"I'm sorry." Vicky reached out and touched the other woman's arm. "I didn't know you were separated."

Marcy shrugged away. "Separated is not how I prefer to think of our living accommodations. We have decided to find our own space." A short pause, then: "Life is a stream, Vicky, rolling relentlessly onward. But there are eddies along the way. I prefer to think of my little house as an eddy, a place where I can emerge into the sacred space of the center." She stopped, her eyes on Vicky's. "Now, why am I telling you this? You came to Denver—what, thirteen years ago?—to find your center."

Vicky gave the carry-on a little swing into the room. "Where would you like me to take this?" she asked, making an effort to conceal the prick of irritation. How easy Marcy made it sound, as if leaving Ben and moving to Denver had been nothing more than a swift glide over an iced-smooth lake, when it had been like cutting herself in half. She had never wanted to divorce her husband, had never meant to break her vows; she had only wanted him to stop hitting her.

Had they lived in the Old Time, she could have gone to her father and his brothers, who were also her fathers in the Arapaho Way, and they would have called Ben to a council and told him, "No more. No more." It would have stopped, or Ben would have been the one punished, and her family would have taken her away from him.

But it was not the Old Time. It was the modern time, and she had been forced to take herself away. Even now she was not certain of the exact moment she had known she must make another life for herself and the kids—Susan and Lucas were so young then. But lately, when she thought about it, it seemed the day had always been arriving, coming toward her like an arrow shot out of her own destiny, when she would have to leave.

She followed Marcy down the hallway on the right, the unbidden memories flooding over her: the long drive across Wyoming and into Colorado, the rush of students on the CU campus in Denver—a sea of white faces surging around her. And Marcy. Appearing from nowhere, chattering like a magpie. Sign up for this class, stay away from that one—walking her through registration. The first white person who had looked at her, talked to her like another human being, as if the differences between them, the shades of their skin, their different cultures, were no differences at all.

Later, when she'd admitted to herself she couldn't wait tables, go to class, and care for her children, and had sent them to her parents on the reservation—when the earth had dropped out from under her—Marcy had been a phone call away. They'd been friends through the endless hours of briefing cases in the law library, the weeks of studying for the bar exam, and the three years at the firm. When she'd decided to return to her people, it was Marcy who had helped her pack up the Bronco. And now, if this fuzzy-headed woman in the flowing kimono had left her husband to find her sacred center, well, they were still friends.

Vicky followed her into a small bedroom. The afternoon sun filtered around the edges of filmy white curtains and slanted across the bed piled high with ruffled pillows, the dresser and mirror, the little nightstand with a phone and digital clock. "May this be a small eddy for you," Marcy said, extending one hand into the room. "I hope you'll find this space comfortable."

Vicky laughed. "I'd have to be dead not to." She propped the carry-on on the bed, unzipped it, and began lifting out the few things she'd packed: another attorney dress, blue jeans, a couple of T-shirts, a pair of sandals. She wished she had brought a few extra changes of clothes. She'd be lucky to get home by the weekend.

Marcy was fitting the dress over a hanger she'd extracted from the closet, chatting about work: she'd left the firm, did Vicky know?

Vicky set her cosmetics bag on the dresser and stared at her friend in the mirror. She didn't know. She had never imagined Marcy would leave the firm.

"A mutual parting of the ways." Her friend wheeled around, hung the dress inside the closet, and shut the door softly behind her. "I like to think I have evolved to a higher consciousness," she explained.

Vicky smiled. She remembered a client droning on about the lousy two mil he'd made when he would have made more if his partner hadn't reneged on a deal, about how he wanted her to nail the bastard's hide to the wall, sue him into next week. And she, wondering how she was paying out her life. It was such cases that had finally sent her to the one-woman law office on Main Street in Lander, buoyed with the hope her life might better be paid out helping her people.

Marcy was droning on: her new job at the West-Side Clinic, so spiritually rewarding. "Even if . . ." A wave encompassing the house. "I have to give up my space here. It depends upon the divorce settlement." She gave a little shrug. "It's a matter of simplifying your life," her friend said, a solemn, earnest tone. "You must learn that you require much less in life if you are to continue evolving."

Vicky stepped back over to the bed and lifted the rest of her clothes out of the carry-on. She wasn't sure what to make of the changes in her friend's life. She said, "I want to hire an investigator. Any suggestions?" Marcy drew in a sharp breath at the abrupt change in conversation. She stared at Vicky a moment, as if trying to refocus her thoughts. Then: "Your old friend Pat Michaels is still the best. Hold on." She brushed past the door, and in a moment she was back, snapping two business cards on the dresser. "Someone else would like to hear from you," she said.

Vicky glanced at the black type on the pair of cards. One read *Pat Michaels, Investigations.* The other, *Steve Clark, Denver Homicide Detective.*

"I ran into Steve yesterday," Marcy was saying, "so I mentioned you were coming to town. Well, I wish you could have seen how his eyes lit up, although, of course, he tried to hide it. But he hasn't forgotten you, Vicky." She prattled on: Steve had given her his card in case Vicky wanted to call. Not that he expected her to call after all this time, but it would be good to hear from her. Talk over the old times.

Vicky slid the card under that of the investigator, a memory shooting past, like an old film on fast forward. Two outsiders. She, an Arapaho woman, divorced from her husband, separated from her kids, and handsome, cocky Steve Clark, fresh from a stint with the Navy Seals. Compared with the other students at CU-Denver, they were grizzled veterans of life. And they were friends, that was all. She had just broken her marriage vows and ended the relationship she had thought would last a lifetime. She didn't want other vows, another relationship. The last she had heard of Steve Clark, he had married a childhood sweetheart.

"He's been divorced awhile," Marcy said, as if she'd seen into the memory. "The marriage didn't work out.

They were never on the same planet. You were the one he'd always hoped—"

Vicky held up one hand. "Thanks for the message," she said.

"You're not going to call, are you?" It was a statement. "He'll be disappointed."

"I'm not going to call." Vicky turned toward the bed with the little pile of clothes beside the carry-on and began unbuttoning the front of her attorney dress.

"Well," Marcy said, backing toward the door. "The pasta awaits." Her footsteps made a soft, padded sound as she retreated down the hallway. Then: "Whenever you're ready" floated back like the last stanza of a song.

Vicky shrugged out of the dress. She pulled on the clean, stiff blue jeans and allowed the soft cotton T-shirt to float over her shoulders. She slipped into the sandals, beginning to feel more relaxed, more like herself, without her lawyer clothes. Leaning toward the mirror, she removed the barrette at the nape of her neck and brushed her hair in long, smooth strokes. Her hair fell about her shoulders, thick and black, still shiny—her best feature, she'd always thought. She was not beautiful. No, she would not describe the face looking back at her as beautiful. It had always surprised her when some man insisted otherwise. She'd always felt she should argue, set the matter straight. Eyes as black as slate, set much too far apart, a too-long nose with that little hump, cheekbones too prominent, and lips much too full. She touched up her lipstick. No, not beautiful, but after seeing so many white faces today, the golden-brown face in the mirror looked . . . well, different, as if it belonged in some other place or time. She clipped back her hair with the barrette and turned away. She was who she was.

Picking up the top business card, she walked over to the nightstand, perched on the edge of the bed, and tapped out Pat Michaels's number.

"Yeah?" The voice on the other end sounded raspy from too many cigarettes and cool nights hunkered down behind a steering wheel, watching shadows.

"Pat, it's Vicky Holden."

The line seemed to go dead. Then: "What're you doing in town, beautiful Indian maiden?"

"Please, Pat."

"Sorry, I forgot you never liked that stuff. Have to keep my thoughts to myself. So, talk to me."

"I'm working on an agreement with the Denver Museum of the West."

"Ah," the investigator said, as if a picture had come into focus. "NAGPRA rears its ugly head. A disagreement, more likely, between the Arapahos and the museum. Tell me I'm right and bolster my confidence."

"I don't know for sure," Vicky said. "I'd like to know more about the curator, Rachel Foster."

Another "ah" came across the line, drawn out and nasal-toned. "A museum curator. One of the upstanding types. Always hardest to uncover anything interesting. No rap sheets. Police never heard of them, except maybe for a prowler call in their neighborhoods. What are you looking for? Anything specific?"

"Anything unusual," she said. "Anything that might drive a museum curator to violate her trust."

"You need the information yesterday, right?"

Vicky smiled. She'd always liked Pat—thirty pounds overweight in rumpled slacks and jackets that looked as if he'd slept in them, which, most of the time, he probably had. She'd worked with him on many cases during her years at the firm. Pat Michaels had always been straight with her. She said, "Yesterday would be fine."

"Get back to you tomorrow," he said. She gave him Marcy's number before pressing the disconnect button. Then she pulled her bag across the bed and fumbled for the little pad on which Annemarie had scribbled the numbers. Flattening the pad on the nightstand, she punched in the number of Todd Harris's grandparents, Doyal and Mary. An intermittent buzzing noise was followed by a click. "Hello?" An old man's voice.

"It's Vicky Holden, Grandfather," Vicky said. Then she launched into the usual pleasantries, the polite dance—how had they been? Fine, just fine. Finally the time was ready. "Have you seen Todd lately?" she asked, her voice calm.

"Not seen him for, oh, a couple weeks," Doyal said, a slow drawl. "Todd's real busy at school."

Another round of pleasantries followed before Vicky ended the call, the sense of alarm growing inside her. She pushed it away. Why couldn't she accept the obvious explanation Doyal had offered? Todd was busy at school, hunkered down in the stacks at some library, trying to finish his thesis. No wonder no one had seen him.

In the kitchen, she found Marcy dropping a wad of linguine into a pot of water. Steam curled up toward the copper pans dangling over the island that divided the kitchen from the living room. Vicky perched on a stool. A TV squatted on the counter behind the island, a newscaster's voice droning softly through the bubbling water.

"Wine?" Marcy hoisted a long-stemmed glass half-filled with deep red liquid and took a long sip. "Or are you still a teetotaler?"

Vicky nodded. She had always been a teetotaler. Ben was the one who drank; she had watched the alcohol steal his soul. When he was drunk, he turned into someone she didn't know or understand, not the man she loved. It was when he was drunk that he'd hit her.

Suddenly Vicky found herself focusing on the newscaster's voice. Another homicide. Latino or Native American male. Early twenties. She was off the stool and, in two steps, in front of the TV. She turned up the volume. "Denver police say the body was found this morning near the confluence of Cherry Creek and the

South Platte River. Exact cause of death is unknown, but the police believe it is homicide."

"My God," Vicky said, half to herself. "I've been trying to reach a young man from the reservation. He's not around. His fiancée is worried he's in trouble."

"This is the city." Marcy shrugged. "People turn up murdered from time to time. Chances are the victim isn't anybody you know."

Vicky was already around the island. She hurried down the hallway, ignoring Marcy's voice calling behind, "Dinner's about ready." In the bedroom, she found Steve Clark's card on the dresser where she'd left it. She carried it over to the phone and tapped out his number.

❮ 7 ❯

The detective sounded both glad and surprised to hear from her: the exuberant tone, the questions tumbling out. How long was she in town? When could he see her? Vicky explained she was calling about the body found in the South Platte River.

There was a slow intake of breath on the other end, a long sigh. "What do you know about it?"

"A young Arapaho, a graduate student, could be missing," Vicky said. She was beginning to feel like an overanxious mother. She had no proof Todd was actually missing. He might even have gone back to the reservation, for all she knew. Maybe he was in one of the cars on I-25 below while she'd flown overhead. And even if he had dropped out of sight for a while, what evidence connected him to the body dragged out of the South Platte River?

She realized Steve had asked if anyone had reported the student missing, that he was awaiting the answer. She said, "I don't believe so. But no one has seen him in the last few days." She told him about stopping by the apartment, about the papers and mail.

"What's his name?" The detective's voice steadied into an official rhythm.

"Todd Harris," Vicky said. Then she blurted out the rest. Twenty-four years old. About five foot ten. Black hair. Dark complexion. Handsome, a nice kid. About to

finish a master's degree in history at CU-Denver. She
was thinking this could be a mistake. Calling police attention to an Indian kid in Denver, when there were
probably a thousand rational explanations for the un-
claimed mail, the stacks of newspapers.

"Physicals could be close," the detective said. "But
we don't have an ID yet. I'll call you as soon as we get
one. You're at Marcy's, right?"

For an instant Vicky had the sense Steve might think
the missing student and the news of a homicide were
just fortunate coincidences she'd seized upon in order to
call him, a way of saving face. Hurriedly she said, "I can
identify the body, if it is Todd."

A clanking noise sounded over the line, as if the detective had just set something down on a hard surface—
a coffee mug perhaps. "You don't want to do that,
Vicky."

"I've known Todd all his life," she persisted. He was
the same age as her own son, Lucas.

"You don't understand." A stern note came into the
detective's voice. "The body was floating in the river at
least twenty-four hours before it got hung up on rocks
and bushes near Confluence Park. And there's something else."

Instinctively Vicky flinched, as if to ward off some
unseen blow. She waited.

"There's no good way to say this," the detective
began. "Looks like he was beaten to death, Vicky. The
face isn't what you're gonna want to see every time you
close your eyes the rest of your life. We'll have a positive ID by tomorrow."

Vicky pressed the receiver hard against her ear,
silently cursing whatever it was that pushed her forward. She could have a relaxing dinner, a long heart-to-
heart with an old friend, and a good night's sleep.
Tomorrow she would know whether it was Todd who
had washed up in the South Platte River or some other

poor kid. Except she knew there would be no eating or sleeping, no respite from the anxiety fluttering inside her. She said, "I want to know tonight."

A soft shush came over the line, as if the detective had taken a pull from a mug of hot coffee. "I was just about to leave the station."

"I'll come right away," she said.

Steve was waiting outside the front entrance to the Denver Coroner's Office, a five-story brick building across from the Denver Health Medical Center in an old, dust-strewn part of the city wrapped in the roar of traffic. Vicky had made the drive in twenty minutes, after leaving Marcy in the kitchen with a platter of linguine swimming in some kind of green sauce, saying she would explain later. Marcy had handed her a house key, which Vicky dropped into her handbag as she slammed out the front door.

A hot breeze plucked at her T-shirt, and the sidewalk burned through the soles of her sandals. Steve came to meet her, hands in the pockets of his tan slacks, the fronts of his blue blazer pulled back. She would have known him anywhere—the squared shoulders and sandy hair—lighter now, about to be invaded by gray—the dark eyes focused and intent.

"You look great, Vicky," he said, his eyes traveling over her.

"I appreciate this, Steve," she said.

He moved closer and took his hands from his pockets. He let them dangle at his sides, as if he had considered putting his arms around her but had thought better of it. She extended her hand. His grasp felt warm and reassuring. "You sure you want to do this?" he asked.

"Let's just get it over with."

Steve stepped aside, ushering her to the glass outer door that gave onto an enclosed entry. She waited as he pressed the button on the intercom in the outside wall.

Suddenly the inner door swung open, and a young woman in a gray pants suit stepped across the entry and opened the glass door. They followed her into an L-shaped waiting room, slabs of beige tile on the floor, and two rows of metal, straight-backed chairs against the green walls. Like a million waiting rooms, arranged for people who had nothing, really, to wait for. The air-conditioning hummed from a metal vent next to the ceiling, belching a stream of cold air that smelled of floor wax and antiseptic. Vicky shivered involuntarily.

"Meet Priscilla DeAngelo, the coroner's investigator," Steve said, taking Vicky's arm and turning her toward the pants-suited woman with short, brown hair and eyebrows penciled into a look of efficiency. Then: "This is Vicky Holden. She might know the homicide we brought in this morning."

Vicky shook the woman's hand and told her she appreciated the opportunity to view the body.

"Not a problem." The investigator gave a quick shrug, as if to say it was a problem—a huge inconvenience to stay late because some woman had a hunch she knew the victim in the latest homicide in the news. But once in a while the hunches, the out-of-the-blue calls, paid off, which was why she had agreed.

Flinging open an inside door, the investigator led the way down a corridor, past a series of closed doors before stopping abruptly and pushing one open. They followed her into a small room, with heavy drapes along the wall on the left, a small sofa on the right. There was a faint chemical odor, like air freshener.

"You sure, Vicky?" Steve asked, placing an arm lightly around her shoulders. Glancing up, she saw the worry behind the focused gaze, the hint of vulnerability that had made her trust him, had ensured they would become friends that day thirteen years ago when she had bumped into him on the steps of the North Classroom building and dropped her books and papers. He had scooped them up, apologizing all the while, when she was the one at fault.

She nodded, and he guided her toward the draped wall as the investigator yanked on a cord. Slowly the drapes parted against a wide window. On the other side, a figure bundled in white sheets lay on a gurney. Only the face was visible.

Vicky gasped. Her vision was filled with the dark face, the mashed cheek, the eye lost in a lump of flesh, the bulge above one ear. With all the outrage, she recognized Todd Harris.

She spun around, past Steve and the investigator, and ran out the door and down the corridor toward a door with the small sign: WOMEN. She barely made it to the row of white enamel sinks before the retching began, shuddering and violent, as if her insides had erupted. Nothing came. She hadn't eaten since breakfast, a fact for which she was grateful. After a moment she turned on the cold water, splashing it over her face. Anger gripped her shoulders and tightened the muscles in her chest, like some force of memory passed to her by the ancestors. Another of the *Hinono eino* slaughtered. Another broken body of a warrior. And for what reason? When would the slaughter stop?

She dipped her face into the water cupped in her hands, allowing the cool wetness to run along her neck and down the front of her T-shirt. Finally she pulled some paper towels out of the holder and began blotting her face. Her hair was wet; a clump had worked loose from the barrette and fallen over her cheek. She pushed it back, surprised at the face that peered at her from the mirror, at the horror in the eyes.

"I've got to ask you a few questions," Steve said as she stepped back into the corridor. He was leaning against the opposite wall, hands stuffed into the pockets of his slacks.

Vicky held on to the edge of the restroom door—

solid and certain in her hand. In an instant Steve was at her side, leading her past the viewing room—the door closed now—and into a larger room with a conference table in the center. The investigator was already seated on the far side. Steve pulled out a chair and waited until Vicky sat down before claiming the place beside her, saying something about it never being easy the first time. She caught the note of sympathy in his voice.

"I've seen death before," she said, her own voice trembling with anger.

Producing a small spiral notebook and pen from inside his blazer, the detective asked, "Who is he?"

"Todd Harris," Vicky said, then repeated what she'd told him earlier on the phone, adding Todd's address and the fact that he was a graduate student at CU-Denver. The detective's pen looped across the page, making a scratchy noise. She told him Todd's grandparents lived in Denver.

Steve stopped writing. "They'll have to identify the body."

Rifling through her bag, Vicky found the little pad with Annemarie's scribblings. She slid it along the table. "They're old people," she said.

"We'll send a car." Steve nodded toward the investigator who lifted herself out of the chair and sidled around the table toward the corridor.

"There's something you should know." He turned sideways toward Vicky after the investigator was gone. "This has all the markings of a drug murder."

"What!" Vicky pushed her chair back and jumped to her feet. She started pacing around the end of the table, down the other side, and back—a full circuit. "You're wrong, Steve," she said, retracing her steps. "Not Todd." She stopped, placed both hands on the table, and leaned toward the man who sat quietly watching her. "You don't know him. He was thirteen when his parents were killed in an automobile accident.

His brother was only eight. They were shifted back and forth among relatives—a couple of years in Denver with the grandparents, back to the reservation with other relatives. That's how they grew up. The only thing Todd wanted was to be a good brother. Everything he did was to show his little brother how to do it. That's why he worked hard and went to college. Now you're saying a kid like Todd Harris used drugs? Is that what he wanted to teach his brother?"

The detective placed one elbow on the edge of the table and rubbed his hand along his chin. "I'm sorry, Vicky," he said. "It's more than a guess."

The room was quiet except for the gurgling of a pipe somewhere, the snap of a shut door. "What do you mean?"

"There was heroin wrapped in dollar bills in his pockets. Either he'd just bought, or he was getting ready to sell. He had a pager on his belt."

Vicky balled her hands into fists, knuckles blanching white, and stared at the man across from her. "This isn't some poor Indian kid who came to the big city and got lost," she said. "This is Todd Harris. There has to be some other explanation."

❮ 8 ❯

It was dark when Father John wheeled the Toyota into the campus of Regis University, which sat on a bluff surrounded by the tree-lined streets of North Denver. The Rocky Mountains rose a few miles to the west, white peaks edged in moonlight. The air was heavy, glazed with shadows under a sky shading into violets and purples. Circles of light glowed from the street lamps scattered across the campus. The curving streets followed the lanes carved out for wagons a century ago, when the Jesuits had started a school in a frontier town of log cabins and two-room shanties housing illiterate gold seekers with wild, preposterous get-rich-quick dreams.

On his left stood the oldest building on campus, a massive red-stone structure, haughty and imperturbable, dominating the modern classroom buildings and dormitories. A slow curve right, and he was in the parking lot behind another building—the modern three-story Jesuit residence.

He climbed out of the Toyota and stamped his long legs against the asphalt, trying to work out the knots in his muscles. He'd driven five hundred miles across the endless stretches of Wyoming plains with the windows rolled halfway down to take the edge off the heat and *Rigoletto* blaring around him. He'd seen only a few more semis, some pickups, and several herds of antelope until he'd looped past Cheyenne and started south toward Denver, traffic, houses, and shopping malls accumulating with the miles.

Exiting the highway, he'd followed the side streets to Regis, a route he always took when the provincial called the Jesuit superiors in the region to a meeting. Except he hadn't been summoned to this week's meetings. He had summoned himself.

He grabbed the overnight bag from the far side of the seat and slammed the door—a sharp thwack that set a dog barking somewhere nearby. As he strode along the sidewalk that flanked the building, he felt oddly confident, even though the provincial's emissary had turned thumbs down on the museum. Father William Rutherford was a reasonable man. A Jesuit trademark—reasonableness.

He let his finger rest on the doorbell at the front entrance. From inside came a muffled buzz, followed by a slow shuffle of footsteps. The door inched open. An old man with cropped, graying hair, twinkling eyes, and a sardonic grin on his Irish face craned forward, peering through the opening. It was Timothy Butler, one of the last of the Jesuit brothers, the jacks-of-all-trades who looked after the thousands of details that kept everything repaired and running smoothly. How many times Father John had wished the Society of Jesus could spare a brother for St. Francis Mission.

"Ah, Father O'Malley. You're looking the bloom of health." Timothy Butler stepped backward, a jerky movement, pushing the door behind him. "Is it you'll be gracing us with your presence awhile?"

"How are you, Timothy?" Father John asked, stepping inside. A soft amber light from the glass ceiling overhead flooded the small entry: the dark, tiled floor, the wooden bench flanked by two doors on the right wall, the staircase on the opposite wall. Quiet seeped through the residence.

"Is it the provincial you're wanting to see?" A grin broke across the brother's face. "We may be graced with yourself for some time, Father."

Father John stifled a groan. He'd promised Geoff he'd be back for the weekend in time for his assistant to spend a couple days, at least, backpacking in the Wind River Mountains. His assistant needed some time off, he knew. He'd been working alone for a month. It wasn't easy, running the mission alone.

Nodding toward the stairway, Brother Timothy said, "You'll be wanting the guest room on the second floor." He reached over and attempted to take the overnight bag Father John held in his hand.

"Save your knees for the races ahead, Timothy," Father John said. He started up the stairs, then stopped, one hand on the wood railing polished glass smooth, and looked back at the old man caught in the circle of amber light. "Is the provincial in?"

Brother Timothy's eyebrows knitted together in a long, thin line. "Well, now, I wouldn't know, Father. His suite is on the third floor. Should I find the man for you?"

"I'll find him." Father John gave a quick wave. He hurried up the stairs and strode down the corridor on the left. Rows of closed doors marched along both sides, and from somewhere came a loud guffaw and the electronic noise of a TV. He let himself into the guest room. A thread of light spilled past the drapes at the window on the opposite wall. He found the light switch next to the door and snapped it on. A dim yellowish light glowed over a desk, bare except for a phone, a chair shoved into the well, a cotlike bed—white pillow, brown blanket stretched taut: a monk's cell.

Just as he dropped his overnight bag on the bed, the telephone jangled, an impertinent sound in the quiet. He reached toward the desk and picked up the receiver, hardly believing his luck. Brother Timothy must have called the provincial after all, and the provincial was in.

"This Father O'Malley?" A man's voice, infused with the politeness of a Native American.

"Yes." He stretched the cord across the narrow space and perched on the edge of the bed, his muscles tensing with apprehension. Something must have happened on the reservation.

"This here's Petey Wilkins. Just come from over at old man Doyal's house. You know him, don't ya? Doyal Harris?"

Father John shifted his thoughts. The call was from Denver and had something to do with Todd Harris's grandparents, the elderly Arapaho couple he always tried to see when he was in town. Good people. He admired them. After their own son and his wife had died in an automobile accident, Doyal and Mary had helped to raise Todd and his brother.

"Are they okay?" Father John braced himself for the reply.

"Wouldn't say so, Father. Them victim's assistance people just took 'em over to the morgue. Looks like maybe that grandson of theirs, Todd Harris—you know him, don't you?—well, looks like he might be dead."

Father John was on his feet. "Dead! What are you talking about?" The words burst forth like a gust of steam.

After a long silence, the voice said, "Looks like Todd might be the kid police fished outta of the river today. I seen it on TV. Doyal seen it, too, and he said it give him a real bad feeling."

It took a moment for the information to work its way into Father John's mind, past the barriers he consciously tried to erect. Todd Harris was a graduate student at CU-Denver. He would be the director of the museum Father John had come to Denver to get approved. And Todd had been at the mission last Saturday. He couldn't be dead. "What happened?" he managed.

"Don't know for sure, Father. 'Cept the story I hear is it might be homicide, and some lawyer lady from the reservation went to the morgue and said it was Todd. So Doyal and Mary had to go give a positive family ID."

Here was another piece of information Father John struggled to locate in the realignment of reality: Vicky Holden was in Denver. He'd spent the last month in Boston praying for the strength to keep his vows and keep her out of his mind. And now she was here. And she had identified Todd! Dear God, he prayed. Let it not be Todd. Let there be some mistake.

The voice droned on: something about Doyal asking him to call Father O'Malley so the priest could give the bad news to the rest of Todd's family on the reservation. But when he'd phoned up St. Francis Mission, he'd gotten some other priest who said Father O'Malley was at Regis. So he'd called up here.

Father John thanked the man and put down the phone. He felt as if he'd just heard a story about someone he didn't know—a character in some novel where the plot takes a strange and terrible twist. How could the story have anything to do with the kid who used to hang around his office after baseball practice and pester him about the past—the long-ago? What was it like before the gold seekers came to the plains? How come they took the land from the Indians? Wasn't it their land?

He'd advised Todd to study history. There was no other way to satisfy the hunger for the past, the longing to sort out what had happened, as if sorting out the past might explain the present. Father John knew the hunger. He was about Todd's age when it had begun gnawing at him. It had shaped his career. He'd spent ten years teaching American history in Jesuit prep schools back East. He'd been working on his doctorate, aiming to-

ward a position at a Jesuit university, when the hunger
had given way to the terrible, implacable thirst that had
changed his life and sent him to St. Francis Mission.

There had been so many compensations. The people, the stories of the elders, and the spring day Todd
Harris had slammed through the office door, waving a
brown envelope and shouting, "I'm in! I'm in!" The
next fall he'd gone off to the University of Wyoming
and, four years later he'd started working on his master's in Denver. Now Todd Harris was dead.

The phone screeched, jarring him out of the memories. Brother Timothy. It seemed the provincial had an
engagement this evening and wasn't aware of an appointment with Father O'Malley. "You had an appointment, did you not, Father?"

He did not. How unimportant it seemed: the long
drive to Denver, the meeting with the provincial, the
pleading and cajoling and reasoning that would take
place. How unimportant, now that Todd Harris was
dead. He thanked the brother and hung up.

Vicky drove through Denver in the gathering darkness, struggling to hold back the tears of anger and grief
welling inside her like thunderclouds building over the
mountains. Once the tears came, she knew, there would
be a flood. She kept the front windows rolled down, allowing the coolness of the summer evening and the
noise of the city to wash over her, as if they might oblit-
erate the picture she had snapped at the morgue and
would carry forever in her mind.

She'd waited with Steve until Doyal and Mary Harris had arrived. Then she'd waited out front in the darkness of the evening while they viewed the body. Several
cars and trucks had streamed into the parking lot across
the street. The moccasin telegraph was alive and well in
the city, Vicky had thought as she watched the men and

women tumble out of the vehicles and gather in shadowy groups, welded together in shock and grief. Finally Doyal and Mary had emerged, and she'd offered to drive them home, but a young man—a spiritual grandson, perhaps—had bounded across the street and ushered the old couple toward a white sedan, the metal grille gleaming under the streetlight.

Now headlights danced toward her, bursting across the asphalt median on I-25. Her mind kept coming back to what Steve had said. Another drug murder. Somebody sells. Somebody buys. Somebody ends up dead. Fighting back tears, Vicky gripped the steering wheel and pointed the Taurus toward the taillights ahead. Todd Harris was not a drug dealer. But whoever had killed him wanted the police to believe otherwise. The killer had planted the drugs and pager on Todd's body.

Why couldn't Steve see that? He'd investigated dozens of homicides. "You get a feeling for what happened," he'd once told her. "The minute you see the body, it's like a film starts rolling, and you see it all just as it took place, and nine times out of ten you're right."

"Nine times out of ten." The sound of her own voice surprised her. What if Steve was right this time? What if she was the one clinging to an idea, fixed and immutable in her mind, that Todd Harris was what he had always seemed? People changed. Maybe she was the one who needed to change, needed to stop being so stubborn.

Suddenly she realized by the green-and-white signs shining overhead that she had missed her exit. She took the next off-ramp, crossed the highway, and entered it again, this time heading north. At Alameda, she exited west onto the narrow, traffic-clogged street lined with warehouses and going-out-of-business furniture stores and empty squares where neighborhood groceries had once stood. She turned into a neighborhood of white frame houses with old trucks at the curbs and people sitting on the sagging front porches—the Indian neighborhood of Denver.

She parked in front of the house where Mary and Doyal lived—a small, white bungalow—and waited a moment, taking some deep breaths, trying to get control. She'd come to pay respects to the old couple, to console them; she didn't want to appear at the door and collapse into their arms in tears.

Finally she gathered her soft leather handbag and got out of the car just as a pickup backed into the space across the street. Headlights flashed over her, fixing her to the asphalt. It was a red Toyota, like the one John O'Malley drove. She caught her breath as the driver swung out—the long legs, the sure, athletic way he walked toward her. She knew him in the darkness.

"What are you doing here?" she asked as he reached her. Only this morning she had learned he was coming back to St. Francis, when for weeks she'd believed he had left for good, that she would never see him again. Now he was here, as if she had conjured him up out of her own pain, her own need.

He said, "I drove down today. I just heard about Todd." He exhaled a long breath before adding softly, "I'm sorry, Vicky."

It was then the tears came, hot and biting on her cheeks, salty in her mouth: tears for the young man on the gurney at the morgue, for the *Hinono eino* who were still losing the warriors—the best, the very best. She felt John O'Malley's arms around her, his breath in her hair, the comfort of his heart beating close to hers.

After a moment he released her. She dug through her handbag for a wad of tissues and wiped up the aftermath of the flood. "I didn't want to do that," she heard herself explaining. "I wanted to be strong for Mary and Doyal."

"I know," he said softly, taking her arm. "Come on. We'll go in together."

❖ 9 ❖

ushed voices floated outside as Vicky and Father
John walked up the sidewalk to the porch that ran
along the old couple's house. Father John rapped on
the thin frame of the screen door. The inner door stood
ajar, and Vicky saw Mary Harris—she must be eighty
now—totter around a group of men. She squinted past
the screen. "Father John and Vicky? That you?"

The door swung open, and they stepped into the
small room thick with the odor of fresh coffee and stale
cigarette smoke. The old woman gave Vicky a quick
hug, as if she'd been expecting her. It was the tall, redheaded priest in blue jeans and plaid shirt setting his
cowboy hat on the small table by the door that she
hadn't expected. "How'd you get here?" she asked,
thrusting both hands into his.

As he began explaining, Vicky glanced about. She
didn't recognize any of the men huddled together, eyes
turned toward the newcomers: a white priest, an Indian
woman. Nor did she recognize the young women moving past the door that opened onto the kitchen, yet not
long ago she had been like them—an urban Indian come
to the city from the wide spaces of a reservation, looking for what? An education, a job, a new life?

Across the room, Doyal Harris was maneuvering
himself out of a recliner wedged into the corner. One of
the men nearby took the old man's arm and pulled him

forward. He was even older than his wife, Vicky guessed, by the gnarled knuckles and wrists, the paper-thin, yellowish skin. He shuffled across the room, eyes on Father John. "Good to see you, Father."

"I'm so sorry, Grandfather," Father John said, shaking his hand. "Todd was a fine young man, a good man."

Vicky saw the tears welling in the old man's eyes, the effort of control in the succession of swallows, the way he squared his shoulders. "*Ho' hou',*" he said softly. There was a mixture of appreciation and gratitude in his voice: this priest understood the Arapaho Way. Only a few—the generous, the kind—could be called good.

Eyes still on Father John, the old man went on: "When that coroner lady called, I said, it's my brother, ain't it? 'Cause he's an old man. His heart's gonna give out on him one of these days. I keep tellin' him, 'You gotta take care of yourself,' but he's so gol-darned busy takin' care of that sickly wife of his."

He stopped, as if he'd found himself on the wrong track and had to devise another route. "Then I thought it's her. That old woman my brother married up with went and died. But the coroner lady says it looks like it might be Todd, and they was gonna send a car for us to come down and identify him." Doyal shook his head, a violent gesture. "I never thought it was gonna be about Todd."

Vicky heard the gasp from the old woman beside her, as if Mary was hearing the news for the first time. She slipped an arm around the woman's thin waist, and the group of men parted to make way as Vicky led her back to the sofa. Settling into the cushions between two other grandmothers, the old woman clasped her hands in front of her chest, as if she were praying or bracing for other blows.

Out of the corner of her eye, Vicky saw Father John ease Doyal back into the recliner. Another moment and

Father John was at her side, just as one of the men in the center of the room broke from the small group and stepped toward them. He was Arapaho, Vicky realized, middle-aged, with short, gray-flecked hair and narrow black eyes.

"I seen it on TV," he said to Father John. "I said to the wife, 'Might be some poor Indian kid caught up with a bunch of no-goods. Sometimes them kids come off the rez and don't have no city sense." His gaze trailed back to the group, as if for confirmation. "No city sense. Get lost here. Take up with the wrong people. Start thinkin' they're gonna get rich, like that's what matters."

"I never thought it was gonna be Todd in that river." This from a younger man who joined them. Probably not much older than Todd, with black hair pulled back into a ponytail. "Todd was a good guy," he said. "Goin' to school. Gonna make something of himself. Gonna help the people. Never hung around with no rough guys."

There was the clap of a back door slamming, a growing chorus of voices in the kitchen. A young woman with black braids stepped through the door and walked over, sidling next to the man in the ponytail. She waited quietly as the man went on talking about how Todd was a good kid, how the old people depended upon him. "Why'd anybody want to murder him?" the man asked.

Father John said, "We should have some answers as soon as the police finish their investigation."

A hopeful notion, Vicky thought. How much time would the police spend on a botched drug deal? A dead Indian?

The young woman who had been standing there suddenly backed away and disappeared into the kitchen. Vicky wished she had added her own comments to the halting search for answers, the hopeful suggestions. Had she spoken, perhaps the woman wouldn't have left, wouldn't have felt she had nothing to contribute. Serious matters were men's business. An image of herself flashed in front of Vicky: she was leaning past the kitchen doorway, straining to overhear what Ben and the other men were saying. The calves lost in the storm, the downturn of the beef market—serious matters that affected her and the kids. Yet she had stayed in the kitchen and waited until Ben called for more coffee, some of those chips, and that hot chili sauce.

Vicky pushed away the memory. "The police will want to speak with you," she said to the man in the ponytail. "They'll want the names of Todd's friends."

"Todd never brought any friends around," he said. Then: " 'Cept for that girl."

Vicky drew in a sharp breath. There *was* a girl. She was right after all. Which meant his murder came down to something simple and stupid—a mugging. She could accept a mugging. She would never accept a drug deal.

"What's the girl's name?" Father John asked. His tone registered the same level of determination she was feeling. No matter what the police said, she and John O'Malley would want to know why a kid like Todd had ended up in the rocks and weeds of the South Platte River.

"Julie somebody," the man in the ponytail said. "Lakota. Todd said she was related to the Wolf people up on the Rosebud."

The screen door opened again and a couple stepped inside, the woman carrying a pajama-clad baby. Behind them came several men. The newcomers moved wordlessly toward the old people and grasped their hands, first Doyal's, then Mary's. From outside came the sound of doors slamming, boots scuffing the sidewalk. Headlights blinked through the curtains at the front window.

Vicky caught Father John's eyes. There was weari-

ness there, a gathering of grief. Without saying anything, they stepped over to the old people and paid their
condolences again. Then they made their way through
the crowded room and out the door.

A shiver rippled over Vicky's shoulders as they
walked down the sidewalk, and she wondered if it was
the evening air or the cold sense of death inside her. She
felt slightly sick, and she realized she hadn't eaten all
day.

"I know a place where we could get a bite," she said,
glancing up at the man beside her.

"I'll follow you," John O'Malley said.

◀ 10 ▶

They settled into a booth with Naugahyde seats cracked from use. Headlights on Sheridan Boulevard streamed into the darkness beyond the plate-glass window. From the kitchen came the noise of dishes and pans clanking together, and every few moments a waitress burst through the heavy swinging doors, a loaded tray hoisted high overhead. Other late diners occupied booths and tables scattered across the restaurant. A couple of men straddled stools at the counter, hunched over plates heaped with french fries and hamburgers.

Vicky turned her attention to the man across from her, scarcely believing he was here. The familiar face: red hair with flecks of gray at the temples; blue eyes filled with light; tiny laugh lines at the corners of his mouth; an almost unnoticeable cleft in his chin. He sat tall in the booth, handsome in a quiet way, a kindness about him, a comforting presence. She had tried hard over the last few weeks to put him out of her mind. How difficult it was to have him in her life as a friend, a dear friend, but only a friend.

A waitress appeared and took their orders. Hamburgers, coffee. How many times had they sat like this in some restaurant, talking about how to help somebody in trouble? A couple trying to reclaim their kids from social services. A kid who had violated probation. And the homicides they'd found themselves involved with—the tribal chairman, the drug dealer in a ditch, the cowboy who'd come home to right an old wrong. Another murder now—a young man they both believed in—and they were together again.

There was so much she wanted to ask him as she waited for the waitress to finish filling their coffee mugs. Why had he returned from Boston? How did he happen to be here at the right moment, when the people needed him, when she needed him? She was still trying to phrase the appropriate questions when he asked what had brought her here.

It startled her to realize their thoughts were following the same track. She took a sip of hot coffee before telling him how the tribe had hired her to recover the Arapaho artifacts from the Denver Museum of the West, how one of the most important objects, an Arapaho ledger book, seemed to be missing.

Father John leaned across the table toward her, eyes narrowing, she thought, into a darker shade of blue. "There must be an explanation."

"I've given the museum until Friday to come up with one," Vicky said. Then she told him the curator claimed she had never heard of the ledger book, yet she knew the exact value—$1.3 million. There was so much else she wanted to talk over with him—her desire to do a good job for the tribe, the museum's exhibit on the Sand Creek Massacre that left out any mention of Arapahos—all the thoughts that had occupied her mind this afternoon and had seemed so important before she'd learned about Todd.

Instead she said, "The police think Todd's murder had something to do with drugs."

"Drugs?" Father John clasped his hands around his coffee mug, his eyes steady on hers. "How could they think that?"

"Steve," she said, then corrected herself. "Detective Clark. An old friend." She caught the brief change of expression in John O'Malley's face as he looked away—how many men had she known in her life? "We were at CU-Denver at the same time." She hurried on, wanting to explain. "He's a good detective, I'm sure. Sharp and very dedicated."

"He's wrong about Todd," Father John said, looking back at her, a hint of anger in his voice.

She said, "They found heroin wrapped in dollar bills in his pockets. He had a pager on his belt."

"I don't care what they found," Father John said. "It could have been planted to make it look like a drug murder."

Vicky smiled. She had missed their talks, the way he always tuned in to the direction of her thoughts, sometimes before she knew where they were headed. She sipped at her coffee as the waitress delivered two plates of hamburgers and French fries, a bottle of ketchup. The moment the waitress turned away, she said, "Todd came to the reservation last weekend. He was upset about something. He wanted to see you."

Father John was shaking the ketchup over his fries. He looked up. "My assistant told me," he said. "Do you have any idea what was going on?"

"That's what I intend to find out." Vicky bit into her hamburger. It was as tasteless as cardboard, not like the food she remembered here. She tried a couple of fries that had the flavor of stale grease, and pushed the plate aside. Then she told him everything else she knew: the stuffed mailbox at Todd's apartment, his failure to see Mary and Doyal in a while—a sign of disrespect.

Father John took a bite of his own hamburger. After a moment he said, "Let your friend the detective sort it out, Vicky. He'll find Todd's friend Julie. Maybe she'll know something."

"That doesn't mean she'll tell the police," Vicky said. "But she might tell me."

Father John took a quick swallow of coffee, eyes

narrowing again. "Look, if Julie does know something about Todd's murder, it could be dangerous for you. Let the police do their job."

"But will they?"

"You said yourself your friend is a good detective."

"A dead Indian washes up on the banks of the South Platte. He looks like a drug dealer, probably dealing to other Indians. Another case of Indians killing Indians, just like the warriors killing other warriors over the best hunting grounds. Only the hunting grounds are drugs. Do the white authorities really care?"

"Of course they care," Father John pushed his own plate to one side. Clumps of greasy fries clung to the rim. "A human life is a human life. Murder is murder."

"I'd like to believe that, John. But unless the police start thinking this wasn't just another drug murder, that's how they're going to handle it. Meanwhile the killer will be busy covering his tracks. Todd's murder might never be solved."

"Look, Vicky," Father John began—the conciliatory tone he always used, she knew, when he was trying to bring her around to the most logical way of thinking. "This isn't the reservation, where you know everybody and understand how things work. Denver is a big city. If you start nosing around and asking questions, you could stumble onto whatever it was that got Todd killed. It could be dangerous."

"Don't tell me you don't want to see Todd's killer brought to justice," she said, an edge in her tone.

"You know better than that." Father John leaned closer. "I just don't want to see anything happen to you."

"Nothing's going to happen to me." Vicky shrugged, picked up the coffee mug, and took another sip, wishing she felt as confident as she hoped she sounded. "I'm going to see if I can find Todd's new girlfriend, Julie, and talk to her, that's all."

"What if Julie is involved?"

Vicky set the mug down hard on the table. This was something she hadn't considered. She closed her eyes a half second, then opened them on this new possibility. "Todd was a great kid," she began, groping for an explanation that would seem logical to the man across from her. "Why would he associate with anyone who might get involved in drugs or murder?"

Father John picked up a fork and rapped it against the table. "You're a difficult woman, Vicky."

"You happen to be a priest, John O'Malley. Your experience, I would suggest, is quite limited."

"You expect me to believe all women are as difficult as you?" He pushed the fork away and smiled at her a moment. Then he reached into the pocket of his shirt and pulled out a small pad and a ballpoint. "Where are you staying?" he asked.

"Are you going to check up on me? Warn me about getting into trouble?"

"I want to satisfy myself you're still alive," he said, the pen poised over a clear sheet of the pad. Vicky gave him Marcy's telephone number and watched him print the numbers on the page and under them, in block letters, VICKY. On another page, he jotted down other numbers. A quick tear, and he handed her the page. "Doyal and Mary asked me to hold a memorial service in Denver, so I'll be at Regis for the next few days. This is the number. Will you call me if there's anything I can do?"

Vicky brushed his hand as she took the paper. Knowing she could call him, that he would be close by, buoyed her confidence and gave her a sense of comfort. She slipped the paper inside her handbag as they slid out of the booth and strolled together to the counter. There was a moment when they argued over the check, a moment when they both tried to force a ten-dollar bill on the woman behind the cash register, another moment when they all laughed.

Outside in the parking lot, he waited as she sank behind the wheel of the Taurus. Leaning toward her, he said, "Promise me something."

She turned toward him, knowing what he was about to say, wanting to hear the words.

"Promise me you'll be careful."

By the time Vicky parked in front of Marcy's house, a cold tiredness had crept through her. It was nearly midnight, and she longed to sink into bed and abandon herself to sleep, but the light falling past the slats of the mini-blinds at the windows told her Marcy was waiting.

As she walked up the sidewalk she heard the soft staccato of drums. The door swung open, and her friend stood in the opening; the flickering light behind her cast fingers of shadows over her face and the long blue-splashed kimono she was wearing.

"You're here!" There was excitement in Marcy's voice.

Vicky walked past her into the living room, where round, thick candles winked from the glass top of the coffee table and the little tables at the ends of the sofas. Another woman, also in a kimono, sat cross-legged on a woven rug, curled over a small drum, like the drums Vicky had seen all her life at powwows and celebrations on the reservation. The woman rapped the drum with both palms—a gentle thumping noise that reverberated across the wood floors, the white walls.

"Come, come," Marcy ordered, taking Vicky's hand and pulling her toward the drummer. "This is my friend Louella Barkley," she said. "Louella has been waiting all evening to meet you."

The pounding stopped as the other woman lifted her eyes. They were blue gray, calm and watchful in a white, doughy face. Her blond hair was caught in two thick braids that hung over her bosom and folded into her lap. She reached one hand upward: squared red nails, gold rings, a row of gold bracelets jangling at her wrist.

"My pleasure," she said. There was a shrill, airy quality to her voice, as if she were blowing a whistle.

"Louella was a Cheyenne princess in her past life," Marcy said. "You must hear her story."

Vicky let herself down slowly on one of the white sofas, numb with sadness and her own tiredness. The drummer's eyes followed her.

"I feel we were friends in the buffalo days," Louella said, air cushioning the words. "When your people came to the village to trade with my people, we used to sit in front of Grandfather's lodge. My grandfather was a great chief."

"Of course," Vicky said.

Louella closed her eyes, perhaps viewing some lost world. "We played with dolls our grandmothers made for us. We were only little girls when we met, but we stayed friends through the summers. Oh, how I remember my older brother watching you. You were very beautiful." She gave a quick shrug, and her eyes flew open. "If only you had belonged to our people, we might have become sisters-in-law."

"Tell me," Vicky began, her voice thick with irritation, "did the spirits give you a vision of our past lives?"

"Oh, yes," Marcy cut in. She had settled in the sofa next to Vicky. "Louella had a dream in which she saw her entire past life. Since then she has been blessed with the ability to dwell in two realities. She has integrated the present with the past. While she's at work in her bookstore—a place of peace, Vicky; I must take you— Louella remains immersed in her other, more authentic life."

The other woman gave a brief, wan smile. "My life is finally meaningful, now that I am one with my past identity."

"I've also been crying for a dream," Marcy said. "I pray the spirits will send one so that I may increase the peace in my own life."

Louella waved one arm above the drum; the bracelets made a clanking sound. "I must warn you, it is very difficult and unnatural to maintain your inner peace in the city." She shifted her gaze to Vicky. "You are so fortunate to have the reservation, where one can exist in close harmony with the spirits."

Vicky was thinking of the three-room houses, the thin-board walls, the bare-dirt yards with white tanks standing on spindly legs and filled with propane gas that never banished the cold, the snow peppering her blanket on winter mornings when she was a kid, and the struggle—the never-ending struggle—just to live.

She said, "Perhaps you should come to the reservation."

"Yes. It would be a wonderful experience."

"You could open a bookstore, one with a coffee shop."

"You mean, move to the reservation?"

"Yes, why not? I could help you work out the legal details."

"Live there permanently? But it's so far away. In the middle of Wyoming, I believe."

"You really must consider it." Vicky got to her feet and turned toward Marcy. "And now you'll have to excuse me," she said. "I'm exhausted." She stepped around the coffee table and walked down the hallway to the bedroom.

Just as she was about to close the door, Marcy appeared. "I'm so sorry if we offended you, Vicky," she said.

Vicky gripped the edge of the door, trying to sort through her feelings. Had she been offended by Marcy and the Cheyenne princess? She didn't think so. She felt sorry at the seeming emptiness in their lives. She said,

"Is there nowhere for you to turn, nowhere to go in your own culture, Marcy, that might help you?"

Marcy jerked backward, as if she had been struck. The color drained from her face. Instantly Vicky regretted the words. But they had been sent into the world, and someday, she knew, their sting would return to her.

"I'm sorry," she whispered as her friend turned and started down the hallway. She watched Marcy retreat into the living room, then closed the bedroom door, shutting out the drums—a hard thump, thump, thump.

◆ 11 ◆

Vicky awakened into a vacant quiet, the sun drifting lazily past the white curtains; she had slept the sleep of exhaustion. Marcy was nowhere about, but she had left a pot of hot coffee and a plate of muffins on the kitchen counter. After showering and slipping into the other attorney dress she'd brought— a soft linen the color of sage—Vicky ate one of the muffins and sipped a cup of coffee in the early-morning coolness on the back patio, grateful for the solitude and the chance to collect her thoughts. She hadn't wanted to call Annemarie in the middle of the night to tell her about Todd. She would call the girl this morning. Although what difference could it make when Annemarie got the news? It would still be the end of plans and hopes, of her life as she had believed it would unfold, and a horrible thrust into a new and unexpected life where, somehow, Annemarie would have to find her way.

Vicky carried the half-empty coffee cup into the bedroom. Rummaging through her purse, she found the pad on which Annemarie had written down her own number under the others. *Call me as soon as you find him*, she had said. Even then, Vicky had detected more fear than hope in the girl's tone.

Vicky dialed the number. The girl picked up immediately, as if she'd been waiting by the phone. Her voice sounded weak and trembling. "Annemarie, I'm afraid I have some very bad news," Vicky began.

"I know," the girl said.

Vicky drew in a long breath. The moccasin telegraph had been busy all night. She explained that she had gone to the morgue, that Todd's grandparents had also gone there—as if it might comfort the girl to know Todd had not been completely alone—and that Father O'Malley would be saying a memorial mass in Denver. As she talked she had the feeling Annemarie already knew everything; the moccasin telegraph was efficient and thorough.

But there was one detail the girl didn't know, Vicky realized the moment she mentioned that the police mistakenly thought Todd was involved with drugs.

"Drugs!" The word came over the line like a wail. "How can they think that?"

"They're wrong," Vicky said, fumbling in her purse for Steve Clark's card. "Look, Annemarie"—she hurried on—"I want you to call the homicide detective and tell him everything you know about Todd." She read off Steve's number.

"I loved Todd," Annemarie said. "The detective might not believe me."

That was possible. "It's important you talk to him anyway," Vicky said.

It was mid-morning when Vicky wheeled into the last available space in a lot across from the Auraria campus, where groups of students toting backpacks hurried along the sidewalks toward the red-brick buildings of CU-Denver. On the west, the city slanted up several miles into the foothills. Beyond was the blue-purple mass of the Rocky Mountains, the peaks and ridges bathed in sunlight.

She hurried past the rows of parked vehicles, bumpers glinting metal hot in the sun, trying to imagine what it must have been like without high-rises and asphalt, without the incessant throb of automobiles and trucks. The land was open in the Old Time, a vast expanse of gentle knolls that rolled toward the horizon. Streams and creeks, hardly wide or deep enough to qualify as rivers, wound out of the mountains and across the plains, like silver paint spilled over a giant canvas. Not far from the corner of Speer Boulevard and Larimer Street, where she waited for the "Walk" light, the village of her people had stood at the confluence of the South Platte River and Cherry Creek, where Todd's body had been found.

Shaking off the sense of accumulating losses, Vicky hurried across the boulevard, past lanes of traffic impatient to grind forward. As she joined the flow of students heading toward the North Classroom building, memories crashed over her. How nervous she had been when she'd walked this pathway the first time—what, thirteen years ago? At the entrance, she stopped to ask a student for directions to the history department, then rode the elevator to the third floor, jammed into the small space with students, briefcases, and books, the smells of perspiration and aftershave.

She found the office in the northeast corner: a long room not much wider than the corridor, with windows on the far wall that framed a view of downtown. A doorway on the right gave onto a small mailroom. Just inside, a rumpled gray-haired woman in a gray blazer and dark, pleated skirt was rummaging through one of the cubicles that lined the wall.

Vicky crossed to the desk in front of the window. A middle-aged woman with a cap of curly black hair sat hunched in front of a monitor, tapping out a furious rhythm on the keyboard.

"Yes?" The woman did not look up.

"I'm here about one of your students," Vicky said.

Slowly the secretary tilted her chin up and lifted her eyebrows, as if she'd expected a student with the usual type of problem and now realized she had to deal with someone else. Her fingers remained perched in midair above the keyboard.

Vicky told the woman her name, that she was a friend of Todd Harris's family.

"What is it you want?" the secretary asked, a flat, noncommittal tone. It was obvious she had seen the article about Todd's murder in this morning's *Rocky Mountain News*, Vicky thought.

She said, "I'd like to speak to Todd's adviser."

"And who did you say you are?"

"A friend of the family." The woman was stalling, trying to slot her into the appropriate category: trustworthy, untrustworthy.

"One moment." The secretary set both hands on the arms of her swivel chair and leveled herself upright. Stepping quickly around the desk, she disappeared behind a door on the right with block letters on the pebbly glass: DEPARTMENT CHAIR.

There was the muffled sound of voices: the secretary's and a man's. Suddenly the man's voice shifted into a tone of authority. Growing more and more impatient, Vicky kept her eyes on the door until finally the secretary reappeared.

"I'm terribly sorry," she said, pulling the door shut behind her. "We are unable to give you any information."

"Perhaps I could speak to the department chairman," Vicky said.

"I'm afraid he's busy." The woman hurried around the desk and sank back into her chair.

Vicky turned and rapped quickly on the door before pushing it open.

"Hey, wait a minute!" the secretary shouted as Vicky stepped into a room twice the size of the outer office. She had surprised herself. How had she come to be so rude? Her grandmother would be ashamed; this was not the Arapaho Way. Was this what she had learned in the white world?

An angular man in a white, short-sleeved shirt with a pen poking from the pocket rose from behind a desk, as if it were a matter of great effort, and fixed her with a look of irritation. His eyes were large behind thick, wire-rim glasses.

"I'm sorry to bother you," Vicky said quickly, "but it's important that I locate someone who can tell me about Todd Harris."

"Yes, my secretary informed me." There was a slight clearing of the throat, a searching for words. "It's unfortunate about the student's"—another clearing of the throat—"accident."

Vicky swallowed back an instant dislike for this department chairman incapable of facing the true story— that Todd Harris had been murdered. "I'm a friend of the family," she said. "I'm also an attorney." She didn't like dropping that piece of information unless the situation called for it. She was here as a friend, not in her professional capacity. The chairman rocked back on his heels, as if to realign his focus, and she saw her professional capacity had gotten his attention.

"My secretary didn't mention—"

Vicky said, "I would like to speak with Todd's adviser."

The chairman cleared his throat again, a loud rumble. "Ms. Holden, please believe me, I would like to accommodate you. However, the police are conducting an investigation about this"—another pause—"unfortunate occurrence. Detective Clark was here earlier this morning. He instructed us not to discuss the student."

Vicky felt a stab of doubt. Steve must have been here when the doors opened. Maybe she'd misjudged him, thinking he wouldn't investigate Todd's murder with the same determination he brought to every other investigation. She said, "Detective Clark was probably referring to the media. I'm not from the media."

"Ah, yes." The man dipped his head, peering at her over the rim of his glasses. "I suppose the family is planning to sue the university for wrongful death. Of course, they would have no grounds whatsoever."

"I hardly think they would do that," Vicky said. "But we would like to know how Todd spent his last days. What was he working on? Who were his associates?" A reasonable story, she thought, hoping the chairman wouldn't suspect she was determined to find out what had happened to the young man.

She saw by the slow smile crossing the chairman's face that her motives were as transparent as glass. "Isn't that the job of the police, Ms. Holden?"

"Yes, of course," she said hurriedly. "My speaking to Todd's adviser would not interfere with the police investigation."

"Well, I'm afraid you'll have to convince Detective Clark." He picked up a folder and slapped it down on the desk. "If the detective gives permission, I suppose we can provide you with the adviser's name. Until then, I must cooperate with the police."

"I'll be back." Vicky pivoted toward the door. She retraced her steps through the outer office and into the corridor, ignoring the secretary behind the desk, the glare in her eyes.

She could be in Steve's office in ten minutes, Vicky was thinking. But what would she tell him? That she intended to conduct her own investigation? That she didn't trust him? She stopped at a window that overlooked the manicured lawns of the campus. A scattering of students walked along the path below. There might be another way to get the information she wanted.

Stepping across the corridor, she turned into the stairwell, a chasm of whitewashed cinderblock walls that rang with the voices of students, the clump of boots on the metal stairs. On the second floor, she turned left and strode down the corridor past a succession of closed doors. She stopped at the one with a small sign in black letters: INDIAN SERVICES. The office was where she had remembered.

Turning the knob, she let herself into a large room with an expanse of windows that framed the top branches of elm trees and the faint, snowy outline of Pike's Peak in the distance. Several easy chairs and desks were scattered about. A group of students with black hair and the features of various tribes sat cross-legged in a circle on the gray carpet, books and papers arranged before them. A girl with black hair hooked behind her ears and a thin, narrow face looked up, then slowly unfolded herself and got to her feet. She came forward, a shy, watchful look about her.

"This looks comfortable," Vicky began, opening the dance of politeness: the indirect revealing of herself, the appeal for trust. "Much nicer than when I was a student here."

The girl pushed back a strand of hair that had fallen forward. She glanced over her shoulder, as if to gauge the reactions of the others. "Are you the police?" she asked, looking back.

Vicky was stunned. How could they think she was the police? She was one of them. She blurted, "I'm a friend of Todd Harris's. I'm Arapaho."

A look of recognition came into the girl's face, as if she knew other Arapahos. They were of good heart. "Tisha Runner," she said. "I'm Ojibway."

"Did you know Todd?" Vicky glanced from the girl to the students on the floor behind her. They shook their heads in unison, looked away, bent closer to the papers. The girl shrugged. "I didn't really know him," she said. "Saw him around campus is all."

She knew him, Vicky thought. Why wouldn't she talk to her? What was she afraid of? That an Arapaho

had been murdered? That the same thing might happen
to her? Or was it simply that Steve Clark had already
been here, too, and had warned the students not to say
anything.

"How about a girl named Julie?" Vicky persisted.
"A Lakota."

"Lakota?" The young woman repeated. Another
glance at the others, as if one might be Lakota and
should take the question.

Suddenly a young man with long black hair flowing
over thick shoulders jackknifed to his feet. He hooked
both thumbs into the pockets of his blue jeans and
stared at her, a cold, defiant look in his eyes. "No Lakotas here named Julie," he said.

"Are you Lakota?" Vicky asked. A guess, judging by
the way he had hurtled to some imagined line of de-
fense, like a warrior riding out to meet the enemy.

He gave a brief nod and rocked back a little, eyes on
her.

Vicky dug into her handbag and pulled out a ballpoint and the leather case that held her business cards.
She jotted Marcy's number on the back of a card and
handed it to the girl. "I'd like to talk to Julie," she said.

"How am I gonna find some Lakota named Julie?"
The girl attempted to hand the card back.

"I'm a friend." Vicky kept her voice low, confidential. "You can trust me. Julie may know something that
would help find Todd's killer." She was thinking Julie
might help convince Steve Clark that Todd wasn't on
drugs.

Tisha Runner slid the card into her pocket, a slow
movement, almost imperceptible. Vicky wondered if the
others had even noticed. She smiled at the girl, then let
herself out the door.

As she rounded the corner near the stairwell Vicky
nearly bumped into the rumpled-looking, gray-haired
woman who had picked up her mail in the history de-

partment office a few minutes earlier. Still clutching a small stack of envelopes, the woman stepped forward. "Ms. Holden?" The voice was tentative. "I'm Professor Mary Ellen Pearson. I was hoping you would stop at Indian Services and that I would catch you."

❮ 12 ❯

Mary Ellen Pearson's office was a windowless cubicle crammed with bookcases, a couple of chairs, a desk piled with books, papers, and folders. She closed the door after Vicky. The air turned heavy and stuffy, suffused with odors of dried paper and stale coffee and a chemical like fingernail polish.

"He didn't tell you anything, did he?" the professor said. For an instant Vicky thought she was referring to the Lakota, then decided it was the history chairman.

"I knew he wouldn't," the professor went on. "I don't care what the police say. Todd's family has the right to know what happened. I saw it all, you know." She crossed the office and sank into a chair pulled back from the desk.

Vicky perched on the hard edge of a straight-backed chair, her complete attention on the other woman—a grandmother, in the Arapaho Way, with lines randomly etched in a colorless face and milky-blue eyes. "Tell me what you saw," she said, her tone soft and respectful, the tone she would have used to ask one of the elders for a story.

"Of course I didn't know it was Todd," the woman began, a mixture of grief and shock in her voice. "Last semester, he was in my seminar on the effect of white expansionism on Plains Indian culture, a very complex subject. . . ."

Vicky nodded.

The old woman took a quick gulp of air and clasped the arms of her chair. "Last Monday night," she began, a slow remembering, "I had just finished teaching a seminar and was walking to the lot across Speer Boulevard. You know the one?"

Another nod. Vicky had left the Taurus there this morning.

The professor went on: she usually walked to the lot with a friend, but that evening her friend had taken ill and left early, so she was alone. Naturally she followed the main sidewalk and the well-lighted path over the little knoll at the edge of the lot.

The woman looked about the room a moment, as if to confirm the memory. She felt perfectly safe, she said, until she saw the man running along the knoll. The next thing she knew, he was running at her! Well, she didn't need to say how it frightened her, a woman alone and, yes, of advanced years, although she never liked to admit how advanced because, don't you know, they are always trying to push you out, even though you stay abreast of the latest research and know more, if the truth were told, than that young man who happens to be head of the department.

Vicky nodded and smiled, fighting the urge to prod the old woman toward the point: what had happened to Todd? Elders told their stories at their own pace, in their own time.

Mary Ellen Pearson rearranged herself in the chair and smoothed the pleated skirt over her knees. "I saw the white car—a four-wheel-drive of some type—speed into the lot. Well, I thought it would run over him, don't you know. But then two men jumped out and started hitting him with something. It might have been a tire iron—the poor boy."

The old woman seemed to slide to the edge of tears. She squared her shoulders and stared at some point beyond Vicky's shoulders. "Terrible," she said. "Terrible."

The anger and sadness she'd felt at the morgue rushed over Vicky again. She took a deep breath. "What makes you think it was Todd?"

"Well, of course, I didn't realize at the time. . . ." Mary Ellen Pearson allowed the thought to trail off, then cleared her throat. "The moment I read about Todd's body being found in the South Platte, well, I realized the poor boy I saw must have been him."

"Have you talked to the police?" Vicky inched forward on the chair.

"Oh, yes. I reported what I saw immediately. I was so distraught. It was terrible. . . ."

"I understand." Vicky reached out and placed her hand lightly over the old woman's.

"And I spoke to the police this morning. A detective . . ." She searched for the name.

"Clark." Vicky withdrew her hand.

"Yes, Detective Clark. I told him everything I had told the officer Monday night, everything I'd witnessed. Two big, burly fellows. Horrible, just horrible men. And the car, a white four-by-four, although I'm uncertain of the type. I wish I had seen more."

"You did as much as you could under the circumstances," Vicky said. "What you saw will help the police."

The other woman pursed her lips and smoothed her skirt again. "The police are wrong, you know."

"Wrong?"

"I daresay I made it very clear to Detective Clark that Todd Harris did not use drugs. Those students are absent half the time, and when they do attend class, it's as if they're not even there. One can tell, you know. One develops a keen sense about these things."

Still the drug angle, Vicky was thinking. She

doubted Mary Ellen Pearson's comments would change Steve's mind. Once he got hold of a notion, he was like a bloodhound pointed in one direction. There would be no turning aside, not without some kind of irrefutable proof that he was on the wrong trail. She said, "I was hoping to find Todd's adviser."

Mary Ellen Pearson scooted the chair into the well of the desk and rummaged through a stack of folders. She pulled out a small booklet and, touching her index finger to her tongue, pushed through the pages. "Aha. Here it is, Professor Emil Coughlin."

It took a moment for Vicky to place the name: Emil Coughlin, the consultant the Denver Museum of the West had hired to verify the Plains Indian objects. What was it Rachel Foster had said? The museum always hired experts. It made sense, Vicky thought. Todd would have wanted an expert to advise him on his master's thesis.

"Where can I reach Professor Coughlin?" Vicky asked, hoping her tone was respectful. The old woman was clearly as appalled by Todd's murder as she was.

Mary Ellen Pearson tilted her head. "Why, his office is down the hall."

"You've been very helpful," Vicky said, getting to her feet.

"Oh, you won't find Emil in his office," the other woman said hurriedly. "He isn't teaching this summer. I believe he leaves for Japan soon."

"Where can I find him?"

The professor slowly lifted herself out of the chair and leaned across the desk, shuffling through another stack of papers, eventually extracting a thin, brown booklet. She flipped it open and, after a moment, read off a telephone number and an address Vicky knew was on Lookout Mountain.

Dropping the booklet onto the disarray on the desk, Mary Ellen Pearson said, "I've only seen Emil Coughlin on campus once since summer session got under way. I don't imagine he will be of any help."

She was probably right, Vicky was thinking. And Steve Clark could have already talked to him. In which case, the professor wouldn't tell her anything he might know about Julie or any other students Todd had associated with. Still it was worth a chance. She debated about calling the professor, then discarded the idea. It would be easy to turn her away on the phone. But Emil Coughlin might find it hard to slam the door in her face if she showed up at his home on Lookout Mountain.

❮ 13 ❯

The Taurus balked on the climb up Lookout Mountain, and Vicky pressed hard on the accelerator coming out of the curves. Denver sprawled below, creeping eastward onto the plains in a blue haze of heat. Rock-strewn hillsides swept past her window, opening occasionally onto views of canyons that led deeper into the mountains—canyons her people had once traveled to hunt buffalo in the mountain meadows. On top of the mountain, she knew, was the grave of Buffalo Bill, a buffalo killer. A hero to whites because he'd helped to destroy the animals that had sustained her people.

She slowed on a straightaway, squinting in the sunlight at the names on mailboxes at the edge of dirt driveways. She was almost past a driveway when she spotted Coughlin. Stomping on the brake pedal, she skidded toward the rim of the road and backed up, then slipped the gear into drive and crawled up the driveway. At the far end, in an expanse of wild grasses and aspen trees, stood a turreted, white stucco house, like a Moorish castle perched on the top of a ridge.

Vicky parked in the graveled circle looping in front. As she got out, a slightly built man stepped through the black-lacquered front door. He was dressed in a yellow polo shirt and white slacks, as if he might have been on his way to the golf course.

"Ah," he said, extending his hand. "The Arapaho attorney from the Wind River Reservation. Good to meet you, my dear."

"Professor Coughlin." Vicky was surprised he knew who she was. The man's grip was strong, the forearms muscled and suntanned. He was probably in his fifties, she decided, with thinning, sand-colored hair combed over his scalp and light gray eyes.

"Please call me Emil. May I call you Vicky?" He was smiling; tiny squint lines burrowed into the suntanned face. "I'm much too old to bother with meaningless formalities."

"You can't be that old," Vicky said, retrieving her hand.

The man patted a strand of hair into place. "Perhaps not, my dear. Although one feels life is quickly passing by, and so much still to do." He nodded toward the door. "May I offer you some refreshments on this stifling hot afternoon? We must refresh the weary travelers who appear at our tipi, must we not, my dear? That is the Indian way, I believe."

He ushered her into an entry swept with white walls and a black-tiled floor. Urns filled with fresh flowers occupied the pedestals at the base of a wide staircase that led to balconies and open spaces overhead. "I hope you won't worry about being alone with a not-so-old man whose wife, I'm afraid, has taken herself off to the boutiques. We leave for Japan in a few days, and she tells me she has nothing to wear. She'll be terribly sorry she missed your visit, I'm sure."

"Emil," Vicky began. "I've come about—"

"I know." The professor tilted the flat of one hand. "My colleague Professor Pearson called. Poor woman! Obsessed with a mugging she saw the other night. Convinced the victim was Todd Harris, when most likely there's no connection." He gave his shoulders a quick shrug. "Muggings occur occasionally, I'm afraid. After all, the campus is part of a modern city."

Another shrug, and the professor led her past the staircase into a sitting room that stretched across the rear of the house. A pair of blue leather sofas faced each other across a marble-topped coffee table. Floor-to-ceiling windows overlooked a patio that ran to the edge of the ridge. Beyond was the city, the glass skyscrapers of downtown winking in the sun.

"A refreshing glass of iced tea for the lady?" Emil Coughlin said, bowing slightly before retreating through a doorway in the side wall. Vicky strolled to the opposite wall, drawn by the Indian artifacts arranged on the glass shelves: parfleches covered with pictographs in muted reds and blues; medicine bags and moccasins covered in beads in geometric symbols.

"Do you like them?"

The professor's voice startled her. She swung around as he set down a tray with tall glasses of iced tea, lemon slices wedged onto the rims. "Please sit down," he said, indicating one of the sofas.

"The artifacts are very beautiful." Vicky let herself down into the soft blue leather. Her hand trembled as she took the glass he handed her. It always gave her a start to come unexpectedly upon objects made by her people.

"Not museum quality, I'm afraid." The professor sat on the sofa across from her and took a long drink from his glass. "I always place the best pieces I find in museums where they can enrich everyone. These pieces"—a little nod toward the glass shelves—"are leftovers, I'm afraid. Hardly representative of the fine craftsmanship of the Plains Indians."

Leaning back into the cushions, his glass balanced on one white thigh, the professor went on: "Tell me, my dear, what is your interest in the murdered student?"

Vicky took a sip of tea: herbal, flavored with raspberries. "I knew him from the day he was born. He and my son were childhood friends."

"My sincere condolences to you," Emil Coughlin said. "And to his family. Please tell them what a fine young man I thought he was. I was shocked to read the article in this morning's paper."

"The police think it was a drug murder," Vicky said, watching for his reaction.

The professor sighed. "Unfortunately ours is a drug culture, is it not? Nevertheless, as his adviser, I knew Todd fairly well. It would surprise me greatly if he had succumbed. Unless . . ." He frowned, furrows deepening in the tanned forehead, as if a new thought had occurred to him, one that required much effort. "Unless he chose drugs as a means of escape."

"Escape?"

The professor stared at her a moment. "Most students figure out how hard they must work to graduate. That becomes the extent of their efforts. But Todd was intent and determined. Worked much harder than necessary, I daresay, which placed him under a great deal of stress. Yes, I would say he was highly stressed. I had been somewhat concerned about him, I must admit."

Vicky took a long sip of the tea, thinking how neatly the professor's theory meshed with Steve's. "Did you know any of his friends on campus?" she asked.

"Oh, my dear, I make it a firm policy not to involve myself in the private lives of students, or allow them to involve themselves in mine." He crossed one leg over the other and swung a brown Docksider along the side of the coffee table. "I believe Todd had a roommate. Someone named Julie. Perhaps if you locate her, she could give you the information you want."

Vicky returned her glass to the tray. The ice made a little clinking noise. No one had mentioned a roommate. Not even the old woman at Todd's apartment building.

"A student?" Vicky asked.

The professor swirled his glass of tea, contemplating it, as if were a snifter of brandy he was about to sip. "I'm afraid I can be no further help," he said finally.

Vicky glanced out the windows at the stalks of meadow grass along the edge of the patio, swayed back in the summer heat. If Julie lived in the apartment, where was she? And why had Todd been working harder than even his adviser thought necessary? What was he working on?

Turning her eyes back to the man across from her, she said, "Tell me about the thesis Todd was writing."

Emil gave his glass another swirl, a nervous gesture, Vicky thought. "Most interesting topic," he said. "Todd set out to identify the exact locations of Arapaho villages and battlefields in Colorado. He did exhaustive research." Another sigh. "Visited every site he documented. About two weeks ago he made a swing through the southeastern part of the state. Quite a few sites there."

"Sand Creek is there," Vicky said.

The professor shook his head. "Ah, yes. The infamous Sand Creek. Todd was determined to document the fact that Arapahos were killed there. I had approved his outline and bibliography. I was looking forward with much anticipation to the finished thesis." Suddenly he threw back his head and laughed—a quick, dry chortle. "It would have destroyed the career of my distinguished colleague, Bernard Good Elk." He gave a little wave—a matter of no importance. "An arrogant man, Good Elk. He's been proclaiming for months now that Sand Creek was a Cheyenne affair. Of course he's wrong, but he's so adamant, he might convince the government bureaucrats who are in charge of allotting land to the descendants of people who were attacked. In any case, I don't know how much luck Todd had. I tried to call him after he got back. Spoke with his roommate. Todd was never in." He shook his head. "Such a hard worker. I did worry about him."

Emil Coughlin drained the last of the tea and sat the glass on the tray. Uncrossing his legs, he leaned forward, a look of conspiracy on his face. "I'm sure you did not come here, my dear, for the sole purpose of inquiring about an unfortunate student. I received a call from Rachel Foster yesterday. She informed me I would most likely hear from you. Evidently you believe the museum has managed to lose an Arapaho ledger book which, if it existed, I can assure you, would be worth a great deal of money."

Vicky held his gaze. "The book was not in the inventory."

"Of course not," the professor said. Suddenly his voice had a harder edge. "The museum never owned such a treasure. Would that it had. It might have sold the ledger book to the Smithsonian or the Field and enjoyed a more secure financial base today."

"The museum exhibited the ledger book in 1920," Vicky said.

The professor shifted back into the cushions. "So you say. I'm sure Rachel Foster explained the museum has no records of the book. Your evidence, I believe, consists of a story told by a very old man."

Vicky tried to curb her annoyance. What he said was true; her evidence was weak. "Charlie Redman is the tribal storyteller. He remembers accurately and tells the truth."

"An old man can make mistakes." The professor was shaking his head. "I spent the last two months verifying the tribal provenance for the Plains Indian artifacts in the museum. In almost all instances, the museum's identifications were correct. We did find a few Arapaho artifacts mislabeled as Cheyenne, however, and vice versa—an explainable error, given the close alliance of the two tribes."

Vicky felt a prick of excitement. She moved forward. "Did you find a Cheyenne ledger book?"

"My dear." Emil Coughlin held up one hand. "Let me quell the fond hope I detect in your voice. What you imagine is not the case. There is no ledger book in the museum."

"Then what became of it?" she persisted.

"May I make a suggestion?" The professor hurried on, as if no response were required or expected. "Several local museums date to the last century. One may have owned an Arapaho ledger book in the past. Perhaps your investigation would bear more fruit were you to contact other museums and ask them to check their records. Undoubtedly your storyteller saw the ledger book somewhere else."

"Tell me," Vicky said, getting to her feet, "is there another museum with white marble columns across the front?"

Emil Coughlin was also on his feet, hands stuffed into the front pockets of the white slacks, a mixture of sympathy and exasperation in his eyes. "I'm afraid, my dear, I have no other suggestions."

Vicky made her way back into the entry, footsteps padding behind her. She opened the door, allowing the afternoon heat to spill inside. Then she faced the professor. "Did Todd Harris help you verify the Arapaho artifacts?"

Emil Coughlin glanced beyond her shoulder, as if to pluck the answer from the outdoors. "He spent a few hours on the project. I'm afraid that was all the time he had."

Vicky thanked the man and hurried toward the car, gravel snapping under her heels. By the time she had backed around the driveway, he had retreated inside.

The closed door gave the house a vacant look, like a prop in some extravagant movie.

The steering wheel felt as hot as a branding iron in her hands as she guided the Taurus down the mountainside, her thoughts on what Emil Coughlin had said. Julie was Todd's roommate. Did that mean she was more than a roommate? A lover? Vicky blinked back the idea. How could that be? Annemarie loved him, trusted him. Whatever Julie was to Todd, there was a chance she might know what had been bothering him; what had kept him so busy he had only a few hours to help identify his own people's artifacts; what had sent him to the Wind River Reservation last weekend.

She curved two fingers over the bottom rim of the searing-hot wheel, trying to put herself in the girl's place. What would she do? Alone in the city; roommate—boyfriend, perhaps—murdered. She would run back to the reservation, Vicky knew. As fast as she could. She would lose herself in the vastness, the endless spaces, and no one, not one member of her family, would tell the police where she was hiding.

She had to find Julie before she left Denver. It might be too late already, she thought as she curved off the mountainside. She pressed hard on the gas pedal and turned onto the highway, heading into the city.

‹ 14 ›

Vicky squinted into the sun rays splayed against the windshield. The mid-afternoon traffic on Sixth Avenue was light but fast, and she clung to the right lane, allowing other cars to hurtle past in a haze of heat and exhaust. Inside the Taurus was cool; the air-conditioning emitted a low hum.

A half block from Todd's apartment building, she spotted the yellow police tape strung around trees and bushes. Two police cars stood at the curb, and as she slowed down, a uniformed officer waved her on, a definitive gesture.

She drove past, then put the Taurus through a jerky U-turn and wheeled into a cramped space. The officer came down the sidewalk as she got out.

"Move on." An order, meant to be obeyed. Waves of heat rose off the asphalt, enveloping her.

Vicky introduced herself. "I'm an attorney and a friend of the victim's family," she said, nodding toward the yellow tape behind him.

He narrowed his eyes, as if to bring her into sharper focus. "What do you want?"

Glancing beyond his shoulder, Vicky saw two other policemen step out of the building and walk down the sidewalk, each carrying a bulging plastic bag—filled with what? Evidence from the apartment? She took a chance: "Is Detective Clark here?"

The officer rocked sideways, studying her a moment. Finally he told her to wait. Stepping across the yellow tape, he strode diagonally to the front door.

Vicky followed as far as the tape barrier and stopped, aware of the other policemen nearby, their eyes on her. After a few moments, the first officer slammed out the door. "Two-B," he said, throwing back his head.

The front door was propped open, allowing the summer heat to fold itself through the shadowy hallway and narrow stairway inside the entry. Vicky climbed to the second floor and started down another hallway sheathed in sunlight pouring through a window at the far end. The second door on the right stood open.

Detective Steve Clark, in pale blue shirt and dark slacks, stood in the center of what looked like an ordinary student apartment. Railroad-flat style: living room, bedroom, and kitchen aligned in a row. Two doors on the left probably led to another bedroom, a bath. Except in this apartment, there was an upended sofa, an upholstered chair rammed against the wall, a bookcase turned on its side, and books and papers strewn across the wood floor.

"My God," Vicky said.

The detective shot her a look of sympathy. "We found this last night after we ID'd the body. Somebody was looking for something. What brought you here?"

Vicky turned her eyes to him, trying to ignore the piles of clothes and blankets littering the floor in the far bedroom, the cabinet doors hanging into the kitchen, the pots and dishes and cans of food tumbling over the counter. "I just heard that Todd had a roommate. Someone named Julie."

Shaking his head slowly, the detective took a step toward her. "I know what you're up to, Vicky. I got a call this morning from the history chairman over at CU-Denver. Why won't you trust me? I want to find the killer as much as you do, and I want to get a conviction.

I don't need well-meaning amateurs like you running around and . . ." he stared at her a long moment. "Well, frankly, you could screw up the investigation."

Vicky said, "She's Lakota."

Steve's eyebrows shot up. "We're talking about the roommate now, are we?"

"She might talk to me. She's going to be nervous about talking to you."

"I don't bite."

"You wear a badge and a gun, Steve."

He raked his fingers through his hair a moment, a weary gesture. "You're too late. She's gone. There's no sign of her in the apartment. Neighbors say she was only around the last couple weeks while Todd was on one of his research trips. She could have been house-sitting, watering plants." He gave a quick shrug.

Vicky glanced about the debris-strewn room. There were no plants.

"Maybe she crashed here awhile," Steve said, following her gaze. "You want my best guess? When trouble started to come down, she hightailed it out of here. Probably back on the reservation by now."

How could she blame the girl? Vicky was thinking. She made a little circle, sidestepping the debris. "What were they looking for?"

Steve pursed his lips. A handsome face, she thought. Strong chin, kind eyes. "Best guess?" he said after a moment. "Drugs, cash, maybe both."

There it was again; the same theory. Another dead Indian. A drug deal. "Oh, God, Steve," she said. "Don't you understand? Whoever killed Todd is going to a lot of trouble to make it look like a drug deal, and you're buying it!"

"Wait a minute." His tone was sharp, the detective tone she'd seldom heard him use. "It looks like he owed some people. After they killed him, they came here for payment. Believe me, Vicky"—his voice softened—"I've seen a hundred cases like this."

Vicky crossed to one of the side doors and pushed it open. Another bed torn apart, another desk with drawers hanging out. Papers littered the floor. Shouldering past the detective, she walked through the kitchen and into the back bedroom. The mattress lay exposed on a narrow, metal frame, clumps of white foam poking through the slits that zigzagged across the top. Against one wall was a desk swept clear of papers or any other reminder a student had once studied there. She stepped closer. A faint trace of dust outlined a dust-free square the size of a computer. "Todd's computer's missing," she said.

"You know for sure he owned one?"

"He was a graduate student, Steve. He was writing a thesis." She glanced back at the desk. The thesis would be on the computer, possibly on backup diskettes. There were no diskettes anywhere.

The detective pinched the bridge of his nose a moment. "The most valuable thing in this apartment is a TV on the kitchen counter that might bring fifty bucks, if some pawnshop felt charitable. So if the victim owned a computer, whoever ransacked this place grabbed it. Next best thing to cash."

"What about copies of his thesis?" Vicky stooped over and picked up a wad of papers—handwritten notes, torn scraps—a jumble of nonsense.

"We found a lot of notebooks and some manuscripts," the detective said. Stepping toward her, he reached out and took her hand. His touch was warm. "Trust me to do the right thing here, will you, Vicky?"

When she didn't reply, he dropped her hand. "If you should happen to find the roommate . . ." he began, an edge to his tone. "I'm not suggesting you keep nosing around, but if you happen to run into her, you'll call me, right?"

Vicky closed her eyes a moment and tried to grab onto the idea at the edge of her mind. Whoever had ransacked Todd's apartment had taken the computer and any back-up diskettes that may have contained his thesis. Why would anyone want a graduate student's thesis? Is that why Todd was killed? For a thesis? It didn't make sense. She said, "I'll do everything I can to make sure the bastard who killed Todd Harris spends the rest of his life behind bars."

"Vicky, Vicky." A patient repetition, a kind of demand for attention. "You'll call me, right?"

"I'll call you, Steve," she said.

He bestowed a long, appreciative smile on her before leading her out of the narrow apartment and down the stairs. Outside they walked past the shade lengthening over the sidewalk and into the bright sunshine at the curb. He held the door as she slipped inside the Taurus. Bending toward her, his face close to hers, he said, "Could we put all this aside for a couple hours and have dinner tonight?"

"I'm sorry, Steve," she began, searching for the words to let him know gently she did not want to reconsider the decision she had made a dozen years ago.

"Level with me," he said. "You're involved with somebody else, right?"

She gripped the handle and pulled the door away from him. She thought of the white man who'd asked her to move to Chicago. A nice man, a company president, but he was not for her, and last week she had told him so. She glanced up at the detective awaiting her answer. "Yes," she said, "I'm involved with somebody else." It seemed the easiest way.

❮ 15 ❯

Father John drove north on Sheridan Boulevard, enveloped in the sounds of Puccini. He had slipped the tape of *Turandot* into the player on the seat beside him, and when "Nessun dorma" began, he nudged the volume so loud that at a red light people in nearby cars were staring at him. For an instant he felt like a kid with a boom box. Didn't everyone love the soaring melody, the force of emotion, the beautiful noise? He often had an opera blaring in the Toyota, but he was usually driving through the open spaces of the reservation.

He was beginning to long for the reservation, the peacefulness of the mission with sunshine mottling the buildings and grounds, the sound of the breeze rustling in the cottonwoods. It looked like it would be a while before he could go home—he thought of the reservation as home. He'd spent part of the morning with Mary and Doyal, reminiscing about Todd, the happy times, the accomplishments in a short life. It was a myth that bereaved families didn't want to talk about the one they'd lost—it was all they wanted to talk about.

Tomorrow he would say the memorial Mass. Then the old people would take Todd's body to the reservation for burial. He would be laid in the Middle Earth, the sacred ground, Doyal had said, although Mary had argued that this ground was also the Middle Earth, the traditional land of the *Hinono eino*. The boy could rest in peace at Mount Olivet cemetery near the foothills.

Doyal had won out, and Father John was glad. Todd should be buried where the earth remained unbound and free. The Holy Old Men would purify his body with the sweet smoke of cedar and paint circles on his face with the sacred red paint that would identify him to the ancestors. There would be singing and drumming to guide his spirit into the sky world. How many times Father John had witnessed the ancient ceremony, yet it always seemed new and comforting, as if he were witnessing the spirit being gently lifted into the next world.

He would say the Mass tomorrow at St. Elizabeth's, the old stone church that stood in the center of the Auraria campus. After leaving Doyal and Mary, he'd driven across the city and made arrangements with the pastor, Father Cyprian. He still had to call his own assistant, Father Geoff—a call he dreaded. It would be a while longer before Geoff could take any time off. One of the priests at St. Francis had to be available in case there were any emergencies. There were always emergencies.

A turn right, and Father John slowed through the streets of North Denver, where there was little traffic and fewer people to stare from passing cars. He exhaled a long breath, remembering. He'd been about Geoff's age—in his fortieth year—when he'd been assigned to St. Francis Mission. Hardly the assignment he'd hoped for at a Jesuit university like Marquette or Georgetown. Perhaps at some point in the future, the provincial had explained. One could never predict the future, could one? And Father John had understood: one could never predict when an alcoholic priest might take the next drink. Best for him to remain at an obscure mission in the middle of Wyoming where he could be hustled back to Grace House, if necessary, with minimum disruptions, the least amount of scandal.

He'd had to ask the location of St. Francis Mission—he was ashamed to think of it. And after he'd arrived in the vast spaces, where the earth and sky melted together on the far horizons, he'd felt more alone, more isolated. He'd spent the first months in a frenzy of work, trying to outrun the thirst that bounded after him, a demon threatening to devour him.

How important it had been to get away from work once in a while and backpack through the Wind River mountains, where he could think and pray. When had he discovered that he did his best thinking and praying in the midst of his work, among the people? That St. Francis Mission was where he belonged?

He guided the Toyota into one of the service roads that ringed the Regis campus and parked behind the residence. Sliding the tape player off the seat, he slammed out of the Toyota. The last act of *Turandot* floated into the afternoon heat.

The Jesuit residence was quiet and cool, a sense of desertion about it. The provincial and his assistants were probably still in the mountains. His boss had hurried past him at the door of the refectory this morning, circled by a group of black suits and white collars. He'd managed to stop Father Stanton long enough to learn that the provincial was on his way to Camp St. Malo near Estes Park. So much cooler there. Do him a world of good.

"I can drive up there," Father John had said.

The other priest had shifted from one foot to the other, glancing over his shoulder at the provincial and his aids moving down the corridor. "Impossible. He'll be tied up all day with various administrators."

"Tomorrow, then."

"Father O'Malley . . ." the other priest had begun while he kept one eye on the retreating figures, "I've spoken to the provincial about your desire to open a museum. He fully supports my decision. We fail to see how a museum at an Indian mission would be either practical or desirable. I suggest you return to St. Francis, where, I'm sure, a great deal of work awaits you."

"I intend to stay in Denver until I see the provincial." Father John had struggled to conceal his irritation.

The other priest had shrugged, muttered something like "As you please," and scuttled after the others.

Now Father John started up the stairway, boots scuffing at the wood, the last notes of *Turandot* bouncing off the stucco walls. Suddenly there was the sharp whump of a slammed door: "Ah, is it yourself, Father?"

He glanced around. Brother Timothy stood at the foot of the stairs, chin uplifted, cheeks flushed, as if he'd been hurrying. "You had a visitor, Father."

Father John turned down the volume. "A visitor?"

"A Native American woman, she was."

"When was she here?"

"You only just missed her."

Father John ran down the stairs and back out the door, leaving it ajar. He saw the Taurus about to turn out of the parking lot, and sprinted after it, reaching the driver's side as the car inched forward.

Vicky turned, a startled movement, like that of a deer caught in a hunter's sights. A look of relief crept into her expression. "I've got to talk to you," she said over the dropping window.

This was not a social visit, he knew. There were never any social visits between them. She was here for a reason. He motioned her back through the lot, a cop directing traffic, then waited as she pulled into the slot she had probably just vacated behind a van. He hadn't seen her car when he'd come in.

She got out and tilted her head toward the grass and shady trees of the campus. "Let's take a walk," she said.

They walked down the narrow sidewalk between the residence and a stand of oak trees. He had the player in hand. The opera began again, the music floating softly around them. She always needed to move, he was thinking—around a room, across a campus, when she was upset, when she was trying to sort through something, as if her whole being were summoned to the task.

Sunshine splashed across the lawn that ran down a gradual slope to the small lake bordering the campus. When they reached the dirt path that trailed around the lake, she turned and faced him. "I just came from Todd's apartment," she said. "The Lakota girl, Julie, had been staying there, but there's no sign of her. She probably took off for the Rosebud. Somebody ransacked the apartment. They took Todd's computer."

"His computer!" Father John understood. Todd's thesis would be on the computer.

Vicky whirled about, took a few steps away, then came back. The shadow of a branch fell over her face, making her eyes even brighter. "Suppose Todd's murder and the missing Arapaho ledger book are connected," she said.

"What are you saying?" Her theories had made sense in the past. Like a laser beam, her instincts had a way of drilling into the center of things.

Vicky went on in an urgent tone that cut through the sounds of music coming from the player: "Todd's adviser told me Todd had been documenting the sites of Arapaho villages and battlegrounds in Colorado. One of the sites was Sand Creek." Her chest rose and fell as she gulped in quick, short breaths.

Father John said nothing, waiting for her to go on.

"Sand Creek," Vicky repeated. "Charlie Redman said his ancestor, No-Ta-Nee, had written the ledger book about the people's last days in Colorado. Don't you see, John? The last days were at Sand Creek. After the massacre, the people fled their lands here. They never came back. What if Todd had found the ledger book?"

Father John gave out a little whistle. If that was true, Todd had found the only Arapaho account of the massacre.

Vicky walked back and forth, carving out little circles in the dirt path, explaining how she'd seen the museum storage space—like a cavern; how the ledger book might have gotten lost on the shelves over the years. Suddenly she stopped, a kind of desperation in her eyes. "Suppose someone didn't want the real story of Sand Creek told. Suppose that person took the book from the museum and sent two thugs after Todd to make sure he wouldn't tell anyone about the book. They found him in a parking lot near campus last Monday night and killed him."

"Hold on." Father John held up one hand. "Even if the ledger book was lost, the museum would have records."

Vicky was shaking her head, staving off any objection. "Whoever took the book would make sure the records also disappeared. The old records are kept in filing cabinets. A lot of people have access to them. The entire museum staff. Rachel Foster, the curator. Or the consultants hired for special projects. Emil Coughlin, Todd's adviser, helped verify the Plains Indian artifacts for the NAGPRA inventories. A Cheyenne historian consulted on the Sand Creek exhibit—Bernard Good Elk. He teaches here at Regis." She tilted her head toward the campus buildings that sloped up from the lakeshore. "Do you know him?"

Father John gave a short nod. He'd met the man a couple of times: black braids and round face, eyes narrowing as they'd appraised him—white man, missionary, failed historian. He said, "Good Elk is highly respected, Vicky. He wouldn't be involved in something like this."

"Even if the ledger book disproves what he's been claiming the last few months? That only Cheyennes are entitled to the Colorado lands promised the survivors of Sand Creek?" Vicky started pacing again. Then, her voice softer, she said, "The book will be destroyed."

"Destroyed? A ledger book?"

"Oh, John." She dropped her head into her hands a moment. "Once it gets into the hands of a dealer, it will be sold page by page."

Father John turned away, his eyes on the lake, the sun dancing across the surface, the ducks floating among the lily pads at the edge. Everything Vicky said made sense. It was possible, even logical—except for the faulty premise. Bringing his eyes back to hers, he said, "There's no proof the ledger book was in the museum."

"What are you saying?" A mixture of alarm and incredulity came into her voice. "The storyteller saw it . . ."

"It's not proof, Vicky," he said.

She stared at him a moment, eyes flashing with anger. Then she pivoted abruptly and started up the slope toward the Taurus. He caught up with her, took her arm, and turned her toward him. The opera was soft between them. "Look," he said. "Maybe we can find the proof." He kept his hand on her arm. Her skin was soft. He saw that she didn't pull away from his touch, but stood there, close to him. He went on: "Whoever has the ledger book won't wait to sell it. The book can link him to Todd's murder. He'll want to get rid of it. There's a place on Broadway, a row of shops that sell rare books and Native American artifacts. I go there every chance I get when I'm in Denver—just to browse. Maybe one of the dealers has heard of an Indian ledger book that's come on the market."

"Let's go talk to them," she said, finally pulling away.

◆ 16 ◆

"We'll need a story," Vicky said, wheeling the Taurus through the traffic, conscious of the man beside her: the plaid shirt, the blue-jeaned legs, the cowboy hat, the faint odor of aftershave. She hurried on: "Todd's killer will have to come up with a good story. Any reputable book dealer will want to know where the ledger book came from. What can the killer say? I stole it from a museum and murdered the kid who found it? Nobody knows about it." Nobody, she was thinking, except a scared Lakota girl named Julie and the man beside her. And herself.

She went on: "How about this? You're a wealthy man. I'm your wife. We collect Indian artifacts, and we've been yearning to own a ledger book from one of the Plains Indian tribes. Preferably Arapaho."

He threw his head back and laughed. "We'll never sell that story. No one would take me for being wealthy. And who would believe a woman like you would lose her mind and marry a man like me?" He gave out another laugh. "We'd better stick to who we are—a brilliant and beautiful Arapaho lawyer and a broken-down, middle-aged priest. Anyway, the minute we walk into a bookstore, the dealer will make up his own story about us. It will probably be more interesting than anything we could do."

Vicky switched lanes, bypassing a bus that burped black clouds of exhaust. It crossed her mind that her story might have been true—could have been true—if only for the moment it would have taken to tell it. Gradually the parking lots and office buildings and stores along the sidewalks gave way to squat, one-story buildings, a mixture of small cafés, vintage-clothing stores, stores selling rare books and antiques. Vicky set the Taurus at the curb, and Father John was already around at her side as she slid out. They waited for a break in the traffic before dashing across the street, ahead of the cars roaring toward them.

The first shop, Vicky saw, was crammed with antiques: oak dressers and tables, gilt-framed mirrors and curved Victorian chairs. The furnishings of rich people from another time—whites her ancestors had never met. There were a few books, fine leather volumes with gold lettering on the spines—decorator items.

They tried the next store: old comic books and magazines on the shelves, red Formica kitchen tables and plastic chairs, low-slung sofas and little triangle-shaped tables. A salesgirl behind the counter dropped the comic book she'd been flipping through and tossed them a hopeful smile. Out of the corner of her eye, Vicky saw Father John nod—an apology for blundering into a store specializing in the 1950s. She led the way back into the sunshine.

They stood on the sidewalk a moment, taking in the shops up and down the street. On the glass pane of the third door down were black letters that blurred in the sun: RARE BOOKS. They started toward the door, as if they'd seen it at the same moment. A bell jangled overhead as they walked into the small space. Books bulged from the shelves lining the walls. "We're looking for rare books on the Plains Indians," Father John told the elderly man scrunched behind the front counter.

The man stared at them, disappointment in his eyes. "Richard Loomis specializes in Indian stuff." He gave a little nod. "Down a half block."

They found the shop near the corner. Black letters on the plate-glass window read: NATIVE AMERICAN BOOKS AND ARTIFACTS. Another bell jangled as they stepped inside. The shop was narrow and dimly lit, with rows of shelves sagging under the weight of books. In a glass case against the wall was a beaded vest, two painted parfleches, a quiver case. There was a heavy smell of dust and dried paper and the metallic smell of old ink in the cool stillness.

"May I help you?" The man's voice came from the rear, and they walked through the dimness toward a desk Vicky hadn't noticed at first.

"We're interested in books on the Plains Indians," Father John said, a matter-of-fact, businesslike tone. So unlike him, Vicky thought.

The man behind the desk slowly got to his feet. "Allow me to introduce myself. Richard Loomis." It surprised her how young he was—mid-twenties, perhaps—with blond hair receding from a long, sloping forehead, and dark, hooded eyes that had a wary look. "Ah." He nodded, glancing at Vicky, as if a Native American seeking books on Native Americans seemed perfectly reasonable. Then his eyes switched back to the white man beside her, and a look of understanding came into his expression. She wondered what kind of story had formed in his mind about the couple who had walked into his shop. "Perhaps I can direct you to something specific."

"We're interested in Native American art," Father John said.

"There are several galleries downtown."

"A ledger book."

The bookman's eyes moved from Father John to Vicky and back again. Was she wrong, or was there the smallest twitch, an involuntary reflex, in the man's face? "You're interested in a ledger book?" His voice was low, confidential, although they were the only people in the shop.

Vicky said, "We understand an Arapaho ledger book has just come on the market."

The bookman gazed at her a long moment, as if he hadn't taken the full measure of her earlier. "What makes you think that?"

"Word spreads very quickly." Vicky shrugged and glanced at Father John.

"I'm Father John O'Malley," he said quickly, reaching out to shake the other man's hand. "I'm opening a museum of Arapaho artifacts on the Wind River Reservation." He touched Vicky's arm. "This is Vicky Holden, my attorney."

She nodded. A good story, she was thinking, with certain qualifications left out. John O'Malley hoped to open the museum, and she was not his attorney. No, she was not his.

There was the sharp jangle, the shush of the door opening. Vicky glanced back at the thick-shouldered young man with black hair and dark skin—an Indian— holding the door, a hesitant look about him, as if he wasn't sure whether to come in. Out of the corner of her eye, she saw the quick movement of the bookman's hand, as if he was flicking away an annoying fly. The Indian wheeled about, pulling the door behind him.

She knew him. The Lakota in the Indian Services office at CU-Denver this morning who had jumped up and denied knowing anyone named Julie. What was he doing here? And why had Richard Loomis motioned him away, as if he'd stumbled into the wrong place?

"Ledger books rarely come on the market," the bookman was saying, as if there had been no interruption. "When they do, they are very expensive."

"Our donors are very generous," Father John said.

The bookman extracted a pencil from his shirt pocket and tapped it against the palm of one hand like a metronome. "One page would be worth . . ." He stopped tapping and glanced at the ceiling, totaling the figures in his head.

Father John said, "The museum is only interested in the book if it is intact."

The dealer looked back, pencil poised in midair. "Most museums are content with one or two pages." He gave a little shrug. "Every page is valuable. But the entire book, well . . ." Another shrug. "No dealer could let a book like that go for less than he could get by selling the pages individually. And I must warn you, foreign collectors are very interested in this material."

"A million and a half," Vicky said.

The man's thin lips curled into a smile. "Would you put that bid into writing?"

"As soon as we see the book." This from Father John.

"Well," the bookman began, a long drawing out of the word, "Should I hear of such a book, you can be sure I will contact you immediately. Where can I find you?"

Before Vicky could reach inside her handbag for one of her business cards, Father John set his hand over hers. "We'll be in touch," he said.

They found a little Italian restaurant around the corner and sat at a table on the patio in back. The air was cool, with daylight slanting past the branches arched overhead. Vicky watched the waiter set two bowls of spaghetti and a basket of garlic bread on the table. She was feeling light-headed, almost giddy. Her theory was right.

When the waiter moved away, she said, "The dealer knows about the ledger book. Probably every rare-book dealer in Denver knows about the book and hopes to get his hands on it." She stopped, suddenly realizing where her thoughts were headed.

Father John gave her a knowing smile. "The book hasn't been sold yet," he said. "Whoever has it is waiting on the highest bid. The police—"

"The police!" she interrupted, an image of Steve Clark flashing before her: the clenched jaw, the determined eyes. Another drug murder, he'd called Todd's death. "We don't have the ledger book, John. All we have is a theory."

They went over the theory again as they ate the spaghetti and finished the garlic bread. Todd had found the ledger book missing in the museum; someone took the book and killed him; and now the killer was trying to sell the book. The more they talked, Vicky thought, the more implausible the theory seemed. A series of stories plucked out of thin air, hardly the kind of evidence to convince a homicide detective—even one who was an old friend.

"We can't prove it," Vicky said, pushing her plate aside—it was almost empty. "Even if a ledger book is on the market, we can't prove it came from the museum." The museum. It always came back to that.

Father John said nothing for a moment. Then: "Museums keep records of the materials researchers use. Maybe—"

She held up her hand. Of course. Why hadn't she seen it? If she could retrace Todd's steps last week, check the materials he had been using when he found the ledger book, she might discover something that would prove the book had been in the museum. She said, "I have a meeting tomorrow with Rachel Foster. When she gives me a story on how there are no records of the book, which I'm sure she's already prepared, I'll ask to see the research materials Todd was using."

The last band of daylight crept along the ridge of the mountains in the distance as Vicky parked in front of Marcy's. She had left Father John at the residence and driven through the quiet streets with a growing sense of confidence and determination. Even if the records were gone, there might be other proof of the ledger book—a sign of some kind—and she would find it. She would not stop until she found it.

She slammed out and marched around the car. The evening was cool; long blue shadows fell over the bungalows and drifted across the front lawns. As she started up the sidewalk she heard a car door snap open. She whirled around. The massive body of a man had emerged from one of the cars at the curb and was moving toward her. "Ms. Holden," he called. His voice came from somewhere deep within the barrel-shaped chest.

She froze, keys clutched in her hand, aware of the stillness, the closed doors up and down the block, the darkness at Marcy's windows. Nobody else was around. The man stopped a couple of feet from her, thumbs hooked into the pockets of his blue jeans. Thick braids rode down the front of his dark shirt.

"Who are you?" she asked. She knew the answer. The round face, the broad cheekbones, and sliver-thin eyes of the Cheyenne—the Shyela, as her people called the tribe with whom they had lived on the plains.

"Bernard Good Elk," he said. "I've been waiting for you. We need to talk."

Vicky kept her place. She said nothing.

"My colleague Emil Coughlin tells me you paid him a visit this morning. Said you got a problem with the inventory of Arapaho artifacts over at the museum."

"The inventory is incomplete," Vicky said.

"So I hear." The man rolled his shoulders; knots of muscles rippled along his arms. "Emil says you think the museum has an Arapaho ledger book." He let out a snort. "I've spent a lot of time in that museum. There's no such ledger book."

Vicky said, "The ledger book was written by No-Ta-Nee. You've heard of him, I'm sure. He rode with Chief Niwot. He was with him at Sand Creek. The book is an Arapaho account of the massacre."

Bernard Good Elk drew in a long breath, nostrils flaring. He moved close—so close she could smell the stale odor of coffee on his breath. "I figured that's what this is all about. Your people want some of the land that rightly belongs to Cheyennes. So you've come up with a cockamamie story about a ledger book that says the Arapahos were at Sand Creek. Well, it's not going to work. Sand Creek was a Cheyenne village. Weren't any Arapahos hanging around." He squared his shoulders and threw his head back. "You're lucky your people weren't there."

Vicky could feel the muscles tightening in her chest, the dryness in her throat. Were the ancestors at Sand Creek to be forgotten? Lost in a new interpretation of history? "Government records prove both of our peoples were there," she said.

The Indian let out a deep laugh. "White people never could tell one Indian from another." Then, eyes narrowing into tiny slits, he said, "Cheyenne tribal officials have heard you people think the museum is holding out, so they've decided to wait before claiming Cheyenne artifacts. A couple of other tribes are doing likewise." He loomed above her. "This story of yours is causing everybody a lot of trouble, Ms. Holden. I strongly advise you to drop the matter so we can all get about the business of reclaiming what belongs to us."

Suddenly he rocked sideways and regarded her a long moment before he started moving backward toward the car. Even in the darkness, she felt his eyes on her. "Forget about the ledger book," he said, flinging open the door. "It doesn't exist." He folded himself inside. In an instant the engine spurted into life, and the

car pulled away and started down the street, taillights
blinking in the night.

Vicky hurried to the front door, fumbling in her bag
for the key Marcy had given her. She let herself inside,
slammed the door with her body, and rammed the bolt
into place, her legs trembling beneath her. Then she
groped for the wall switch. A white light flooded across
the walls and wood floors. Little specks of light
sparkled in the chrome legs of the chairs, the glass coffee table.

The Shyela! Did Bernard Good Elk really think he
could intimidate her? Scare her into advising her tribe to
sign off on the inventory and forget about the ledger
book? Forget about the lands that belonged to them as
much as to the Cheyenne? Why did he think it would
work? Because the Cheyennes were warriors, while her
people were traders and diplomats? Well, her people
were also warriors. They fought for what was theirs.

In the bedroom, Vicky found a note from Marcy on
the dresser. *Pat Michaels called. Meet him at eight tomorrow morning. Said you know the place.*

◀ 17 ▶

Pearl Street hummed with early rush-hour traffic, but the sidewalks were vacant. Most of the shops and restaurants wouldn't open for another couple of hours. The only activity, Vicky saw as she parked the car, were the customers going in and out of a small, white-brick building with BAGELS arched across the plate-glass window. Several people sat at round metal tables on the sidewalk, drinking coffee, peering at folded newspapers.

Vicky recognized the man at the far table—the slight, muscular build, the hawklike nose and thick glasses in pinkish frames, the cropped gray hair. Pat Michaels threw her a smile as she walked up. Pulling himself halfway to his feet, a kind of bow, he said, "You haven't changed, beautiful."

"I was thinking the same about you, Pat." Vicky slid into the chair across from him.

"Yeah, I'm still beautiful," he said, dropping back onto his seat. He nodded toward the Styrofoam cups and plastic bag bulging with bagels. "Hope you brought your appetite."

Vicky reached for one of the cups, popped the tab, and took a long sip before pulling a bagel out of the bag. There was the clean, light feeling of morning in the air, with columns of sunshine and shadow lying across the sidewalk. The sun felt warm on her arms.

Pat took a sip from his cup before reaching into his shirt pocket and bringing out a small notebook. He pushed the glasses down over the hook in his nose and began flipping through the pages, peering over the rims at the cramped writing. Finally he stopped. "Found what you want," he said. "Rachel Foster. Born Rachel Wentworth, Denver, 1943." He glanced up, eyebrows raised. "Name ring any bells?"

Vicky swallowed a bite of bagel and shook her head.

"One of Denver's oldest families. Owned half the town at one time. Cyril Wentworth came to Denver in the Gold Rush. Figured out he'd make a helluva lot more money selling supplies to the other fool gold seek ers than he was gonna make panning gold in some freezing mountain stream." The investigator looked down, checking his notes. "Opened store on Larimer Street in 1859. Died thirty years later. Left only son good chunk of downtown property." A glance upward. "That would be Rachel's grandfather."

Vicky let out a long sigh. "You're telling me the curator came from a wealthy Denver family. I could have guessed as much."

"Hold on," Pat said, still peering over the glasses. "*Used* to be wealthy."

"What do you mean?"

"Real-estate crash decade ago pretty well wiped out the Wentworth fortune." He gave a little shrug. "Rachel's brother started speculating. Leveraged the family properties to develop skyscrapers and shopping malls. Took a major bath. Lost everything old Cyril had worked his butt off for."

Vicky was quiet a moment. Then: "How did Rachel take it?"

Nudging his glasses back into place with an index finger, the investigator said, "Had a little chat with a friend of hers who let it slip how Rachel was mad enough to kill her brother. Turned out he beat her to it.

Shot himself. Then Rachel's husband of ten years divorced her. Cash cow had gone dry." The investigator closed the notebook and slipped it inside his pocket. "Rachel moved to a little apartment and went to work as a research assistant at the museum. Worked her way up to curator. She's no dummy."

Vicky washed down the last bite of bagel with another sip of coffee. She'd met women like Rachel Foster—wealthy women who had lost their wealth. The big house and car, the designer clothes and country clubs— gone. It was as if they had awakened in a strange country where they didn't know the customs, couldn't understand the language. What would such a woman do if she saw the chance to reclaim her wealth and rightful citizenship, her identity? If she came across a ledger book lost for years in the museum? A ledger book worth $1.3 million?

"What do I owe you, Pat?" Vicky said.

"Next time you're in town, you can take me to breakfast." The investigator crumpled the bagel bag and tossed it into a nearby trash can. "Or you could tell me what you're looking for."

Vicky leaned back and drained the rest of her coffee, eyes on the man across from her. Always the investigator. Curious about everything. "An Arapaho artifact seems to be missing from the museum." she said. "A ledger book."

"No kidding?" Pat bit his lower lip a moment. "A ledger book would bring some big bucks over on Book Row. But I don't see Rachel Foster involved in anything like that. She's got a good record. Might be hard to work for—couple of staff people say she's a real dictator—but she's efficient and organized. Since she came on board, the museum's increased its collections and gotten a lot of grant money. Trustees love her. Just gave her another five-year contract."

As Vicky started to get to her feet Pat reached out

and took her hand. "This got something to do with that Indian kid they found in the river?"

"I'm afraid so." She pulled back her hand.

"Good God, Vicky." The investigator was on his feet. "Stolen ledger book. Murder. Whoever's behind this is gonna be a determined and vicious son of a bitch. Police get paid to hunt down sons of bitches. Stay out of it! You get in a killer's way, you don't know what could happen."

He was wrong, Vicky thought. She knew exactly what could happen. She had seen Todd's body at the morgue. "Thanks for the warning, Pat," she said as she turned and started for the car, ignoring the alarm and frustration in his eyes.

A few people occupied the pews at St. Elizabeth's Church—a scattering of mourners, Vicky thought as she slipped into a back pew. Sunlight filtered through the stained-glass windows on the side walls, casting a tinge of orange, green, and brown over the wooden pews, the tiled floor. A faint smell of lilacs hung in the air, which was hot and stuffy, despite the fan softly whirring on the right side of the altar.

Vicky let her eyes roam over the people ahead: Doyal and Mary in the front pew, several grandfathers and grandmothers around them, a group of older white men who looked like professors. She spotted Emil Coughlin among them, arms folded across his chest, head turning from side to side as he glanced about. The rest looked like students—a few whites here and there, clusters of Indians. It struck her that Julie could be among them, but she had no idea what the girl looked like.

Then she spotted the young black-haired woman sitting alone in a side pew near the front, head bowed over something in her hand—a missal, perhaps. Suddenly the head jerked up, and Vicky saw it was Tisha Runner, the girl she'd met yesterday at the Indian Services Office. The girl who claimed she didn't know Todd Harris. Why was she at a memorial Mass for someone she didn't know? If she had lied about Todd, maybe she'd also lied about his roommate.

Vicky decided to join the girl. She started to slide out of her pew just as the drums began pounding—a steady *thump, thump, thump,* like that of her own heart. She remained in her place. Three old men had taken seats around the small drum near the altar. There was a shuffling noise, a shifting of atmosphere, as people got to their feet and two elders started up the aisle. Behind them was John O'Malley, tall and redheaded, wearing a white chasuble embroidered at the edges in geometric designs—the Arapaho symbols of life. His hands were pressed together in prayer.

The elders gave little bows before slipping into a front pew while Father John walked to the altar and faced the congregation. "We've gathered here to pray for the soul of Todd Harris," he said. His voice resonated through the church.

Vicky kept her eyes on the priest as he began the prayers of the Mass, head bowed, hands clasped. She was glad he had returned to the people, that he was here when Todd's grandparents needed him, that he would be at St. Francis Mission when others needed him. She didn't want to think of what it might have been like if he hadn't returned, if she never saw him again: a kind of death.

Voices rose around her: Lord, have mercy. Christ have mercy. Lord, hear us. Christ, graciously hear us.

Then quiet filled the church, broken by the whirring of the fan, the clearing of a throat, a little cough. "The souls of the just are in the hands of God," Father John said. Then he began talking about Todd, how he'd gloried in his life and used the talents God had given him to serve others, how he had touched everyone who knew him. A low sobbing noise came from the front pews where the grandmothers and elders sat as Father John walked over to a chair angled next to the altar and sat down.

"Father, I want to talk." An elder's voice mingled with the whir of the fan. A commotion followed as the old man worked his way into the aisle. Now, Vicky knew, was the time for the criers—like the men who had gone through the villages in the Old Time, crying out the news, telling what had happened, urging the people to be of strong heart.

The old man stood in front of the altar, gazing out over the church, thin brown arms dangling from the sleeves of his plaid shirt. "This was a good boy," he said. "Just tryin' to do right. People shouldn't forget him, now he's gone to the ancestors."

The next elder was already beside him. Then a line of old men, one after the other, walked to the altar and cried out the same message. A good boy. Don't let your heart get discouraged. Gotta keep going on. Finally they filed back into the pews, and Father John resumed the Mass.

When he finished, the drums started again, loud thuds in the hushed quiet as Father John walked down the center aisle. Vicky watched the pews empty behind him, people following him toward the door. Suddenly she realized she'd lost sight of Tisha Runner. The girl wasn't in the crowd. She must have gone out a side door.

Darting out of the pew, Vicky hurried up the side aisle. She found a door inside a small alcove. On the other side was a hallway that led past the sacristy to an outside door. She pushed it open and stepped onto a shady stretch of lawn next to the church. People were already getting into cars and pickups on the street; a brown pickup pulled out in a grating of gears. The girl was nowhere.

Vicky walked across the lawn to the front, where students and elders pressed around Father John, stretching out their hands. She saw the way he took each hand and held it a long moment—a comforting touch, she knew.

Emil Coughlin seemed to be awaiting his turn, standing back, surveying the crowd. He had the look of a professor about him—the dark blazer over a blue shirt and loosely knotted tie, the wrinkled slacks. Catching her eye, he walked over. "Nice to see you again, my dear," he said, extending his hand. His grip was as firm as she remembered.

He smiled at her. "Any luck finding that roommate of Todd's?"

"Not yet," Vicky said, taken back by the question. The professor had said he had no interest in the personal lives of his students.

"I hoped she might be here." His eyes went to the group hovering around Father John. "The police say some fool broke into Todd's apartment and stole his computer. Must have had the only copy of his thesis, since they didn't find it in any papers. Todd did some solid work. I would hate to see his research disappear. His roommate might know if he kept a backup disk somewhere else. Smart thing to do, you know. And Todd was a smart kid. Trouble is, the roommate seems to have disappeared."

Vicky was quiet a moment. They had reached the same conclusion: Julie might know something about the thesis. She said, "It's possible Todd found some very significant information."

"Absolutely!" The professor nodded. "He was a first-rate researcher."

"He may have discovered the Arapaho ledger book in the museum."

"My dear," Emil began in a pleading tone, "I've explained to you there is no such book—"

Vicky interrupted. "It exists, Emil. And it tells the story of Sand Creek."

The professor rocked back on his heels. "That would be a significant discovery, indeed," he said. Raising his head, he gazed at some point beyond her. "It would have changed the entire thrust of Todd's thesis. I find it quite puzzling that he did not mention such a find to me."

"I think he was scared," Vicky said. "Someone didn't want the ledger book found. That's why Todd was killed."

A smile cracked at the corners of the professor's thin mouth. "Oh, my dear, I'm disappointed at your obsession over this so-called ledger book. I'm afraid my worthy colleague Bernard Good Elk may be right about you. This is just a ploy, a smoke screen that you insist upon raising in an attempt to prove Arapahos were involved in the Sand Creek debacle. A fantastic story. Well . . ." He glanced at the last cars pulling from the curb. "It must be difficult for Todd's family, all this speculation on why the poor boy was killed. The police know why he was killed. The evidence seems clear. Shouldn't you content yourself with trying to reclaim the Arapaho artifacts in the museum?"

"Not until I find the ledger book," she said.

"I see." Emil exhaled a long breath. "And how do you propose to conjure up this ledger book?"

Vicky turned away. The crowd was thinning out. A few elders talking to Father John, grandmothers waiting in parked cars. Looking back, she said, "I'm not sure. But if Todd found the ledger book, I can find it. I intend to follow his footsteps."

Giving the professor her best professional smile, she started toward the crowd thinning out around Father John just as a blue Honda rounded the corner, Tisha Runner at the wheel. "Tisha, wait!" she called, waving both hands overhead, running into the street. The

Honda gathered speed as it swung around a corner. In another instant it was lost in traffic on Speer Boulevard.

Vicky stepped back onto the curb. There was shock and disapproval on the faces of the grandmothers staring at her from the cars. So undignified. And she, an Arapaho woman.

She walked toward the dwindling crowd in front of the church. Emil Coughlin was gone. She waited until the last students had turned away and started down the sidewalk. Father John was alone. She told him that the Mass was beautiful and comforting; that she was glad he had returned. Then she said, "I had a surprise visitor last night. Bernard Good Elk."

Father John left his eyes on hers a moment. Without saying anything, he took her arm and gently propelled her back into the church and down the center aisle. A musty odor filled the air, a residue of perspiration and grief. They genuflected—a sign of respect for the Blessed Sacrament—and walked through the side door into the hallway where, a few minutes ago, she'd run after Tisha Runner. The door outside stood partway open, and cool air floated toward them. They stepped through the door on the right into a small sacristy walled with cabinets and shelves. An old man puttered about: Mass book here, chalice there.

"Meet Father Cyprian," Father John said. The other priest shot her a sideways glance before going back to arranging the shelves. These younger priests. Drums at Mass. A woman in the sacristy. Vicky felt out of place, as if she'd blundered into the center of the male universe.

Father John had already shrugged out of the white chasuble. "What did Good Elk want?" he asked, hanging the garment inside a small closet.

"He claims the Arapaho ledger book doesn't exist," Vicky said. "It's a figment of my imagination, a story I've made up. Emil Coughlin agrees wholeheartedly."

"The man outside." Father John nodded toward the front of the church as he pulled on a black suit jacket over his black shirt. The garb of a priest, Vicky thought, so different from the blue jeans and plaid shirts, from the way she was used to him on the reservation.

"Look, Vicky," he went on. "We don't know who may be involved in Todd's murder. It's time you talked to the police."

Suddenly the old priest stepped between them. "What's this? If either of you knows something about the murder of this young man, it is my moral duty to remind you that you must tell the police."

Father John took the old man's arm and guided him aside. "Of course, Father," he said, glancing at Vicky. "We're going to do just that."

"Of course." Vicky fixed the strap of her bag into the crook of her shoulder. Looking past the old priest, she gave Father John a little wave and hurried out the side door.

Before she took her theory to Steve Clark, she intended to have another meeting with the curator at the Denver Museum of the West.

❮ 18 ❯

Vicky wheeled the Taurus around the southern edge of downtown Denver, catching a one-way street in the wrong direction, making a series of turns before she was heading in the right one. She'd frequently gotten lost in the maze of old downtown streets that followed the banks of the South Platte River. New sections of the city had grown up in a straight grid, which left the downtown streets angling into thoroughfares and butting into dead ends.

Finally she passed the white marble columns marching across the Denver Museum of the West. She drove the car to the same parking lot where she'd left it two days ago.

Inside the museum, the same elderly woman sat at the horseshoe-shaped desk. She frowned in disapproval as Vicky approached. "The curator has been trying to reach you," she said.

Vicky made her way to the third floor, where she found the office door open, the curator staring at the computer screen. She looked up just as Vicky was about to rap on the doorjamb. "Do come in," she called. The hint of a smile played on the red-lipsticked mouth. "We've solved our little mystery."

"Mystery?" Vicky crossed the office and took one of the chairs facing the desk. She kept her handbag on her lap, the leather cool in her hands.

"The mystery of how one of your elders could have seen a ledger book in the museum. The answer is quite simple." Rachel Foster's smile widened into a grin, exposing a row of perfect, white teeth.

Vicky felt a profound sense of relief tinged with confusion. If the ledger book was in the museum after all, why had the book dealer seemed to believe one was about to come on the market? She wondered if Rachel Foster had made inquiries, then had decided against trying to sell the book. Was it their meeting two days ago, when she had told the curator she knew about the book, that had changed the woman's mind? It didn't matter. Now the book could be returned to her people. "I'm glad the ledger book is safe," she said.

"No, no, no." The curator raised both hands in protest. "I'm afraid you misunderstand. We do not have a ledger book in our collections. We've checked the records from the day the museum opened through 1920. There is no record of an acquisition. We did find this, however." The curator opened the center drawer and withdrew a small red booklet. She handed it across the desk.

On the cover, in smeared black type, were the words: *Bulletin of the Denver Museum of the West, June 1920.*

"Your storyteller may be correct," Rachel Foster said as Vicky opened the booklet. "The museum had an exhibit on Plains Indian art during the summer of 1920. It's possible the ledger book was part of the exhibit. We did not own the book, however."

Vicky glanced up. The bulletin felt light in her hand. "What are you saying?"

Another wide smile. "A private collector must have loaned the book for the special exhibit." She nodded toward the bulletin. "It's all there."

Vicky slowly turned the pages. At the top of page four, in bold type was the heading: *The Unique Art of the Plains Indians.* A short paragraph told of the painted tipis, war shields, women's dresses, and warrior shirts on exhibit throughout the month of June. There was no mention of a ledger book.

"Museums often borrow items for special exhibits," Rachel Foster explained. "Two collectors loaned us some of the weapons for our current exhibit on Sand Creek. Obviously the curator in 1920 borrowed the ledger book." She waved one hand—a pesky matter settled.

Laying the bulletin on the desk, Vicky said, "I believe an Arapaho student found the ledger book in the museum last week and was using it for his thesis. His name was Todd Harris. Perhaps you read about him. He was murdered Monday night."

Rachel Foster gripped the edge of the desk and pulled herself forward. "What possible evidence could you have to link this museum with that horrible murder? You are dangerously close to slander, Ms. Holden." She picked up the bulletin and rapped it hard against the edge of the desk. "This was in the library stacks. This is what your graduate student found." Another whack. "He must have jumped to the conclusion that the exhibit included a ledger book."

"Ms. Foster," Vicky said, getting to her feet, "I would like to know which research materials Todd worked with last week. Could I see the sign-in sheets?"

The curator stood up, still gripping the desk. "This is outrageous. You are persisting with this . . . this"—she reached out one hand, as if to pull the appropriate expression from the air—"preposterous theory. Do you have any idea of the trouble you are causing? The Cheyennes and Comanches say they won't agree to the list of artifacts we supplied, since the Arapahos are contesting their list. You have ruined our reputation among the tribes. Why? Because some student found a bulletin and concocted an elaborate story. Well, this has gone far enough."

Vicky stepped closer to the desk. "I can ask for a court order to see the sign-in sheets," she said. A bluff, she knew. What she had was a theory. A theory wasn't evidence. The museum records were public record.

The curator drew her lips into a thin, red line. Her cheeks took on a paleness. After a moment she picked up the phone, tapped out some numbers, and cradling the receiver in her shoulder, huddled over it. She spoke quickly. Vicky Holden, Arapaho attorney, sign-in sheets, Todd Harris. Turning back, the phone still in hand, she said, "The research librarian will help you."

The young woman with the wedge of brown hair, the watchful eyes behind tiny, round glasses, sat at the desk inside the library. She picked up a file folder and handed it to Vicky. "The sign-in sheets you requested." Her voice was a whisper.

Vicky thumbed through the typed sheets. There were three—dated Tuesday, Wednesday, and Thursday of last week. Under *Patron's Name* on each sheet was a sharp, angular scrawl: Todd Harris. Under *Materials Requested*, the same scrawl: Smedden Collection.

"What is the Smedden Collection?" Vicky leaned across the desk, her index finger underlining the words.

The librarian swiveled toward a computer on a small table next to the desk. A few keystrokes, and she was squinting at the monitor through the little glasses. "Collection donated by James J. Smedden and family in 1903. Miscellaneous documents pertaining to Kiowa County, late 1800s."

Vicky felt the muscles clench in her stomach. Sand Creek was located in Kiowa County. "May I see the collection?" she asked.

The librarian seemed to gather herself inward, hesitating. "The file contains a complete list of all documents in the collection." She nodded toward the wall of filing cabinets beyond the stacks.

"The collection, please," Vicky said.

Sighing, the young woman got to her feet, a slow unfolding. "The collection is in storage. It will take a few moments."

Vicky walked across the reading room and sat down at a vacant table. An elderly man at the next table was running a magnifying glass across a yellowed newspaper. He turned watery blue eyes on her a moment before peering again through the glass. There was the quiet jangling of the phone, the soft scuffing of footsteps somewhere in the stacks. Finally the librarian appeared with a brown carton the size of a large hatbox. She set it in front of Vicky and handed her a pair of white gloves. "Will that be all?" she asked, as if she'd just delivered a hamburger.

"I would also like to see the past year's sign-in sheets for Todd Harris," Vicky said.

"The past year?" The woman blinked behind the glasses. "That information's in the database. It will take a while to print it out."

"I'll be here," Vicky said, raising the lid on the carton.

"We are trying to cooperate with you people."

Vicky glanced up. The remark surprised her. "My people appreciate it," she said. After the young woman had turned away, she pulled on the gloves and began lifting out the documents—a collection of deeds tied in faded blue ribbon, a brown envelope stuffed with old maps, stacks of envelopes with folded letters, edges crinkled and brown, several small, bound books, a handwritten manuscript.

She sank back against the hard chair rungs and stared at the manuscript. The writing was faded and smeared. Across the first page were large, capitalized words: MEMORIES OF J. J. SMEDDEN. Quickly she flipped through the other pages, glancing at the headings: *Boyhood in Missouri. Sergeant in Civil War. Soldiering on the Plains. Ranching Days.*

Setting the manuscript aside, she leafed through the small books: journals telling of the weather, the cattle sold at market in Denver, the cattle lost in the storms of the 1860s, 1870s. She stood up and lifted the rest of the documents and papers from the carton. More manuscripts. More journals. And then she saw it: a gray ledger book pressed against the bottom. It was probably six inches wide and twelve or thirteen inches long. Her hands shook as she brought it out of the carton. Slowly she dropped to the chair and pushed the carton aside. She laid the book on the table. A faint red stripe ran down the front cover, which was roughened with age. She opened it carefully. On the first page, inked words precisely formed: *Accounts. Double D Ranch. James J. Smedden, proprietor.* Down the left were notations: feed, chickens, harness, halter. On the right, columns of figures. With a sinking heart, she turned the rest of the pages—similar notations, similar figures.

A ledger book. A common ledger book kept by every rancher and farmer, every store owner in the West. The same kind of ledger book kept by the government agents to the Plains Indian tribes. How the warriors prized them! Would trade buffalo robes or ponies for a simple, gray-clothed ledger book with empty pages and a couple of pencils—colored pencils were best. Precious possessions with which to write the stories.

It felt stuffy in the reading room, as if the air had been sucked away, and Vicky leaned back into the chair. Was this where Todd had found the ledger book? Pressed against the bottom of the carton, under the other ledger book? What had he done? Did he lift it into the air, scarcely aware of the precious possession he held in his hands? Open the cover, study the first page, the following pages, reading from right to left, the way ledger books were meant to be read, getting a sense of the story. At what point did he realize the story was about Sand Creek? What clues did he find? The uniforms of the soldiers? The detailed drawings of the rifles? The guidons of the Third Colorado Regiment? The village in the big bend of the creek bed. The name *glyph*—a red bull—above the pictograph of No-Ta-Nee, the storyteller.

Vicky let her eyes roam about the room. The elderly man peering through the magnifying glass; other patrons engrossed in old books and manuscripts, the librarian bent over a printer behind her desk. Did anyone notice a young man at one of the tables, hunched over a ledger book?

Three days Todd had come to the museum to study the ledger book, the account of the massacre. Another voice, another point of view that would expand and shape the story of that terrible day. How could he contain his excitement? Whom did he tell?

Vicky rummaged through her bag for the small pad and a pen. She opened the pad and jotted *adviser*. It seemed logical, yet Emil Coughlin had denied knowing about the ledger book. He'd claimed he hadn't talked to Todd after he'd gotten back from his research trip to southeastern Colorado. She drew a black line under the word. She had interviewed clients who, with a mountain of evidence proving their guilt, had claimed they were innocent.

She made a large question mark after *adviser*, trying to think what she would have done had she found the ledger book. Her eyes scanned the room. She would have taken the book to the librarian: "Did you know . . . ? Do you realize . . . ?"

Is that what Todd had done? Had the librarian called Rachel Foster? Is that when the ledger book disappeared?

Vicky wrote down *curator* and underlined the word.

Then she slipped the pad and pen inside her bag. Carefully she set the documents back in the carton, the flush of anger warm in her face. Something had alerted Todd that the ledger book was in danger—that he was in danger because he'd found it. What happened when he came back to the museum on the third day? Was that when he found the ledger book missing? Did he fear he would be accused of taking it? Is that why he drove to the reservation to see Father John, the only man he knew he could trust?

Vicky fixed the strap of her bag over her shoulder and walked to the desk. The printer made an intermittent shushing noise, like a broom pushing against dry leaves. Scooping up a stack of paper, the assistant handed it to her. "Copies of the sign-in sheets," she said.

Vicky rifled through them. There was no mention of the J. J. Smedden Collection before last week. Not until last week had Todd used the collection. Not until then had he found the ledger book. She said, "Did Todd Harris tell you about the ledger book he discovered?"

The young woman's head jerked backward, as if she'd been slapped. Her eyes blinked rapidly. "Ms. Foster said you believe the museum owns a ledger book. It's not true." The hint of a smile began to play at the corners of her mouth—a kind of embarrassment. "All of us here wish it were true."

Vicky wondered about the inducements that would cause a young librarian to lie. A hefty bonus paid under the table from the sale of a ledger book valued at exactly $1.3 million? Enough to risk a career? A reputation? A criminal charge? She said, "I would like to see the file on the Smedden Collection after all."

A mixture of relief and eagerness crept into the young woman's face. This was firm ground—the retrieval of materials and files. She gave a quick nod and dodged into the stacks. When she didn't reappear after a few minutes, Vicky started back along the rows of metal shelving, past the spines of old books, the cartons jutting forward. She found the assistant at the filing cabinets, stooped over an opened drawer. "I don't understand," the woman said, her voice tense. "It should be here. It must have been misfiled." After a moment she slammed the drawer and yanked open the drawer below.

Vicky watched the thin fingers combing the folders. Whoever had taken the ledger book had removed all the records, every possible trace, just as she had suspected.

Abruptly Vicky swung around. She retraced her steps through the stacks and out into the corridor. The light flickered above the elevator: Three. Two. One. She felt as if she couldn't catch her breath; her heart raced. The ledger book was on the market. A dealer could have bought it today. How long before the pages would be in expensive frames on the walls of collectors willing to pay thousands of dollars for an example of Plains Indian art?

There was so little time. But she had something now. She knew where the ledger book had been lost in the museum; she'd found the dealer waiting to handle it, waiting on the highest bid. Steve Clark would have to take her theory seriously.

◄ 19 ►

The lawns and pathways of Regis seemed familiar, Father John thought as he pulled into his usual parking spot behind the Jesuit residence. The sun dipped toward the mountains, an orange ball of fire suspended in a sky as blue and clear as a mountain lake.

He'd spent most of the afternoon at Doyal and Mary's, eating a bologna sandwich and a piece of white cake, sipping hot coffee, while he visited with the grandmothers and elders who had sat in the front pews at Mass this morning. Neighbors and friends, cousins of cousins, blood relatives and spiritual relatives—a gathering of Indian people. How many gatherings had he attended on the reservation? So many funerals; he could no longer keep count. And afterward he was always the guest of honor—the priest whose prayers accompanied the spirit into the sky world.

He knew that later today Mary and Doyal would fly to the reservation. He also knew, although no one had told him, that everyone at the house had chipped in—hard-earned dollars, carefully counted out change—so the old couple could take their grandson to the Middle Earth for burial.

He mounted the front steps at the residence, wondering what Vicky had learned at the museum, if she had gone to the police, if she had called. He'd felt a stab of worry as he remembered the determination in her eyes when she'd walked out of the sacristy this morning. What was it that drove her? As if she could right past wrongs—a lone woman. How appropriate the grand-mothers' name for her: *Hisei ci nihi*. Woman alone.

He was about to let himself inside when the door swung open and Father Stanton appeared. "So, you've finally returned," he said. "I believe your memorial Mass was over at eleven this morning. Where have you been?"

"What's going on?" Father John had no intention of accounting for his time, even though the black-suited man blocking his way was his superior.

The other priest squared his shoulders. "The provin-cial had a break in his schedule this afternoon, and I convinced him to meet with you. You were nowhere to be seen, however."

"I can meet with him now."

Father Stanton threw his head back and gave a little laugh. "The provincial left thirty minutes ago. He has a busy schedule, a great many matters to deal with while he's here. If this museum of yours is so important, you should have made yourself available."

"What about this evening?" Father John asked. "To-morrow?"

"The provincial has meetings through the noon meal tomorrow, after which we will depart for the airport. I'm afraid you have missed your opportunity, Father O'Malley." He shook his head, an expression of mock sorrow in his face. "Perhaps the next time the provincial comes this way."

"I intend to see him," Father John said. "You're going to have to squeeze me in."

The other priest stepped back, a startled look in his eyes—the alcoholic priest; one never knew what to ex-pect. "Your attitude is highly inappropriate," he man-aged. "Need I remind you—"

"I'll be in the provincial's office first thing in the

morning," Father John said, brushing past the other priest.

The air was stuffy in the entry, faint with the odor of fresh fish and brewing coffee. From somewhere came the clatter of dishes and pans, the usual preparations for dinner. Before starting up the stairs, Father John checked the small table against the back wall. There was a folded sheet of paper with *J. O'Malley* scrawled on top. He picked it up. *One P.M. Professor Good Elk called.*

Father John glanced at his watch: nearly half-past four. He might catch Good Elk before he left his office. Crumpling the paper into the little wastebasket next to the table, he walked back outside, past Father Stanton, who was leaning against the railing, staring at the blue rim of mountains in the distance. He cut across the campus, walking around a group of students lounging under a tree, papers scattered about.

Inside the Main Classroom building, he took the stairs two at a time and strode down a corridor to the history department office. The secretary looked like one of the students he'd passed—white T-shirt, blond hair tucked behind her ears. She glanced up from the book in front of her. "You're the mission priest!" she said, eyes wide in surprise, as if a strange new creature had happened along. She babbled on: Oh, she'd heard he was on campus. The tall man in the cowboy hat. All the students were wondering—

"Is Professor Good Elk in?" Father John interrupted.

Before she could reply, a barrel-chested man with dark, slanted eyes and black hair combed back from a round, puffy face stepped through the door behind the desk. "Well, Father O'Malley." His voice boomed into the quiet office. "Come in. Come in."

Father John stepped past the door, and the professor gave it a shove—a loud thwack. "Have a seat, Father."

He motioned toward a chair at the corner of a desk that reminded Father John of his own: the papers and folders that seemed to reproduce themselves in front of his eyes, the endless matters demanding his attention.

He perched on the edge of the chair, where, he imagined, students usually sat, supplicants awaiting favors— a different class, a better grade. The professor folded his large frame into the chair behind the desk. He swiveled slowly from side to side. "Your friend has caused a lot of unnecessary trouble on Indian reservations."

So this was why Good Elk wanted to see him: to convince him to talk Vicky into giving up her search for the ledger book. He said, "I take it we're talking about Vicky Holden."

Good Elk stopped swiveling. "I made a few inquiries. Didn't take long to find out you and Vicky Holden work on the Wind River Reservation. I figured you gotta be friends." He shrugged. "Point is, Father O'Malley, Cheyennes are refusing to acknowledge the inventory from the Denver Museum of the West. Same with Lakotas, Kiowas, and Comanches. Everybody waiting to see if the museum is hiding a ledger book that belongs to Arapahos. Everybody saying, what's the museum hiding that belongs to us? Nobody trusts the museum. Whole NAGPRA process has dropped in its tracks like a shot coyote."

Father John held up one hand. "An Arapaho ledger book on Sand Creek is missing," he said "As soon as she finds out what happened to it—"

"There's no Sand Creek ledger book," Good Elk cut in. The chair squeaked as he leaned back. "There was one written by a Cheyenne warrior, but it was destroyed years ago. Only one page is extant, and it's in a museum."

"Todd Harris, the student who was murdered, found the book." A theory, Father John knew, but it

made sense, and he had learned that Vicky's theories—
her instincts—had a way of being right.

"Yes, yes." The professor waved one hand. "Rachel
Foster has told me what Vicky Holden claims. How
could an Arapaho warrior write about Sand Creek? No
Arapahos were there. Sand Creek was a massacre of
Cheyenne people."

"The Arapaho Chief Niwot and his band were there.
Fifty of them were killed." Father John felt the hard
knot of anger in his throat. Was this what drove Vicky?
The flare of anger at each new injustice?

The professor fixed him with a cold stare. "You're
out of the history field, Father O'Malley. A lot of things
have happened since you got stuck at a mission in the
middle of Wyoming. Obviously you're uninformed of
the new scholarship. The Arapahos missed the party
Colonel Chivington and Governor Evans threw for my
people at Sand Creek."

Father John drew in a long breath. "How much is
the land worth that the Cheyennes hope to reclaim?
Enough to rewrite history?"

Good Elk brought one fist down hard on the desk.
Little piles of paper jiggled and slid sideways. Levering
himself onto his feet, he said, "This isn't about land."

Father John was on his feet. "Don't give me that,
Good Elk. You've staked your reputation on a piece of
revisionist history that you hope will force the government to give all the land to the Cheyenne tribe. The last
thing you want is a ledger book that proves Arapahos
were also at Sand Creek."

The professor shifted his massive bulk over the desk,
eyes black with rage, cheeks mottled with angry red
splotches. "Let me tell you what you want, Father
O'Malley." Little specks of spittle landed on the papers.
"A museum at St. Francis Mission. Well, the provincial
happens to be a friend of mine. He knows what you're
after. Yesterday, at the meeting in the mountains, he

asked me what I thought. You know what I told him? The whole idea stinks. Arapahos didn't leave behind enough artifacts to fill up a garage." He stopped. Pulling himself upright, he drew in a long breath. "The provincial takes my advice. I am, after all, a Native American. Tomorrow when I meet him, I can tell him I've changed my mind. That the museum at St. Francis Mission would be a fine idea. I guarantee you'll have your museum this summer."

"Let me guess," Father John said, struggling to contain his fury. "All I have to do is convince Vicky Holden to give up any notion of a Sand Creek ledger book."

The professor nodded. "Soon as Arapahos give up this preposterous notion, the rest of us can get on with the business of reclaiming our artifacts. I'm offering you a good deal, Father O'Malley."

"No deal." Father John swept one hand across the desk. A pile of books thudded against the floor. He turned and walked out of the office.

◀ 20 ▶

Vicky hurried through the patterns of sunshine falling across the plaza in front of the Denver Police Department complex. Two buildings of sand-colored brick, massive and impersonal symbols of authority, formed an L along the plaza. A young couple—Hispanic, perhaps, faces grim—exited the wide glass doors of the building on the right. Vicky let herself into the other building, nearly colliding with a couple of uniformed policemen on their way out.

The stretch of lobby across the front was dim and cool as a vault. A murmur of voices floated from the roped-off area in the far corner where a sprinkling of people sat hunched in metal-framed chairs. Straight ahead was a reception counter, and beyond, a four-foot-high wooden railing that blocked off access to a bank of elevators.

Digging through her black bag for a business card, Vicky crossed to the counter, heels clacking against the brown-tiled floor. She handed the card to a policewoman behind the counter and asked to see Detective Clark.

"Gotta have a look at your driver's license," the policewoman said, examining the card.

Another fishing expedition in her purse, and Vicky slid the license across the counter.

The policewoman studied the miniature photo, glancing up at Vicky several times. Then: "Detective Clark know what this is about?"

"Please ring him," Vicky said, using her lawyer tone.

The policewoman picked up the telephone. There was a quick exchange of information, followed by a nod toward the roped-off area. "Wait there."

Vicky took a seat offering an unobstructed view of the elevators. A couple of young women in cutoff jeans and T-shirts slouched on chairs to her left. Across from her were three middle-aged men, bony, roughened hands clasped between knees, red-rimmed eyes staring at the floor, exuding an air of resignation and hopelessness. What had brought them here? she wondered. What terrible events?

There was a loud ping, and the elevator doors parted. Steve Clark stepped out. Vicky jumped to her feet and hurried over to the gate in the railing that he held open. "A social call, I hope," he said.

"I've got some new information," Vicky said, her arm inadvertently brushing his as she walked past.

Steve snapped the gate into place and hit the elevator button. "I'm in the information business," he said as the doors splayed open and they stepped inside. He pushed another button and leaned against the side wall, smiling at her.

They exited on the fourth floor and walked down a carpeted corridor past a series of closed doors. The air felt warm and close, as if the air-conditioning didn't extend into the corridors. From somewhere came the soft clacking sound of a keyboard, the muffled screech of a phone. Another policeman in civilian clothes, a thick file folder in hand, came toward them. There was the typical hurried male exchange, Vicky thought, that had nothing to do with communication: "How's it going? Can't complain."

Steve opened a door and motioned her into a large room with about a dozen desks arranged in rows, a chalkboard covered with white scribblings on the left wall, and on the far wall, windows that framed a patch of blue sky and the white peaks of the mountains. The room was deserted except for two men huddled together at a desk in the center, voices low and intense. Neither looked up as Steve led her over to the desk against the window.

"This is where I ponder the world," he said, one fist thumping the desktop. Neat stacks of folders and papers trailed around the edges. In one corner, the photo of a little girl with long blond hair looked out from a small silver frame. "Kathy, my daughter," he said, following Vicky's eyes.

Vicky smiled at him. She didn't know Steve had a child. Fatherhood suited him, she thought. She took the chair he'd pulled over for her.

"So what do you bring me?" The detective dropped into the swivel chair behind the desk and leaned back toward the window.

"A theory." Vicky felt the jittery flutters in her stomach that she always felt when she was about to sum up a case before the jury, pull together scattered pieces of evidence, weave a story that made sense. She launched into what she had pieced together: a graduate student documenting the sites of his people's villages and battlefields, stumbling across a ledger book lost in a museum, recognizing the story of a massacre that occurred more than a hundred years before, ending up murdered because he had found the book.

Little furrows came into the detective's forehead and questions flashed in his eyes. The story sounded farfetched even to her own ears, a tale as thin and insubstantial as the pages in an old ledger book. She hurried on, explaining how the government had promised lands in Colorado to the people of Sand Creek—lands never actually allotted—and how the ledger book proved Arapahos had been in the village.

Steve ran his fingers along the edge of his chin. "If what you're telling me is true, the museum will have records."

"They're gone," she said. "Anything that connects the ledger book to the museum is gone. That's why the killer ransacked Todd's apartment and took his computer—to destroy any reference to the book."

The detective swirled sideways and glanced out the window a moment. "Let me get this straight," he said, looking back. "Todd Harris was murdered over an old Indian ledger book and a massacre that happened way back in history."

"A ledger book worth more than a million dollars." Vicky kept her voice steady, firm. "A ledger book that proves Arapahos are entitled to lands worth even more." She jumped to her feet and walked over to the window. Traffic threaded along Thirteenth Avenue below, a silent procession broken by the occasional squeal of brakes.

She turned back. "Suppose the museum curator saw the chance to make a lot of money from an artifact everybody had forgotten existed. I happen to know Rachel Foster could use some money." There was resistance in his eyes. She plunged on: "Suppose a scholar by the name of Bernard Good Elk claims that only Cheyennes were at Sand Creek. What would he do if a ledger book that proved otherwise suddenly surfaced?"

Steve was tapping a pencil against the edge of the desk, a hard, steady rhythm. "Okay," he said. "Let's assume this million-dollar ledger book exists, and Todd Harris discovered it. There is another possibility."

"Don't say it." Vicky held up one hand, fingers outstretched. If he spoke the words, they would take on the weight of truth. "Todd Harris is not the one who took the book."

"You don't know that."

That was true. She had no proof, only a sense of

what was true, of what Todd would have done. She said, "Todd would have shown the book to someone in the museum—the research librarian, maybe the curator herself. He would have expected the museum to protect the book. That's what museums do."

Steve held her gaze a moment before sliding a folder off one of the stacks. "A million dollars buys a lot of heroin, Vicky," he said, weariness in his voice. "It could pay off a lot of drug suppliers." He opened the folder and lifted out a printed page. "The autopsy report," he said. "I didn't want to have to tell you. Todd Harris's system was full of heroin."

Vicky was standing behind her chair. She grabbed the top. The wood grain felt rough against her palms. "There has to be some explanation, Steve."

"Why?" An irritation in his tone now. "Because Todd Harris was Arapaho, and Arapaho kids never do drugs? Let me tell you, I've seen dead kids of every color and stripe shot up with heroin and a lot of drugs you haven't even heard of. Why should Todd Harris be any different?"

"I knew him," Vicky said slowly, measuring the words.

Steve leaned forward. "There were needle tracks on his right arm."

"Right arm?" Vicky stepped around and dropped onto the edge of the chair. "Todd was right-handed, Steve. Somebody wanted it to look as if he'd shot heroin."

"You're a stubborn woman, Vicky." The detective slipped the report back inside the folder and stared at her a long moment. Then: "Okay, there's the possibility the tracks were fresh."

"What? You knew this?"

"It's a possibility. We don't know for certain. The body was in the water at least twelve hours. It was pretty bruised."

Vicky gathered her handbag and got to her feet.

What was she thinking? That she could send a homicide detective on a wild-goose chase after a ledger book when the evidence he needed—the evidence he wanted—was at his fingertips? "You're not going to look into the ledger book, are you?"

"Look into a ledger book that's not in the museum and for which there are no records?" Steve pushed his chair back and stood up. "It would help to have some proof the damn book exists." He came around the desk toward her. "But I'll see what I can find out. Okay?"

She was about to thank him when the phone at the far edge of the desk emitted a screech. "Look, I've been thinking," he said. "I don't care if you are involved with somebody else. We could still have dinner tonight, couldn't we? Two old friends." Stepping back, he picked up the receiver, mouthing the words, "Think about it." Then, into the receiver: "Detective Clark here." There was a long silence broken by the sound of his pencil scratching on a sheet of paper.

After a moment Steve snapped the receiver into place. "Before you turn me down again, I'm withdrawing the invitation. We've got another homicide victim just washed up in the South Platte." He reached toward a coat tree near the window and lifted off a blue blazer.

"Who?" Vicky heard the fear in her voice.

"Hispanic or Native American." He pulled on the blazer. "A lot of bruises and contusions on the body."

"My God," Vicky said. "Just like Todd."

"Wrong, Vicky." He came around the desk. "This homicide's a woman."

Vicky followed him across the room, past the other two detectives still huddled over the desk, intent on the papers spread before them. "Let me come with you."

"No way," he said. "You don't need this."

They hurried down the corridor. "It might be a friend of Todd's," Vicky persisted. "It might be someone I know."

"You don't want to see another body." Steve punched the elevator button and stared at the closed doors, as if he could will them to open. Another moment and the doors parted. They stepped inside the small space filled with a faint odor of cigarette smoke. She felt the floor dropping beneath her. Then the hard stop, and they walked out toward the railing. He took her arm and pulled her out of the way of two uniforms coming through the gate.

"Where did they find the body?" she asked.

He leaned toward her. She could smell the after-shave, the trace of coffee on his breath. "Okay," he said. "I can't stop you from going, but I'm not going to take you. The victim's at Confluence Park."

A large crowd had already gathered as Vicky wheeled into a dirt lot behind three police cars, an ambulance, and a white Blazer with a gold City and County of Denver insignia on the side doors. Not far away, the rush-hour traffic streamed along I-25, tires crying out against the asphalt. She ran toward the crowd of bikers and joggers blocking the pathway along the South Platte River. Shouldering past the perspiring, Lycra-clad bodies, the handlebars and spoked wheels, she reached the top of a little hill overlooking the placid, gray-blue river. Below, a line of yellow police tape marked off a half circle on the rock-strewn bank. Inside the tape was another crowd—medics, uniformed policemen hovering over what looked like a small, twisted bag of rocks caught among the boulders.

Steve Clark stood in the middle, like a bandleader—directing, admonishing—as the medics lifted the body onto a stretcher and started up the slope, huffing with the weight, although the girl was small, scarcely more than a child. Vicky saw the face, the red marks, the swollen eyes. A black braid fell loose over the edge of the stretcher.

The crowd climbed up, Steve in the lead. He veered toward her. "One of the officers found a wallet over there." He nodded toward the clump of wild grasses spiking the rocks. "Could be the victim's. Name is Julie . . ."

Vicky closed her eyes a moment. *The face isn't what you're gonna want to see every time you close your eyes the rest of your life,* Steve had told her when she had insisted upon going to the morgue. Todd's face had been in her mind since. And now there would be another. She turned away and started back to the lot.

"Last name's Clearwater," the detective said, walking alongside her. They waited as the white Blazer backed up, then turned into the street, bound for the morgue, Vicky thought, where Todd had been taken. And who would claim the body, who would grieve for Julie Clearwater? A grandmother somewhere on the Rosebud Reservation? A brother or sister? A friend?

Vicky swallowed back the lump forming in her throat. She would not cry again, she told herself, hurrying toward the Taurus, the detective beside her.

"What do you know about Julie Clearwater?" he asked.

Sliding inside, she gripped the steering wheel—the solidity, the steadiness. *Nothing,* she thought, staring through the windshield at the police officers milling around the lot, the bikers starting to roll down the path. She knew nothing about the girl. Except . . . "There's a student at CU-Denver. Tisha Runner. I met her at Indian Services. She might know something." Drawing in a long breath, Vicky turned toward the detective. "Todd told Julie about the ledger book. So they killed her."

Steve dipped his head. She couldn't see his eyes, couldn't gauge his thoughts. She heard the quick intakes of breath—in and out, in and out. Slowly he brought his eyes back to hers. "They were doing drugs together, Vicky. They met up with some bad people, the kind that beat kids to death if they try cheating the dealers, start thinking they're smarter. Both murders have drug-deal-gone-wrong written all over them. I've seen enough to know. Forget about your ledger-book theory. There's no proof."

Vicky gripped the wheel harder, nails biting into her palms. "You're wrong," she said.

"Did you see the victim's arms?" His voice was softer. "There were needle tracks all over them."

Vicky wasn't sure how she'd gotten to Marcy's, what route she'd followed. She'd driven through the dusk on automatic. Stop. Go. Turn here. Turn there. Slow for brake lights ahead. On automatic she had wheeled through the drive-in, picked up a hamburger and Coke, feeling the hollowness inside, the light-headedness. Her thoughts on two dead Indian kids, so like her own kids, Lucas and Susan. About the same age, the same black hair and dark eyes, the same caramel-colored skin. It might have been them; what was to keep such unspeakable horror from her own kids trying to make their way in a city—in Los Angeles—where there was no one to look after them, no one to protect them?

She let herself into the man-made coolness of Marcy's house. From out in back came the slow, rhythmic sound of drums. Through the patio doors beyond the kitchen, she could see a group of women sitting cross-legged in a circle—long hair falling across shoulders and backs, loose, robelike dresses billowing over the patio. Marcy curled over a small drum.

Suddenly the tapping stopped, and before Vicky could escape down the hallway, Marcy sprang to her feet and slid back the patio door. "Come join us," she called.

Vicky held up one hand and began pleading exhaustion, work to do. She would have a bite to eat in her room, she said, and then fall into bed. She didn't mean to be unsociable; she was sure they were having a good time—how should she put it—a meaningful experience. She was rambling, grateful that Marcy finally broke in. "You could be so much help to us."

Vicky stared at the woman framed by the patio door, like a butterfly pinned to the glass. She was thinking she'd been no help to anyone lately—not to Todd, not to a Lakota girl. Certainly not to the police.

She forced her mind back to what Marcy was saying: something about tapping into the strength and courage and endurance of Native American women. "You have endured, Vicky," her friend said. "Through centuries of pain and disruption because of your spiritual strength." Marcy stretched out her hand, as if she might reach across the space between them. "If you would just talk to us. Tell us how we, too, can tap into our spiritual strength and become whole and vibrant."

In her mind's eye, Vicky saw the broken body of Julie Clearwater. She had to fight the urge to run, get in the Taurus, and drive—across the city, across the plains, back to the reservation. She said, "It will have to be another time, Marcy."

Ignoring the disappointment in her friend's face, Vicky walked down the hallway to the bedroom. As she closed the door she heard the patio door slam into place, detected the little ripple through the floorboards, and felt a wave of regret that she was not the kind of friend Marcy seemed to need.

She sank into the pillows propped on the bed and tried to concentrate on the yellow legal pad and pen in her lap. What was she missing? Why couldn't she see it? Somewhere there was proof the ledger book existed, that it had been in a carton stacked on shelves amid hundreds of other cartons.

She wrote in block letters: TODD. Under the name, SMEDDEN COLLECTION. And under that, LEDGER BOOK. She drew long, black lines between the words, around the words, trying to find some kind of connection. What was she missing? Why couldn't she see the connection? She made more slashes—a series of lines nearly cutting through the paper. Then she threw the pad aside and dug into the white bag for the hamburger. The filmy curtains moved at the window in the faintest stir of air; the drumming was light and muffled, a barely perceptible tapping, like a small animal nibbling at the side of the house.

She had only eaten half the hamburger and taken a few sips of Coke before she fell asleep to the sounds of a drum beating in a faraway place and time.

◀ 21 ▶

The jangling noise came from far away, and for a moment Vicky thought she was on the reservation, where dancers were approaching the powwow arbor. Suddenly she jerked upright. A faint light from the street lamps outside drifted through the window. There was the soft shushing noise of the air conditioning. She was at Marcy's, and the phone was ringing on the night stand.

She lifted the receiver.

"It's for you, Vicky." Marcy's voice came over the line. Her friend had already picked up an extension.

There was a soft click, and another voice, more desperate. "Vicky Holden?"

"Yes," she said, a slight sense of disorientation still present.

"Tisha Runner. You probably don't remember me."

"I remember you," Vicky said, her senses alert now.

"Can you come over?" The thud of drums echoed in the background.

"Where are you?"

"I'm at the powwow. Denver Indian Center."

Vicky glanced at the digital clock on the nightstand: 9:45. She'd dozed off for more than hour. "I'll be there," she said.

In five minutes she had splashed cold water on her face, touched up her lipstick, and was back in the car, sipping on the Coke—it was lukewarm now. Another twenty minutes and she parked in the last vacant space in front of the white, low-slung building—an elementary school at one time—that housed the Denver Indian Center.

Spreading from the center, like spokes from a wheel, were streets clogged with old pickups and trucks in front of small, frame houses—the Indian neighborhood in the river bottoms of the long-dried-up tributaries of the South Platte. Doyal and Mary lived only a few blocks away.

The muffled *thump, thump, thump* of drums floated into the night air. Vicky followed the sound around the building to what had once been the gymnasium. Inside, the drumming reverberated off the cement-block walls, filling the cavernlike space. Indian families sat on folding chairs arranged in a wide circle around the dancers: a group of men and boys swirling and dipping, bare feet pounding the tiled floor.

Vicky stood inside the door a moment, transported into another time and place. The dancers wore buffalo headdresses covered with matted brown fur, horns curving upward. They danced as her people had always danced, to ask the buffalo to share his qualities with the people: strength, courage, endurance, and generosity.

"You wanna stay? Three dollars." The voice startled her, brought her back to herself. An old man sat at a small table next to the door. In front of him was an open cigar box with dollar bills and coins stacked neatly inside.

"Yes, Grandfather," Vicky said. She removed three dollar-bills from her handbag and handed them to the old man, then started past the circle of folding chairs, her eyes searching the brown faces for Tisha Runner. She didn't see the girl anywhere.

She walked down a wide hallway, fluorescent lights casting shiny circles over the green-tiled floor. Smells of hot grease and charred meat drifted toward her. At the end of the hallway, a scattering of people lined up in front of a counter stacked with bowls of potato chips and buns, plates of hamburgers. On the other side several grandmothers scurried about the kitchen.

Vicky let herself through the door next to the counter, aware of the grandmothers' eyes on her—the stranger. A Native American by the black hair, brown skin, and almond-shaped eyes, but not one of them. Not someone they knew. She stopped next to the old woman scooping coffee grounds into an oversized metal coffeepot. "Excuse me, Grandmother." she began, "I see you're very busy, and I'm sorry to interrupt you." The dance of politeness must always be observed. "I'm supposed to meet someone here. Her name is Tisha Runner."

The old woman shook her head and went back to scooping the coffee. Out of the corner of her eye, Vicky saw another woman set a bowl of potato salad on the counter and start toward her. "Come with me," the second grandmother said.

The sound of drums faded behind them as they walked down another corridor past doors that had once led into classrooms. Small signs read: LITTLE EAGLE PRESCHOOL, CIRCLE DAY CARE, HEALTH CENTER. The old woman stopped at a door with the sign OFFICE. "You wait in here," she directed.

The office was narrow and small, probably carved out of an adjoining classroom. Shoved against one wall were two desks cluttered with papers and notebooks. A couple of metal chairs were propped against the opposite wall. The drumming sounded far away, an echo of her own heartbeat.

After a few moments there was a shuffling of footsteps in the corridor; the door swung open and Tisha Runner walked in. She looked the same: the black shiny hair falling toward her face, the blue jeans and T-shirt.

She carried a small brown envelope. Without saying anything, she sank into one of the metal chairs, a tenseness in the way she moved.

"Police found a body in the river this afternoon," she said. The words were clipped, abrupt. "It's been on the TV. I'm scared it's Julie."

Vicky perched on the edge of the desk. "Is Julie a friend of yours?"

The girl shook her head, a stiff, deliberate motion. "She was staying with me the last couple days, that's all. I didn't want to say anything at school yesterday 'cause she was real scared. She asked me not to tell anybody where she was."

"Tell me about her." Vicky tried to conceal her anger and frustration. If Tisha Runner had told her about Julie yesterday, maybe the girl would be alive.

"I don't know much." A quick shrug. "She's Lakota from up on the Rosebud. She got here a couple weeks ago and was looking for someplace to stay till she got a job. So she came to the center. I work here part time, over in day care." She tilted her head toward the hallway. "Julie seemed real nice, kinda lost, you know, 'cause this was her first time off the res. I would've let her stay over at my place, but I only got a foldout. So I said I'd ask around, which I did over at school."

She stopped a moment, gazing at some point beyond Vicky's shoulder. "Somebody said Todd Harris had an extra bedroom. He was gone a lot, and he might like somebody watchin' the place. So I gave her Todd's number, and it all worked out, you know, except Todd was murdered, and now . . ."

Vicky gripped the edge of the desk and leaned forward. "Why did Julie leave Todd's?" she asked.

"She didn't want to leave," the girl said. "He told her she had to get out."

"When?"

"Last Sunday." Another shrug.

Sunday, Vicky was thinking. The last time the old woman at the apartment building had seen Todd was Sunday.

"He told her it was too dangerous for her to stay in the apartment," the girl went on. "He called me up and asked if Julie could stay at my place a few days. I said okay, a few days." Tisha pushed back in the chair; the legs squeaked along the tile. "Next thing we know, Todd gets murdered, and Julie freaked out. I mean, she went nuts. Said she had to find some way to get to the reservation."

"She wanted to go back to the Rosebud," Vicky said. A confirmation. It was what she had expected.

"Rosebud? She was trying to find a ride up to the Wind River Reservation."

"What?

"Todd gave her this." Tisha held up the brown envelope. "He made her promise if anything happened to him, she'd get it to Father O'Malley. Then she heard how Father O'Malley was gonna say the memorial Mass, so she wouldn't have to go to Wyoming. She could give him the envelope at St. Elizabeth's. But she didn't show up for the Mass. When I went back to my place to look for her, I found the envelope still in the closet where she was hiding it. And now she might be dead, and I don't know what to do with this." Another thrust of the envelope into the air. "I don't know how to get a hold of Father O'Malley. I can't go all the way up to Wyoming."

"He's staying at Regis," Vicky said. She reached toward the phone. "I'll call him."

"No, wait." The girl was on her feet. She handed Vicky the envelope. "Just give it to him, okay? I don't wanna be involved." She started for the door.

"Tisha." Vicky caught the girl's arm. "I was there this afternoon when the police found Julie."

The girl blinked, pulling away, head shaking, nostrils flaring.

"You are involved," Vicky went on. "The police will have to talk to you. There's a detective—Steve Clark—he's a friend of mine. You can trust him."

Still backing up, the girl groped behind her for the doorknob. "I don't want anything to do with murder. I didn't know Julie very long. I didn't know Todd real well. I don't know what they were involved with, but I don't want anything to do with it." She found the knob and yanked open the door.

"You could be in danger," Vicky said as the girl darted out the door. Vicky followed. "You've got to go to the police," she called, but the girl had already disappeared around a corner.

Vicky stared down the empty corridor a moment. The drumming had stopped; in its place, the rustle of footsteps, the spike of voices coming from the serving counter. She turned back into the office and slowly opened the envelope. Inside was a diskette. It didn't surprise her. She had expected Todd to keep a backup diskette. She slipped it back into the envelope and stuffed the package into her handbag. Then found the little sheet of paper on which John O'Malley had scribbled down the number at Regis.

◄ 22 ►

Father John heard the phone ringing as he came down the corridor. He'd taken a walk along the lake after dinner, trying to sort his thoughts. He'd missed the chance to talk to the provincial this afternoon; the museum was beginning to seem like an impossible dream. The whole trip had been a waste of time—except he'd been here to say Todd's memorial Mass, and he'd spent time with the old people. He was glad for that. He should go back to St. Francis tomorrow, but he didn't want to leave yet.

The air had been cool, tinged with the violets and blues of evening, and he'd stared at the moonlight shimmering on the lake a long time, knowing he could not go back yet. Not with Vicky determined to find a ledger book that was in the possession of a killer. Not until he was sure she would let the police handle the matter. Not until he was sure she was safe.

As he opened the bedroom door he realized the ringing phone was his. In a couple of steps he was at the desk, the receiver pressed against his ear. "Father O'Malley," he said.

"I wouldn't be bothering you, Father." It was Brother Timothy. "But someone named Vicky's on the line. Says she has to talk to you, and with the time getting past ten o'clock! I tried telling her to call at a respectable hour."

"It's okay," Father John told him. "Put her on."

There was a soft click, then the familiar voice. "John, I've got Todd's thesis," she said.

Father John was waiting when the headlights flickered across the parking lot. He opened the driver's door and Vicky slid out. Moonlight slanted across her face; he saw the agitation in her eyes. "Julie's dead," she said. "They found her body this afternoon. Beaten and thrown into the South Platte, just like Todd."

"Dear God," Father John murmured. Another Indian kid who had come to the city and, somehow, gotten lost. He'd been hoping the Lakota girl was safe at home on the Rosebud.

"Todd asked her to give this diskette to you." Vicky handed him the envelope. "He knew he was in danger, so he gave the diskette to the girl who had been staying in his apartment less than two weeks. She wasn't a friend; she was just somebody who needed a place to stay. He must have hoped no one would think he would trust her with the thesis. He arranged for her to stay with a student, Tisha Runner. Tisha got scared when she heard the police had found a woman's body in the South Platte. She wanted to get the diskette to you, but she didn't know where to find you. So she called me."

Father John took her arm, and they crossed the campus, in and out of the circles of light, to the Math and Sciences building. Light splashing along the first-floor corridor confirmed what he'd guessed: the computer lab never closed. A humming noise, like the swarm of bees, greeted them as he opened the door with the small sign LAB. The room was the size of two classrooms, bathed in white light, computers marching along the tables. A student about Todd's age, Father John thought, was tapping at a keyboard on the far table.

Vicky sat down in front of a monitor and snapped the disk into a slot. Pulling over a chair, Father John sat down beside her. He hadn't used computers much lately; St. Francis Mission didn't even own one, but it would be the first thing he would buy if by some miracle the provincial approved his plans for the museum.

He stared at the scrolling screen as Vicky's fingers clicked rapidly on the keyboard. In half a second several lines of type appeared: *The Colorado Presence of the Arapaho People: An Inventory of Sites of Arapaho Villages and Battlefields. A thesis prepared by Todd Harris for the faculty of the University of Colorado in Denver in compliance with the requirements for a master's degree in history.*

There was a stillness about Vicky, a focused quiet. He heard the soft intakes of her breath as she leaned toward the screen. Several other clicks and they were staring at the table-of-contents page. The first line read: *Sites of Arapaho Villages.* A list of familiar places followed: Denver, Boulder, Niwot, Longmont, Fort Collins, Golden, Lamar, LaJunta, South Platte River, North Platte River, Cherry Creek, Arkansas River, Smoky Hill River. At the top of the next page: *Sites of Arapaho Battles*, followed by another list—Julesburg, Cheyenne Wells, Fort Morgan, Brush, Sand Creek.

In half an instant Vicky had called up a page with the heading, *The Sand Creek Massacre.* He leaned close; they read the paragraphs together. A familiar story, one he'd read before in history books and heard from the elders, their voices filled with mourning as they talked about the men, women, and children who had died at Sand Creek. November 29, 1864. The earth, frozen; snow blowing across the plains, the Indian village sprawled along a creek in the vastness of southeastern Colorado—the No Water Land, the Arapaho elders called the area. It was dawn, with the sun lifting out of the east, and the sky blazing red, when the soldiers came.

They read on: the soldiers riding into the village, the

ponies' hooves beating on the earth, guns retorting in the icy air. And the shouting and screaming, the whinnying of the ponies in the corral, the people running up the creek bed, half-naked, stumbling and falling, bare hands digging out holes in the rock-hard banks, shielding the children with their bodies against the guns that never stopped.

And then the frozen silence broken by the occasional scream of a horse, the moanings of the wounded as the soldiers went about their work, hacking and slicing at the fallen bodies: a woman's breast, a scrotum—aha! Such trophies to carry back to Denver!

Vicky sat back in her chair. Father John placed one arm around her shoulders, and she allowed his arm to rest there a moment before she raised her hand and threaded her fingers into his. The warmth of her flowed through him, staving off the cold chill of death.

After a moment her breathing became quiet. Removing her hand, she bent toward the keyboard and scrolled to the bibliography page. *Manuscript Materials* appeared at the top. Halfway down the page: *Ledger Book, by No-Ta-Nee, Arapaho. Denver Museum of the West Collections.*

Father John felt the rim of his chair hard against his ribs. The student had left. They were alone in the lab, alone with the proof that No-Ta-Nee's ledger book had existed last week. "You've got what you need," he said, his voice soft. "We'll take this to your detective friend tomorrow. He'll find whoever killed Todd and Julie. We've got to trust him to do his job."

"Trust him?" A note of hysteria sounded in Vicky's voice. She shifted in the chair, turning toward him. "Steve is looking for the drug connection. As far as he's concerned, the Sand Creek ledger book is a fantasy, a story that exists in the mind of an old man and a graduate student who wished it were true. Rachel Foster, Bernard Good Elk, and I don't know how many other experts will convince him the ledger book doesn't exist. There are no records, and Steve wants proof. I've got to find it."

"No, Vicky," he said. "It's dangerous. Two people have already been killed. You should go back to Lander. Wait until the police complete the investigation. Sooner or later they're bound to stumble onto the truth."

Vicky shook her head. She pushed the save key; the computer made a soft rumbling noise. Then she pulled out the disk and slid it inside the envelope. Setting the package inside her bag, she pushed back the chair and got to her feet.

He hadn't convinced her, he knew. There were no words to convince her. He walked her back across campus, aware of the low rumble of traffic from the highway a mile away. As she got behind the steering wheel he leaned toward her. "Will you call me and let me know what you decide to do?"

She gave her head a little nod before she pulled the door shut. It was some consolation.

‹ 23 ›

Father John had slept badly. The dreams were jarring and nonsensical, urgent and demanding, propelling him toward some idea he couldn't grasp; something he should know, should understand. Why didn't he understand? The closer he came, the farther away he was from the key that would help him understand. He'd awakened in a sweat, gotten out of bed, and cranked open the window, breathing in the cool air, his thoughts switching between the horror he'd read of in Todd's thesis and the meeting earlier with Bernard Good Elk. A man capable of murder to keep a ledger book secret? He couldn't imagine it, but then he couldn't imagine murder. It always took him by surprise, the ugly and unexpected twist in the logical unfolding of human life.

But what if Good Elk were responsible for Todd's murder? Father John forced himself to move on to the logical conclusion looming dark and terrible at the edge of his mind: Vicky was also in danger. She knew about the ledger book; she wouldn't stop until she proved what had become of it. And who would help her? A homicide detective who had convinced himself Todd was killed over drugs?

He wasn't sure how long he'd stayed at the window, but the first red light of dawn was flickering in the dark sky when he laid down again, propping his hands behind his head. He would call Vicky first thing, he resolved. Try to convince her to return to Lander. Two murders already—enough! If they were right—if Todd had been killed over the ledger book—the detective would eventually figure it out. He was a good detective—Vicky said so herself.

It was still early when he'd given up all pretense of sleep. The air floating through the window was cool with the smell of pine that reminded him of the reservation. He'd showered, dressed, and shaved, then eaten a bowl of cold cereal and downed a mug of hot coffee in the dining room. Except for Brother Timothy, he'd been the only one up at that hour. Afterward he walked to the lake again, his thoughts on Vicky. If anything happened to her—he couldn't make his mind grasp the possibility. He couldn't imagine a world she was not in.

He tried to call her when he got back to his room. A woman said Vicky had left, and when he pressed for answers, she insisted she had no idea where Vicky had gone. He'd set down the phone, his thoughts a pool of worry. Where was she? She'd promised to call and let him know what she was up to. He felt angry and helpless.

Now he waited outside a closed door down the corridor from the dining room. The sounds of the other priests at breakfast—the clanking of dishes and scraping of chairs, the occasional laughter of Jesuit camaraderie—floated around him. Behind the closed door was the provincial. Before Father Stanton had stepped inside, Father John had made it clear he intended to wait until he saw their boss.

Suddenly the door opened. Father Stanton—black suit, puffy red nose, and thick neck—filled the doorway. "Five minutes, O'Malley. That's all you get."

Father John moved past him into a room as large as the living room in a well-to-do home, with twin sofas angling toward a wall of windows that overlooked the grassy slope he'd walked across earlier. Beyond was the lake, striped in blues and whites in the morning sunshine.

He crossed behind the sofas to the dark wooden desk where Father William Rutherford sat hunched over a paper of some sort. Almost twenty-five years earlier, they'd been in the seminary together. Two young men, ambitious and idealistic, eager for the careers ahead. A teaching position in philosophy at Georgetown for Rutherford; a position in history at some equally prestigious Jesuit University for him. It was a goal Rutherford had achieved, until the father general in Rome had made him a provincial in charge of his fellow Jesuits.

While Father John—well, he'd never made it to a university faculty. He had found himself on a different path, shunted there by the terrible thirst that, even now, had a way of coming over him at unexpected moments.

"How are you, John?" the provincial said. He did not look up.

"There's an important matter I'd like to discuss with you," Father John began. "I want to open a museum in the old school building at St. Francis."

William Rutherford lifted his eyes. There was tiredness, a kind of disillusionment in his expression, and for an instant Father John wondered if he had also found himself on an unintended path. "So I've been given to understand," the provincial said. He waved toward an upholstered chair next to the desk. "Have a seat."

Father John sat down and began explaining the importance of a museum large enough to hold collections now scattered about the reservation, the importance of their history to the Arapahos. He was about to explain the importance of the old school when voices erupted outside. The door burst open.

"Beg your pardon, Fathers." Brother Timothy shuffled into the room, Father Stanton behind him. "I tried to tell him," the priest said.

"What is it?" This from the provincial in an irritated tone.

"A visitor for Father O'Malley," Brother Timothy said. "She says it's urgent."

Father John was on his feet, striding past the two men and down the corridor toward the entry, vaguely aware of Father Stanton's voice behind him. "This is highly irregular, O'Malley. Highly irregular."

Vicky stood inside the door, dressed in blue jeans and T-shirt, black hair hanging loose and brushing her shoulders, not pulled back the way he was used to seeing her. The voices of Father Stanton and Brother Timothy burst from the corridor, an angry chorus, and he took her arm and led her outside. It was quiet. The parking lot below lay dappled in the morning sunshine.

"I'm going out onto the plains," she said. "To southeastern Colorado."

"What?" This woman was full of surprises. He could never guess what she might do; it was never the logical, the most prudent course.

She said, "I've been awake most of the night, trying to figure out the missing piece. Suddenly it hit me. Emil Coughlin said Todd had gone to southeastern Colorado to talk to ranchers about two weeks ago. When he got back he immediately went to the museum and requested the Smedden Collection. It wasn't luck, John. He knew exactly where to look, which means he found out about the book on his trip. Someone told him. Someone down there knows the book was in the museum. All I have to do is follow Todd's footsteps."

Father John shook his head. There were probably dozens of ranchers in the area; how would she ever find the one who knew about the book? And what if she did find the right person? She might seal her own fate, and probably that of the rancher. The whole idea was crazy.

"Do you want to come?" she asked.

Father John kept his eyes on hers a long moment.

What she was proposing could get her killed. The kid who knew about the ledger book was dead; so was a girl who might have known. Yet Vicky was determined to find proof the book existed.

He took his eyes away and stared out over the campus. Inside the building behind him was the provincial he'd come to Denver to see, and he'd only begun his argument for the museum. It was entirely possible he would never have another opportunity, even more possible his boss would consider him unredeemable—a man who would walk out of a meeting, a recovering alcoholic, never to be trusted, never to be counted upon.

He looked back at the woman beside him. She had pushed herself away from the railing: a bird poised for flight. There were no words to make her reconsider, no sensible, logical argument to steer her away from danger. He said, "Let's go."

Vicky drove the Taurus—an unaccustomed situation, someone driving him around—but she'd balked at his suggestion they take the Toyota. The rental car had air-conditioning, she'd pointed out, and the early-morning sun already burned with ferocity. It would be even hotter on the plains.

They caught I-70 and headed east across Denver, sunshine streaming over the stockyards and coliseum, the miles of block-shaped buildings on both sides of the highway. Vicky kept her eyes straight ahead, talking about the two dead kids, the ledger book that would be destroyed, pages cut out and sold around the world. If it hadn't already happened. "We've got to find the proof it was in the museum," she said, taking one hand from the wheel to push back her hair. "Before anyone else is killed."

Exactly, Father John was thinking, which was why he was here. All they had to do was retrace Todd's steps.

That could be hard. He let out a long sigh, and Vicky glanced at him. He gave her a smile of encouragement.

Gradually the city fell away and traffic became lighter: a few semis and pickups ahead, an occasional car whipping by in the passing lane. The plains stretched around them—a great expanse of flat, grass-stubbed land. Outside his window, Father John could make out the gentle dips and swales, the arroyos that broke the earth into jagged pieces, like the shapes of a jigsaw puzzle.

They sped on. The air-conditioning hummed softly; the car felt cool and comfortable, but the sun created sparkling mirages on the asphalt ahead. At Flagler, they stopped for gas and bought a couple of sandwiches and two cups of coffee. Then they drove down the wide, shady streets to a little park where they ate lunch at a picnic table under the sprawling branches of an oak tree. At a nearby table sat another couple. Several toddlers tumbled over the grass, giggling and squealing. Across the park, a baseball game was going on. He watched a kid in a white uniform race around the bases. A shout went up from the grandstand behind home plate. This was how other people lived, he thought. Saturday in a small town. Picnic in the park. Coach the Little League game.

When they got back to the car, he took the wheel and turned south onto a ribbon of asphalt flung across the open plains. It looked like the reservation—Indian country. An occasional ranch house, a clump of barns rising against the horizon. Vicky seemed relaxed beside him, her breathing quiet and regular. For a long time he thought she was asleep. He switched on his tape of *La Traviata*, glad he'd gone up to his room for the tape player and his cowboy hat. He'd need the hat on the plains. He was used to the opera on long drives.

Vicky stirred beside him, and he took his eyes off the road, glancing at her: she had been awake all the time.

"Every time I cross the plains," she said, her voice mingling with the music, "I imagine warriors riding in the distance, and great buffalo herds, and tipis in the cottonwoods along the streams. Sometimes I think I see children playing, the women fetching water or gathering wild fruits. Sometimes I think I'm with them." She shifted in the seat; he could feel her eyes on him. "I know it doesn't make sense."

Father John glanced at her again, meeting her eyes a moment. "It doesn't have to make sense."

A sign rose on the highway ahead: EADS. He let up on the accelerator. In another moment they were gliding down the wide street with pickups and trucks in front of squat, flat-roofed stores and cafés. Down a side street, he glimpsed a stone building that looked like the libraries in small towns across the country. He swung around the block and parked in front.

Inside was a reading room with tables and chairs on either side and a counter jutting from the back wall. Except for an elderly man poring over a newspaper at one of the tables, the library was empty. They walked to the counter, and Father John tapped a little bell. It jangled into the quiet.

Almost at once a door behind the counter opened and a middle-aged man in a short-sleeved white shirt with a black bolo tie at the collar stepped out. "Didn't hear you," he said. His eyes fell on Vicky a moment—an appreciative gaze—then moved to Father John. "Visiting our fair town, are you?"

"We're looking for a family that ranched in this area around the turn of the century." Vicky clasped her hands on the counter. "The name was Smedden."

The librarian picked up a pencil and gave his front teeth several taps. "Doesn't ring any bells," he said. Then: "Hold on." He disappeared behind the door. In another moment he was back with a thick, green-bound book. He flipped it open. "This old county directory might tell us something," he said, pushing through the pages.

He stopped. An index finger ran down a page in the middle of the book. "Aha. J. J. Smedden ran a ranch out near the county line in 1900." Another flip through the pages. "Still there the next year, and the next." *Flip. Flip.* "Aha. Not listed in 1904." He slammed the book shut. "There was a bad drought about that time. A lot of ranchers didn't make it. Just picked up and left."

"Where exactly was the ranch?" Father John asked.

The librarian motioned them to the right of the counter. He reached up and pulled on a cord. A large map rattled down over the shelves of books. "Kiowa County," he said, sweeping one hand across the width of the map. "East county line over here." He tapped a black line on the far right. "Ranch was probably about here." Another tap halfway down the line.

"Who owns the ranch now?" Vicky asked, expectation and excitement in her voice.

"A corporation." The librarian snapped the map back up into its holder. "Lot of ranches in that area are agribusiness. Tough for families to compete with corporations."

Vicky whirled around and walked back to the counter. The air was thick with her disappointment and frustration. Suddenly she turned back. "Look," she said, eyes flashing, "about two weeks ago a graduate student at CU-Denver came through here. He was talking to people, trying to find the sites of Indian battles and villages. Did he come to the library?"

Nodding slowly, the librarian moved back behind the counter. "Todd Harris," he said. "I helped him many times. A fine young man. I could hardly believe the article in the paper about his murder. It's getting so nobody's safe anymore. Can't walk down the street without getting killed."

Father John was at Vicky's side. "Can you tell us which research materials he was using?"

"Same as usual." The man gave a little shrug. "Old county maps. He was rechecking data, I suppose. Said he was about to finish his thesis and had a job at a museum somewhere up in Wyoming. I wished him luck. Next thing I heard, he was dead."

Father John was quiet, aware of Vicky leaning into the counter beside him. "Did he say anything about Sand Creek?" she asked in the same tone of hope.

The man raised his eyes to the ceiling—remembering. "He said he was going to run up to Sand Creek and take another look around."

Outside, the afternoon heat hung in the air like invisible smoke. Father John could feel the sun burning through the shoulders of his shirt as he followed Vicky to the Taurus nosed against the curb. "I've never been to Sand Creek," she said, crawling into the passenger seat. "Would you drive?"

‹ 24 ›

As they headed east Vicky kept her eyes on the narrow, dusty road ahead. What route had the soldiers followed, she wondered, as they rode through the ice-filled night, fortifying themselves with whiskey for the killing ahead? The bluffs, the Indian village below, Chief Niwot and the Arapahos camped in the big bend of the creek. The story was seared into her mind. She was immensely grateful that John O'Malley was here. "I'm not sure I could go alone," she told him.

Father John nodded and gave her a quick glance. There was sympathy in his eyes. "We don't have to go," he said.

Vicky was quiet a moment. "Something at the site—maybe the site itself—led Todd to the ledger book." It sounded crazy, but the man next to her was taking her there anyway, guiding the Taurus down the dusty, gullied road.

Ahead was a large sign, an intrusion on the plains. As the car slowed Vicky caught the block letters: SAND CREEK BATTLEFIELD. It amazed her that anyone would call the massacre a battle. They were heading north now, the sign behind them. After several miles—an interminable number of miles—they made a left past a small ranch house and slowed onto a bluff. Suddenly the car stopped.

Vicky let herself out into a pervasive stillness,

vaguely aware that Father John had started walking toward the ranch house. She moved to the edge of the bluff, feeling cold despite the sun on her face, the hot breeze rippling the air. Below lay the site of the village, the winding dry creek bed, the old cottonwoods, leaves shimmering in the sun. This was where the soldiers had halted their horses before the attack.

After a few moments Father John was back, and they started down the bank, sliding in the dry earth. She had to catch herself from falling into a clump of grass. He took her hand, steadying her until they reached the bottom. Together they started across the field, wild grasses crumpling beneath their steps. At the big bend in the creek bed, she stopped. "My people were here," she said, sweeping out one arm. "They heard the gunshots and ran out of the tipis. They were running every which way; they didn't know where to go. And Chief Niwot called out—run up the creek—while he walked forward to meet the soldiers. He held out his hands in peace."

Vicky swung around and headed for the dry creek bed, a wide, flat indentation in the earth. Father John was beside her, walking north in the soft earth, the direction the people had taken that morning. Running, running from the soldiers galloping behind. Vicky started walking faster, sensing something behind her, a great malevolent force pushing her forward. And then she was running full out, a sharp stitch in her side, gulping in air, arms flailing, the sound of horses' hooves beating like drums in her ears.

"Vicky! Stop, stop!" She felt John O'Malley's arm around her, slowing her. She was stumbling, nearly falling, and he pulled her toward him and held her. Her heart was thumping; she fought for breath. Together they slumped down against the soft bank. She heard his voice again, steady and soothing. "You're okay. You're okay." For an instant a sense came over her—a kind of remembrance—that they had been in this place before. In that other time. Together.

"It's only some men on horseback," he said.

"What?" She turned toward him, trying to focus on what he was saying. And then she saw six or seven cowboys riding across the bluff. They nosed the horses down the bank and came across the field. Father John was already on his feet, pulling her upright, and they started retracing their steps, walking toward the riders.

"This is private land," one of the men called as they rode up.

"Sorry," Father John said, his eyes on the man who seemed to be in charge. "I stopped at the ranch house. Nobody was around."

The man laid the reins lightly against the horse's neck. "You'll wanna be gettin' on outta here."

Vicky said, "A young man—a student—came here a couple of weeks ago. Did you happen to see him?"

"We throw people outta here every day," one of the other riders said.

"He was looking for some of the old-timers around here," Vicky persisted. "Do you know who he might have talked to?"

The first man shrugged. "Don't know as I ran into him."

"Hold on there." The second man again. "I seen him wandering around here. Yeah, about two weeks ago it was. Indian fellow. Seemed harmless enough, but I tol' him to clear on out."

Father John took a step toward the man. "Did he say why he was here?"

"Well"—the second man shifted his weight in the saddle—"like the lady here says, he wanted to know if there was any families around that went all the way back to the battle. So I sent him down the road a piece to talk to some folks."

"Smedden?" Vicky heard the hope in her tone.

"Lawler's the name. Been around a hundred years, I guess. Nobody goes all the way back to the battle. Nothing but Indians around then."

"Don't forget the soldiers." A man sitting a gray mare in the rear spoke up. There was a little guffaw from the others.

"Smedden," the first man said, pushing up his cowboy hat and staring past them, as if he'd caught a glimpse of something in the distance. "Name has a mighty familiar ring. Ran a big ranch on east of here a long time ago. The old grandma that lives with the Lawlers is one of 'em, if I remember rightly."

"Where can we find the ranch?" Father John asked.

"Keep on goin' down the road," the second cowboy said. "Ten miles or so. Big white place. You can't miss it."

It took twenty minutes over back roads to reach the two-story ranch house shining in the sun on top of a rise, like a white whale beached on the plains. A gravel driveway ran along the house to a cluster of barns and sheds beyond. Father John parked close to the house and they walked up the steps to a porch that sprawled across the front. Vicky pushed a small button by the door. Somewhere inside, a bell jangled—the only sound except for the high whinny of a horse out back.

"Be here," she whispered, then glanced up at Father John. She'd done a pretty good job today of convincing him she was nuts. Now she was talking to herself. He smiled at her—a reassuring smile—and she pressed the doorbell again.

Minutes passed. They were close now, she could feel it. This was where Todd had come. This was where he'd found out about the ledger book. Behind the door was someone who knew . . .

The door cracked opened and a fleshy-faced woman with a cap of gray hair peered around the edge. "Yes?" she said in a tentative tone.

Father John introduced himself, then Vicky, and the door widened. The woman stared at them, curiosity and incredulity in her expression: priest in a cowboy hat? Native American woman?

"A friend of ours, Todd Harris, came to see you about two weeks ago," Vicky said.

"Todd Harris." The door was wide open now. The woman ushered them inside. "I felt so bad when I read about what happened. Such a nice young man. I can't believe the police think he might've been mixed up with drug dealers. What rubbish. If they'd ever met him, they'd know he wasn't the type."

They were standing in an large, sun-filled entry. The living room opened on the right, and a stairway angled upward on the left. Straight ahead was a hallway leading to the back of the house, where a TV was blaring— laughter and applause, a game show. "How can I help you?" the woman asked, closing the door behind them.

Vicky said, "We understand Todd spoke with your grandmother."

"Yes. Yes. A nice long visit. Grandma was so pleased. We don't get much company out here."

"Could we meet her?" Father John's voice was soft.

The woman led them down the hallway. "No guarantee she's awake," she said over one shoulder. "Spends most days dozing in front of the TV."

They followed her into the large kitchen ringed with cabinets and counters on which an array of gadgets were lined up in neat order. On the other side of the kitchen was a little room where an old woman lay back in a recliner, white sneakers propped in front of a large-sized TV.

"Grandma, you got some more visitors." The woman walked over and turned off the TV. Quiet fell across the room as the woman in the recliner seemed to snap herself awake and glanced sideways at them.

"Come closer," she said, motioning them forward.

"They're friends of Todd Harris, that nice young man who came to see you a couple weeks ago," the other woman said.

"You look tired and thirsty." The old woman turned to her granddaughter. "Where's your manners, Doris? Get some cold lemonade."

"Go on in and sit down," the other woman said, brushing past them and into the kitchen.

Vicky walked over to the recliner, introduced herself, and took the old woman's hand a moment. It was rough and knobby with age. Then Father John did the same, and they stepped past the large wicker trunk that served as a coffee table and settled on a sofa.

Leaning toward the old woman, Father John said, "Can you tell us what you and Todd talked about?"

"The old days." The old woman shook her head against the recliner. "Imagine, a young man wantin' to know the old stories. Well, it did my heart good. So I told him about my granddaddy, James J. Smedden, comin' out on the plains after nearly gettin' hisself killed fighting for the Yankees. Just a kid, he was, but a good soldier. So the army sent him out to Wyoming to fight Indians."

"Wyoming?" Vicky scooted forward on the cushion. "We understood he ran a ranch here in Colorado."

"Over on the county line." Doris sidled past the recliner and set a tray with four glasses of lemonade on top of the wicker trunk. Passing out the lemonade, she said, "Might've been a good soldier, but he sure wasn't much of a rancher." She sank into a straight-backed chair on the other side of the trunk. "Lost the place after a few years."

The old woman's head jerked forward. "Lots of folks lost places in the drought. Lucky for you, my mama married into the Lawler family, and they had enough money to hold on to this place, or you wouldn't be sitting here, missy."

Turning toward Vicky, the old woman went on: "When granddaddy was clearin' out things, gettin' ready to give the ranch back to the bank, he give a lot of his stuff to that museum up in Denver. But I still got some of his things. That young man thought they was real interesting." Waving toward her granddaughter, she said, "Go get me Granddaddy's box."

Doris lifted herself slowly out of her chair, set her glass on the tray, and disappeared: a soft patter of footsteps down the hallway.

Vicky sipped at the lemonade. She hadn't realized how thirsty she was, or tired. Yet every part of her felt awake, on edge, as if her nerves were wound tight, ready to spring. The old woman was bent forward in the recliner, talking about her granddaddy as if the man might walk through the door, dusty and sunburned from riding across the plains. He'd spent two years in Wyoming. Rough duty it was, chasing Indians onto reservations. Couldn't blame them Indians for not wanting to be penned up, but he had his duty. Killed some of them, she guessed.

Vicky set her glass back on the tray. A story was taking shape in her mind—beginning, middle, end. No-Ta-Nee dying on a battlefield in Wyoming two years after Sand Creek. The ledger book—his most precious possession—dangling from a cord around his neck or strapped to his body where Smedden had found it.

Doris reappeared, carrying a small box that she deposited on her grandmother's lap. The old woman began rummaging through papers and small books. After a moment she pulled out an old newspaper and handed it to Father John. "Real interesting," she said. "Tells about the bank takin' over Granddaddy's ranch."

Father John asked, "Is there anything about the time your grandfather spent in Wyoming?"

Vicky held her breath, awaiting the answer, realizing that John O'Malley had tuned in to her own thoughts.

The old woman bent lower over the box—rummaging, rummaging. Suddenly she pulled out a gray ledger book and handed it to Father John. Vicky caught her breath. The ledger book had been here all the time! Rachel Foster was right. J. J. Smedden's family must have loaned the book to the museum in 1920. But if that was true, why did Todd's thesis say the book was in the museum?

She moved closer to Father John, her heart tumbling as he lifted the cover. She heard herself gasp. The top page was covered with words and numbers, not pictographs. As Father John flipped through the other pages she saw they were the same.

"Sad, isn't it?" Doris took her chair on the other side of the wicker trunk. "Record of everything he sold to pay off the bank—furniture, dishes, tools, animals. Last page lists the stuff he give to the museum. Like he couldn't bear for everything to go without a trace. Like he wanted some part of the ranch safe up in that museum so it could witness to what he'd tried to do."

Father John had already found the last page. Black squiggles covered the lines. At the top was *Donations, Denver Museum of West, 1903.* The list below took up two columns. Even before he'd set an index finger on the entry, Vicky's eyes had found it. *Indian ledger book. Colored pictures. Taken from Arapaho brave. Sweetwater Battle, 1866.*

Vicky couldn't take her eyes away. Finally she turned to the old woman. "This record book of your granddaddy's is very important," she said. "It could help the police find whoever murdered Todd Harris. Would you trust us to borrow—"

"I should say not." Doris was on her feet. She leaned across the wicker trunk and grabbed the book from Father John's hand. "This is one of Grandma's treasures. All she has left of the past." She waved the book over the table. "You don't know the hours she spends going through that old box, pulling out papers and books, just gettin' the feel of them 'cause it makes it seem like her people—her granddaddy and her ma and pa—like they're still with her, like she's not the only one left."

Father John and Vicky both stood up. "We'll see that the book is returned," he said. "You have my word."

The old woman pushed down the footrest. It squealed like a trapped animal. "Give them the book," she said.

"You don't mean that, Grandma." Doris moved backward toward the kitchen, clutching the ledger book to her chest.

"Like hell I don't, missy. It's my book, and I can do whatever I please. And what I please right now is doin' whatever's gonna help find the no-good snake that killed that nice young man."

Slowly the other woman came forward and held out the book, a tentative, reluctant gesture. Father John reached across the wicker trunk and took it, then handed it to Vicky.

Dusk was settling over Eads by the time they drove down Main Street. The sun glowed orange in the distance where the earth met the sky, and a hint of coolness tinged the air, as if the night had already begun to dispel the heat of day.

They ate dinner in a small café that catered mostly to locals, Vicky guessed, judging by the trucks in the parking lot and the attention they received from the waitress. "Where you from?" she'd asked the instant they'd sat down. Later, pouring coffee: "Nice to see new faces around here." And again, when she brought the plates of chicken-fried steak and mashed potatoes—the special of the day: "What brings you around these parts?"

"Just out for a little drive on the plains," Father John assured her.

The waitress had shot him an I-don't-buy-it smile. "Most folks come to Colorado and take a little drive to the mountains," she'd said before swinging away. Then, leaning back: "Strikes me you two got headed the wrong direction."

"It wouldn't be the first time," he said. Vicky had caught his eye, and they both laughed. She was thinking she'd spent her entire life headed in the wrong direction, always trying to get back on track, not ever sure if she was there.

They chatted about Smedden's records—the proof Steve Clark had demanded. How the detective would have to turn his attention to whoever had stolen the ledger book. When he did, he'd have Todd's murderer. Every once in a while Vicky had found her fingers wandering to her handbag on the seat beside her, tracing the hard contours of the record book and Todd's diskette through the leather, reassuring herself that they were both there.

On they chatted, but in one part of her mind, Vicky kept thinking about the strange sense that had come over her at Sand Creek. Now, more relaxed with each bite of hot food, each sip of coffee, the experience seemed crazy—*Nohoko*. She was feeling more and more embarrassed. She said, "I'm not sure what happened at Sand Creek. You must think I'm nuts."

Father John took a draw of coffee and regarded her a long moment. "What I think is you've heard the story of the Sand Creek Massacre all your life. It's part of you. Out there this afternoon, you imagined what it had been like, that's all." He sipped at the coffee again. "Stories are very powerful."

"I imagined you were there, too," Vicky blurted.

He set the coffee cup into its saucer. "I know."

She was quiet a moment. "We don't have to go back

tonight. We could stay here. In separate rooms, of course," she said hurriedly. "I'm pretty tired. You must be, too." She was groping for words, selecting, avoiding what she wanted to say: no one here knows us. She hurried on, "We can drive back first thing tomorrow and still get in early enough to catch Steve the minute he comes to work." Rambling, stumbling over the words.

She stopped breathing as he took his eyes away and glanced around the café: the waitress talking to two cowboys at the counter, the couple at a nearby table. Finally he looked back at her. "I'll drive," he said. "You can sleep all the way to Denver."

◀ 25 ▶

Vicky curled up on the passenger seat, drowsiness overcoming her before they were out of town. At some point she was aware of soft music—an unfamiliar aria—and once she awoke and stared at the headlights streaming into the darkness ahead. Then she dropped off again into a kind of half-sleep, lulled by the music, the rhythm of the tires on the asphalt, the motion of the car, the quiet, steady breathing of the man beside her. He was different from the other men she'd known; they were the ones who made the offers. She wasn't surprised he had turned her down. It was as it should be. She felt an odd sense of calm, of acceptance. At another time, in this place, it had been different.

The car stopped, and Vicky opened her eyes. The headlights played over the steps of the Jesuit residence, and Father John was asking if she was awake. She sat up, willing herself awake, blinking at the dimness inside the car. Marcy's house was only a few blocks, she told him. She wanted to tell him how grateful she was he'd come along, how grateful for everything that had happened. She said, "*Ho'hou'*."

He let himself out, and she slid over behind the wheel. "Why don't you let me keep the diskette and the record book," he said.

In the glint of the dashboard light, she saw the worry in his eyes. She wondered what difference it made which one of them had the proof. If the killers came after her and didn't find what they wanted, they would go after him. He was in as much danger as she was. She smiled at him. "I'll call you tomorrow. We can take them to the police department together."

She waited as John O'Malley walked through the headlights and up the steps. He turned at the door and gave her a quick wave. She rammed the gear into drive and started forward.

She drove through the deserted streets of North Denver: the stop sign here, the turn there—familiar to her now. The houses on Marcy's street were dark, except for Marcy's. Light burst through the front windows, forming a crazy-quilt pattern of light and shadow on the front lawn.

Vicky parked and cut the engine, wondering if Marcy was having some kind of New Age celebration of light. She groaned at the thought of a houseful of Marcy's friends, a part of her mind readying the excuses, the exhaustion she would plead. Yet there was only one car parked ahead: Marcy's.

Gripping her handbag, she slammed out of the car. At the front door, she halted, one hand on the knob, straining to catch the beat of a drum, the scuffle of a chair, voices raised in *oms*. It was quiet. Light glowed steadily through the windows. And then she heard the sobbing.

She twisted the knob and pushed on the door. Locked. Remembering the key, she dug through her bag until her fingers closed on the small piece of metal. She jammed it into the tiny slot. The door fell open, and she was inside.

It looked as if the room had tumbled down, spilled across the wood floor: books, pictures, shards of pottery and china. The twin sofas lay on their backs, seats jutting upward in a grotesque parody. The glass top on the coffee table had been smashed; slivers of glass hung like icicles around the chrome frame. Huddled on the floor near the corner where the hallway emptied into the living room was Marcy, knees pulled to her chest, head buried in the circle of her arms.

Vicky crossed the room, stepping around the detritus of her friend's life. She squatted beside her, placing an arm around the fleshy shoulders, the knobs of her spine: so fragile, she was taken by surprise. "Marcy," she said, "are you okay?"

Slowly Marcy's face came upward; a mixture of wetness and makeup striped her cheeks. Her eyes were blurred and watery. "Oh, Vicky," she said, swaying sideways, falling against her, "look what they've done."

Vicky held her as if she were a child. "Who, Marcy? Who did this?"

Raising a hand, Marcy swabbed at her face, as if her fingers were a cloth. "I don't know," she said in a kind of whimper. "I went out to my encounter group. When I got back . . ." She flipped her hand toward the room. "I found this."

Vicky exhaled a long breath. At least Marcy was all right, at least she hadn't been here when they'd come. But what if her friend *had been* here? She said, "Did you call the police?"

A quick nod. "They just left." The sobbing started again, a loud, racking noise. After a moment Marcy said, "All I wanted was some space where I could belong. When Mike left, there was this big black hole, and every time I tried to crawl out, I fell back in. So I found this house, and it sheltered me. I was just learning how to climb out of the hole, Vicky. I was almost out."

"I'm sorry," Vicky said. A wave of guilt and regret washed over her. It hadn't been a stroll through the park, Marcy's separation from Mike; it was a wrenching apart of something that had once been whole, just like her own divorce from Ben. She'd fled to Denver, throwing herself into classes and term papers, trying to climb out of the darkness, grasping for that space where she could be whole again, while Marcy had come here, to a circle of new friends, new ways. Grasping, grasping.

Marcy pulled away, her eyes wide as if she were seeing the destruction for the first time. "Who would do this? Why would anybody tear my house apart? What were they looking for?"

Vicky leaned against the wall, numb with exhaustion and fear. Whoever had ransacked Todd's apartment had been here this evening, ransacking the house where she was staying. What were they looking for? The diskette with Todd's thesis? The link to the Sand Creek ledger book? Had Julie told them about it while she could still talk, before they finished beating her to death?

Was that what they were looking for? A diskette that experts could explain away? Is that what drove them to a frenzy of murder and rampage—beating two kids to death, trashing an apartment and a house, tearing up books and papers, pulling shelves off the walls?

Vicky leaned against the corner, the edge burrowing into her back. Slowly the realization came over her. This wasn't about a diskette. This was about a ledger book. A ledger book worth $1.3 million.

Why hadn't she seen it before? Todd must have taken the ledger book from the museum. Steve Clark had suggested the possibility, but she'd shrugged it away, not wanting to believe Todd would do such a thing. But what if he'd suspected the book was in danger? Suspected someone would destroy it? He knew the controversy over the Sand Creek massacre, knew the claims of at least one Cheyenne scholar. How could he not know? He passed the exhibit on Sand Creek every time he went into the museum. Something had filled him with so much fear he'd taken the book.

And they'd come after him. But he hadn't given up

the book. So they'd gone after the girl who'd been staying in his apartment. And now—Vicky blinked at the debris strewn over the living room—they had come after her.

She helped Marcy to her feet and gently steered her down the hallway and into the bedroom. Whoever had broken into the house had been here, too: sheets and blankets thrown across the floor, the naked mattress askew on the bed frame, clothes and shoes heaped in front of opened closet doors.

Marcy stood in the middle of the room, like a patient waiting for the nurse to prepare the bed, while Vicky shoved the mattress into place and spread a sheet on top. Then she helped Marcy over to the bed and settled a blanket over her.

"They did this because of me," she said. "I'm so sorry."

Marcy rolled over, wrapping the blanket around her. She didn't say anything, and Vicky let herself out of the room, snapping off the light and closing the door softly behind her.

She walked through the small house, locking doors and windows, turning off lights. She found her handbag and clasped it to her. In the kitchen, the same disarray: cabinet doors flung open, drawers hanging out, pots, pans, and dishes tossed about. Nothing untouched. She lifted a butcher knife from the floor and carried it down the hallway. If they returned, she told herself, she would fight them with all her strength.

In the bathroom, she had to step around towels and bottles and shards of glass to turn on the tub. The smell of lavender filled the room as she sprinkled in bath crystals from one of the intact bottles. Stripping off her clothes, she let them fall over a wad of towels before sinking into the hot, creamy water. She lay back, the water lapping at her shoulders. The handbag lay on a little table next to the knife, close enough so she could reach it.

First thing in the morning, she would take Smedden's records and the diskette to Steve. Father John would be there—a logical, reasonable man. A priest. Together they would present the evidence that the book had been on the museum shelves last week. And the ransacked apartment, the girl's murder, and now Marcy's place ransacked—further proof that whoever had killed Todd was looking for the book. Steve would have to listen. And then a homicide detective would be looking for the killers. They would no longer be calling the shots.

She felt herself relaxing. The Sand Creek ledger book was still intact, still capable of telling its story. The killers didn't have it yet. They didn't know where it was. But she knew. The moment she'd realized Todd had taken the book, she knew. He had placed it in the safest possible place, and tomorrow she and John O'Malley would go and get it.

The water had faded to lukewarm when she lifted herself out of the tub, toweled off, and pulled on a clean T-shirt, letting the soft cotton fall over her body. She fixed her watch back onto her wrist: she would get up early.

Picking up the bag and the knife, she turned off the light and made her way to the bedroom. In the dimness of a light shimmering through the bedroom window—a passing headlight, perhaps—she pushed aside the messed blankets and pillows, making a small space for herself. She shoved the knife under a pillow, then pulled a blanket over her, the handbag at her side. She fell into an exhausted and dreamless sleep.

Something hard pressed against her arm; fingers dug into her, shaking her. She blinked herself awake, groping under the pillow for the knife. Where was it? Then her fingers found the hard, cold metal, the indentations on the handle. Gripping the handle, she roared upward, swinging out of bed, gulping in air, the knife in hand.

The figure looming over her jumped back. "My God!" Marcy screamed. "What are you doing?"

Vicky dropped the knife on the bed and sank down next to it. She was shaking. She made herself take several deep breaths, trying to calm herself, aware for the first time of the morning sunshine drifting past the window, Marcy holding a portable phone. She started to explain, to apologize.

Marcy interrupted. "Steve wants to talk to you." She handed Vicky the phone and walked out of the room.

Vicky could feel her heart still pounding. She checked to make sure the handbag was in the bed before pressing the on button and muttering a good morning she didn't feel.

"Where the hell were you last night?" The detective was shouting.

She told him she'd gone to Sand Creek.

"Sand Creek? For God's sake, Vicky. Why didn't you call me when you got back?"

"It was late, Steve."

"You think whoever trashed Marcy's house was after her? They were looking for you, Vicky, and whatever they think you might have. You were nowhere around. Marcy didn't know where you'd gone. I've been worried as hell."

"I know what they're after," Vicky said. "They're looking for the Sand Creek ledger book."

The line went silent. Then: "That's what I figured you'd say."

She was quiet a moment, debating whether to tell him she knew where it was. Last night, she'd been so certain, but now she saw the certainty for what it was: a hunch, an instinct. And this was a man who wanted proof. He didn't even believe the ledger book existed.

(*Show me the proof*, he'd told her). She would find out first if the book was where she thought it was.

She said, "I've got the proof the ledger book was in the museum collections last week."

"I'm at my desk," he said.

Vicky pushed the disconnect button, then punched the numbers for Regis. Brother Timothy's voice came on the line, and she asked to speak to Father O'Malley.

"Ah"—a long drawl—"the good father has left us to return to his mission."

"He left?" Vicky blurted.

"I'm afraid the good father's assistant was called away yesterday. A death in his family, I believe. There was no one at the mission. Naturally Father John felt it incumbent to return. He asked me to explain to you. Oh, yes. He said you would know what to do."

"When did he leave?" Vicky asked.

"An early riser, Father O'Malley. He was gone at dawn."

Vicky thanked the old man and hung up, trying to hold back the sense of abandonment flooding over her. He would not have left unless it was an emergency, and St. Francis without a priest was an emergency. She glanced at her watch. Almost nine o'clock. He could be halfway home by now, provided the Toyota pickup didn't break down. She made a couple more calls. In a few moments she had a reservation on the noon flight to Riverton. She would be there by one.

She dressed in jeans and T-shirt, pulled on her sandals, and threw the rest of her things into the carry-on. Barring any major traffic holdups, she could drive downtown, meet Steve, give him Todd's diskette and the Smedden record book, and still get out to DIA in time to turn in the rental car and catch the plane. She picked up her carry-on in one hand, her black bag in the other, and hurried down the hallway.

Marcy was in the kitchen pointing out the damage

to a young man with a clipboard—an insurance adjuster, Vicky guessed. She waited for a break in the conversation, then told her friend she was leaving.

"Hold on a minute," Marcy said to the young man. Then she walked out front with Vicky. The sun blazed yellow out of a startlingly blue sky. A dog barked somewhere, a lawn mower whined—neighborhood sounds.

"I've been a terrible guest," Vicky began.

Marcy shook her head and placed a hand on Vicky's arm. "It's okay," she said. "I wish we'd had more time to visit, but last night—well, at least last night we had a little heart-to-heart."

"I'm sorry about your house, Marcy." Vicky kept her voice soft. "And about you and Mike."

Tears welled in Marcy's eyes. She turned away a moment, running one finger along both cheekbones. She looked like an overweight child, Vicky thought: shoulders hunched inside a baggy blue shirt, blond curls springing out of a clip on top of her head. After a moment she looked back. "I didn't sleep much last night. All this"—a wave toward the house—"is a big bother, but at least it's fixable. But Mike and I, well, that's Humpty-Dumpty. I can't put it back together, so I'm going to have to go on. There isn't any safe space I can crawl into and hide, is there?"

That was true. There was no safe space. "You'll be okay, Marcy," Vicky said, laying one hand on her friend's arm. She gave Marcy a smile and hurried down the sidewalk to the Taurus. She'd lost precious time—it couldn't be helped. She'd have to drive like hell to keep to her schedule.

‹ 26 ›

A few uniformed officers milled about, telephones jangled, and the monotonous hum of conversations drifted from the roped-off area where a couple huddled with a teenage boy: Sunday-morning noises at the Denver Police Department. Vicky stood at the gate, staring at the elevator beyond. Lights flashed overhead: "3", "2", "1". There was a loud ping, and the doors parted. Steve Clark stepped out, hurried over, and snapped the gate open.

"You don't know how glad I am to see you," he said, ushering her toward the waiting elevator. A policewoman brushed past and entered ahead of them. Vicky stepped inside, and Steve planted himself beside her, one hand on her arm. She could sense his wanting to tell her something, but he was quiet. They were not alone.

The elevator bumped to a stop, and he guided her into the corridor. A familiar route now: left turn through the door marked HOMICIDE. There was no one here. The office had a vacant, musty smell, like a church that had just emptied out. They crossed to Steve's desk, footsteps clattering into the quiet.

"What happened?" Vicky asked. She perched on the edge of the chair where she'd sat two days ago. Her handbag felt heavy on her lap.

Sinking into the swivel chair, Steve glanced out the window a moment. A cloud as jagged as the mountain-tops drifted through the clear blue sky. He looked back. "Night before last, somebody paid Tisha Runner a visit. Tore up her apartment."

Vicky brought one hand to her mouth. Her breath felt hot in her palm. "Is she okay?"

"She's dead, Vicky," he said. "A friend dropped by yesterday morning and found her tied up on a kitchen chair." He stopped. The sound of a telephone ringing somewhere floated into the quiet. "It didn't take much," he went on. "She probably died with the first blow."

Vicky closed her eyes. The image formed in her mind, like a color photograph floating up from the chemicals of a darkroom—the girl with black hair falling over her face, the girl who didn't want to be involved with murder. Snapping her eyes open, she jumped to her feet and walked to the window. Tisha Runner—racing out of the Indian Center. Why hadn't she run after her? Who had been waiting for her?

Swinging around, she said, "The killers are after the Sand Creek ledger book. Todd wouldn't tell them where it was, so they killed him and ransacked his apartment. Then they went after Julie Clearwater, who just happened to have stayed in Todd's apartment. And then Tisha Runner."

Steve placed both hands on the arms of his chair and leveled himself upright, leaning across the desk toward her. "And then you, Vicky. And if they'd found you . . ." He brought one fist down hard on the desktop. A ballpoint skittered to the floor, making a sharp clack against the tile. "They would have done the same thing to you they did to the others. Whoever these thugs are, they're vicious and they're getting more and more desperate." He stopped, nodding toward her vacant chair. "Sit down and tell me everything you know."

Vicky dropped back onto the chair. She reached inside her handbag and pulled out the Smedden record book and the brown envelope with Todd's diskette. She handed them across the desk. "Here's the proof you wanted," she said. She explained what was on the diskette, what he would find on the last page of the record book.

His eyes on her, he picked up the book and flipped to the last page. " 'Indian ledger book, colored pictures, taken from Arapaho warrior. Sweetwater Battle, 1866.' " He peered over the book. "This the proof you're talking about?"

"A rancher named James J. Smedden gave the ledger book to the museum in 1903, along with other papers and documents," Vicky said. "Before he started ranching, he was a soldier. He was at the Battle of the Sweetwater."

Steve dropped the book on the desk. Questions and disbelief flashed in his eyes. "Who's to say this ledger book is the so-called Sand Creek ledger book?"

Vicky went over it again, the same story she'd tried to tell him two days earlier when his mind had been on drug deals gone bad. While she talked he picked up the book again and turned to the last page. When she had finished, he said, "And the Indian ledger book with colored pictures that rancher Smedden found is worth a million dollars?"

"It's worth one-point-three million," she said, reminding him that the museum curator had known the exact value, all the while claiming the museum had never owned the book. "It's the only Arapaho record of Sand Creek. It proves some of my people were massacred there, along with the Cheyennes."

Still the questions in his eyes: "What does this matter today? A massacre more than a hundred years ago?"

She explained again how the Cheyennes were trying to obtain reparation lands in Colorado, how the ledger book would prove Arapahos also had a right to the lands.

Steve tossed the record book onto the desk and leaned back, staring at her. "So we're talking about a ledger book worth a million dollars in its own right and probably worth a lot more as a historical record. And somebody decided to make it disappear—"

"Todd may have taken it," Vicky cut in. "He must have known it was in danger."

"Jesus, Vicky," Steve said. "Danger from whom? I need names." He picked up a ballpoint and pulled a pad across the desk.

Vicky was on her feet again, pacing: chair, window, chair. There was the scratching sound of pen on paper as she told him about Bernard Good Elk, the reputation he'd built for himself on a false claim. Then she mentioned Rachel Foster again. "I happen to know she could use the money."

"You happen to know?" Steve looked up, pen poised over the pad.

"An investigator friend." Vicky shrugged. "Look, Steve, there's no telling who Todd told about the book after he found it. He probably showed it to the research librarian. It would make sense; he pulled it out of the papers in the Smedden Collection, realized what it was, and called the librarian over right away."

"Librarian." Another scratching noise, like that of a tiny mouse working its way over the desk.

"He might have called his adviser, Emil Coughlin," Vicky went on, "although the man says he hadn't talked to Todd in the last couple weeks. He claims he never heard of the ledger book."

Steve nodded. "Yeah, well, looks like three people are dead because of a ledger book nobody heard of."

Vicky stopped in front of the desk. "Whoever killed them will destroy the book," she said.

"A million-dollar book?"

"There's already a buzz among the dealers on Book Row. The killers have gotten out the word; they're angling for the best price." Vicky heard the rising emotion in her tone. "And after the dealers get the book, how long—days, hours?—before the pages are cut out and shipped to collectors around the world? The collectors are waiting, Steve. That's why the killers are desperate. They have to find the ledger book before we find it."

"We?" Steve jumped to his feet. "There have been three homicides. I appreciate the ground work you've done and"—he drew in a long breath—"obviously I should have listened to you sooner. But we'll handle this from now on. I don't want you involved. I don't want any more nights like last night, wondering"—he stopped again, took another breath—"if yours was going to be the next body I fished out of the South Platte. I don't want anything to happen to you, Vicky."

That's when she told him she knew where Todd had hidden the ledger book.

A mixture of frustration and worry gripped Father John as he pointed the Toyota down the gray strip of asphalt receding ahead. The plains crept into the distances and melted into the rinsed-clean blue sky. Overhead, the sun hovered in a yellow-white blaze, clamping the earth in a vise of heat. The wild grasses swayed in the breeze. To the west, he could see the faint outline of the Wind River mountains against the sky. He was almost home.

He had found the message on the table in the entry when he'd gotten back to the residence last night. Father Geoff had been called home to Chicago; his father was dying. It was still dark when Father John pulled out of the parking lot and headed north on I-25 as the sun rose out of the east, flooding the sky with purples, violets, and reds. He'd turned west at Cheyenne, going deeper into Wyoming, the sun blazing behind him, piercing the rearview window and glinting in the mirrors. The soaring notes of *La Traviata* rose around him, and when the opera had ended, he'd fished through the glove compartment and extracted another tape—*Don Giovanni*—and turned north, plunging through the emptiness to the music of Mozart.

He wished he wasn't going home empty-handed. He'd left Father Geoff to deal with everything at the mission while he'd gone off on a wild-goose chase. Eventually his assistant would hear through the Jesuit grapevine how Father John himself had sealed the museum's fate by walking out on the provincial.

Yet he would do it again. He did not regret yesterday. What he regretted was leaving Vicky in Denver, where she was likely to continue searching for the ledger book. He could only hope she would do the most sensible thing and take the Smedden record book and Todd's diskette to Detective Clark first thing this morning. And then she could come home—he hoped she would come home. She would be safe at home; the killer was in Denver.

"Il mio tesoro" filled the cab as Father John slowed into the outskirts of Riverton. He switched his thoughts to what they had accomplished. The diskette. The record book. A book dealer waiting for the ledger book. The kind of evidence certain to get the attention of a homicide detective. What, then, was the unease, the sense of incompleteness that nagged at him? As if there were something he'd missed, some notion of an idea demanding his attention. He drew in a long breath and gave himself up to the music—opera always helped him to sort his thoughts—and went back over the last few days. Vicky's search for the ledger book. The killers' search . . . Suddenly the missing piece snapped into place.

They'd been wrong, he and Vicky. They'd completely missed the point, gone off on tangents. They'd assumed the killers went after Todd and Julie because they knew about the ledger book. Or maybe the killers had been after the backup diskette. But anybody could challenge a thesis on a diskette. That's not what the killers wanted. They wanted the ledger book itself! Father John gasped at the obvious conclusion: Todd was the one who took the ledger book from the museum.

He resisted the idea. Todd would never have done that. Unless . . . unless Todd had felt that the book was in danger, that he had to protect it. And he had protected it with his life.

The last pieces were tumbling together, like confetti floating down and forming a perfectly logical shape. He and Vicky had followed Todd to southeastern Colorado, where they had found the Smedden record book. And they had stopped, even though Todd's footsteps were as clear before them as the first prints on a wave-washed beach.

He thought about pulling into a gas station to call Vicky, but a quick check of his watch told him she would have left Marcy's by now. She had probably already met with Steve Clark. She could be anywhere in Denver. He'd have to wait until evening to call.

He turned onto Highway 789, racing toward the mission where Todd had gone after he'd found the ledger book. He'd been distraught, upset Father John wasn't there. Wasn't there because he'd gone to Boston to straighten out his own life, renew his own vows, set himself back on track. But if he'd been there—dear God, if he'd been there—maybe Todd would be alive. Together they would have gone to Ted Gianelli, the local FBI agent. He trusted Gianelli. He was a friend. Gianelli would have kept the ledger book safe, while whoever was after it, whoever wanted to destroy it, would have been stopped.

But he hadn't been there. Todd had hung around, Father Geoff said. It had surprised him to step out into the corridor and find Todd still there. Still there, Father John thought. Outside the door to the small room that housed the mission archives, where Todd had left the ledger book—on a shelf, tucked in a carton with other old books, unobtrusive, safe.

He was speeding down Seventeen-Mile Road, hoping there were no patrolmen lurking on a side road, waiting for drivers like him. He was always getting pulled over and warned—"Father, you gotta watch it." But there was no other traffic, nothing but the long, empty road ahead and turned into the mission.

He strained against the speed limit all the way to the turn into the mission.

The mission grounds were filled with Sunday-afternoon quiet: a breeze rippled the branches of the cottonwoods and played over the grasses. There was no sign of the new Blazer Father Geoff's father had bought him a couple of months ago. The residence had a vacant look about it. Elena, the housekeeper, had probably stayed home today—with no priests about, there was no reason to prepare the usual Sunday chicken dinner.

He was alone. He could look for the ledger book alone. He stopped the Toyota in front of the administration building, turned off the tape player, and let himself out. The door made a sharp *thwack* into the quiet. Sunshine streamed across the mission; the hot breeze pressed against his shirt. His legs felt cramped and stiff as he hurried up the familiar stairs.

Even as he opened the front door he sensed he was not alone after all. A small creak in the old wooden floor, a faint smell of something—aftershave?—the unmistakable signs of a human presence. Slowly he made his way across the entry to his office door. It was closed. He stood at one side, listening. Nothing. A forced stillness. Whoever was there had heard him drive up, would have confirmed his arrival by looking out the window.

He grabbed the knob and flung open the door. Inside, the killers were waiting for him.

‹ 27 ›

Vicky read the "Departures" signs. The plane to Riverton left in fifteen minutes. She started running, weaving past the other passengers, the roll-on luggage, her own carry-on bumping against the sides of the moving walkways. The signs pulled her to the last gate on the DIA concourse.

She stopped at the desk, handed her ticket and driver's license to the attendant. "You'd better hurry," the woman said, handing back the license with a stamped ticket. She rushed past a second attendant who was starting to close the door and hurried down the gangway, her heart thumping against her ribs, dimly aware of the footsteps clumping behind her.

The meeting with Steve had taken longer than she'd anticipated. He had gone over and over her theory, examining each detail until she'd wanted to scream: "I've got a plane to catch." Finally she had grabbed her handbag, announced she would call the moment she found the ledger book, and fled from his office.

"If it's there," he'd called after her, and she'd realized he was still unconvinced; still believed her theory was concocted out of thin air, out of a wish that the Sand Creek ledger book existed and that Todd Harris had not been involved with drugs.

She'd driven as fast as she dared to DIA, one eye on the rearview mirror, dreading the sound of a siren, feeling as if everything was moving in slow motion: the long drive, the line at the rental-car checkout, the shuttle to the airport. Slow motion, even as she'd run through the airport.

The plane was almost empty—a few businessmen in suits near the front, laptops on extended trays. Other passengers sat scattered about the small plane. She found her seat near the center. No one claimed the seats around her.

As she stuffed her carry-on into the overhead, she sensed a presence behind her, pressing toward her. She gave the carry-on another push and ducked toward the window, realizing someone was following her into the seat. As she sat down she stared in surprise at Emil Coughlin. A casual, relaxed look about him, in khaki slacks, a blue polo shirt opened at the collar. He might have been going on a cruise.

"I hope you don't mind a seatmate for the short trip to Riverton, my dear," he said, settling beside her.

Vicky felt herself stiffen. "What are you doing here?" Even as she asked the question she realized with a sickening sense that she knew the answer.

"Joining you for a lovely flight to Riverton on this beautiful Sunday," he said. "I was on the phone in the concourse when you whizzed by, and I was delighted to discover we were to take the same plane. There are so few passengers." A nod around them. "I decided to join you. We can use this opportunity for a little chat. Save some time later, perhaps."

Vicky kept her eyes on him. "I don't know what you're talking about."

The professor held up a thin, suntanned hand, his attention on the flight attendant going through the safety drill. They were pulling back from the gate, a slow, rocking movement. And then the drill was over and they were rolling across the pavement, taxiing down the runway, lifting off.

He turned toward her. "I have you to thank, my dear. When you said you were going to follow Todd's footsteps, I realized I had been wasting my time. I could follow his footsteps to the ledger book. I told myself, I'll simply go where he went after he took the book from me."

Vicky gasped. "From you!"

The professor seemed to study her a moment. "Ah, I see I've told you something you didn't know. Yes, of course he took the ledger book from me. Came right into my office like a common thief and removed it from my briefcase." He gave a little laugh. "Well, I suppose I must give him credit for figuring out I was the one who removed it from the museum."

Vicky realized her first instinct had been right. She said, "Todd told you immediately that he'd found the ledger book."

"Oh, my, you've misjudged the poor boy." The professor drew in a long breath, as if he were about to enlighten a particularly dim student, then went on: "Todd didn't tell me at all. Todd and I had a bit of a misunderstanding some time ago. In fact, I believe he was most unhappy to have me as his adviser, but he was so far along on his thesis, he was reluctant to start with someone new. At any rate, he seemed of the opinion that several Indian artifacts I had come across in the most out-of-the-way places—forgotten towns across the West where no one else goes—well, he seemed to think they belonged in museums, that I didn't have the right to dispose of them as I saw fit. But museums have so much, they can't possibly display everything they own. You have seen the storage basement at the museum, have you not?"

Vicky said nothing, and he hurried on: "A vast storehouse of treasures that can never be fully exhibited. Who can blame private collectors for wanting to enjoy something beautiful within the confines of their own homes? Collectors are willing to pay a great deal of money for such privileges and"—he gave a little shrug— "I married a woman with very expensive tastes. Hardly the tastes I could afford on a professor's salary. I'm sure you understand."

He glanced across the aisle at the empty seats. "Unfortunately Todd did *not* understand. I'm sure that's why he neglected to tell me about the ledger book, but I found out anyway when Rachel Foster called to inquire as to the value of a ledger book on Sand Creek that had been found by a graduate student. I told her, of course. One-point-three million dollars, uncut. Probably more if sold page by page. I knew immediately that Todd had stumbled across the definitive evidence about Sand Creek he'd been looking for."

Vicky could feel the anger and disgust colliding inside her: Rachel Foster had known about the ledger book all along.

"What a blow when the book turned up missing!" Emil Coughlin gave a little laugh. "After all, Rachel Foster has a reputation as the most organized curator in the nation." Another laugh. "She would be the first to tell you. How could she admit the museum had owned such a treasure and had managed to lose track of it? And then, adding insult to injury, had allowed the book to disappear?"

The professor shifted in his seat, turning toward her. "I'm sure she suspected I took it, but how could she ever prove it? She's smart enough to realize that inevitably suspicion would fall upon her and her protégé, Bernard Good Elk. Oh, how she adores that blustering fathead. Considers him the definitive authority on Native American ethnohistory. And there they were, she and Good Elk, with an exhibit on Sand Creek that denies Arapahos had been there, and a ledger book that proves otherwise. Between you and me"—he dropped his voice to a conspiratorial tone—"she was probably most relieved to have the book disappear. She would not want to see her protégé's career in ruins."

Emil Coughlin threw his head back and emitted a series of snorts, a parody of laughter. Then, glancing at the attendant in the aisle, he cleared his throat and ordered a Scotch on the rocks. The attendant set a small bottle and a glass of ice on his tray. Turning toward Vicky, he said, "And you, my dear?"

Vicky shook her head. She watched him unscrew the bottle cap, splash the clear liquid over the little cubes in the glass, and take a long draft. After the attendant had moved down the aisle, Vicky said, "So you went into the stacks, found the Smedden carton, and removed the ledger book. Then you took the records from the filing cabinet."

Emil Coughlin drew his lips into a thin line. His eyes took on a vacant look, as if he were seeing himself in the museum library, approaching the bank of files. "How foolish of the museum not to have transcribed the old records into the data system. It was Rachel's every intention to do so, of course, but like so many executives of public institutions, she must work with limited funds. Those pitiful scraps of paper with notations scribbled all over them comprised the only record of the Sand Creek ledger book."

Another sip of the Scotch, a long, satisfied sigh, and Emil Coughlin went on: "It was so easy. I had free access to every part of the museum, of course. The staff was used to me poking around after the weeks I had spent verifying the Plains Indian artifacts. A fine job I did." He held up the glass of Scotch, a toast to himself. "You owe me a debt, my dear."

Anger curled inside Vicky, like a rattlesnake ready to strike. "How many other Arapaho artifacts did you help yourself to?" she asked.

"Another misjudgment on your part." The professor gave her a long, appraising look. "I would hardly remove any item stored in full view of every staff member. Besides, most of the artifacts had been collected recently enough that records are on computer. Much more difficult to deal with, although . . ." He set the glass on the tray and rubbed his chin a moment. "The idea of destroying computer records intrigues me, my dear. It is worthy of consideration."

He lifted the glass. "May I propose a toast to the end of a painful journey for both of us? I was rather fond of Todd Harris, you know."

"You killed him."

Emil Coughlin took a long sip. "Well, not technically. I'm afraid I must leave that sort of thing to my associates. Unfortunately they sometimes get carried away with their work. If only Todd hadn't been so stubborn. If he had been willing to cooperate and return the ledger book to me, I would have made it worth his while. I am a reasonable man. It was all so unnecessary."

He leaned back and gave the glass a little shake. The ice made a tinkling noise. "At least my associates understood the necessity of planting heroin on the boy's body. Even shot heroin into his arm, I believe. The girl, also. I must say, it had the desired effect of sending the police chasing their tails in the wrong direction. The other girl . . ." He gave a little shrug. "Well, we didn't bother with the drugs. What difference would it make? I had started thinking about what you said, and it came to me in a flash, one of my most brilliant breakthroughs. I knew exactly where Todd had hidden the book."

He drained the glass and waited as the attendant cleared his tray. When she was gone, he said, "And now we will go to St. Francis Mission, where Todd left the ledger book."

"Why would he take it there?" Vicky asked, struggling for a reasonable tone. She might convince him otherwise.

"The most logical place, my dear. His roommate admitted readily—well, after a bit of persuasion—that he went to the reservation last weekend. Now, why would he do that? To seek advice from that mentor of his, Father O'Malley, of course. Todd spoke of him often, how much he admired and respected him, trusted his advice. Imagine the poor boy's ideal—a washed-up history teacher." The professor gave his head a quick shake, mock sadness in the gesture.

Vicky turned toward the window. Riverton lay in the distance, streaked in sun and shadow. Surrounding the town were the open, rolling plains of the reservation.

"I can scream," she said, bringing her eyes back to the man beside her. "I can tell the attendant you are a murderer and a thief, and you have threatened me. The Riverton police will meet the plane when we land."

"Oh, my dear!" Emil Coughlin let out a guffaw, as if he'd just heard an exceedingly funny joke. "A highly respected professor such as myself? Without a weapon of any kind?" He glanced down—the polo shirt, the khakis. "How could I have gotten on the plane with a weapon? What threat could I possibly be to you? I'm afraid you would appear quite hysterical."

He stopped, his eyes traveling over her now. "On the other hand, the police might take your story seriously. In which case, I would have to invent a more likely story. Let me see. I would simply explain we'd had a lovers' quarrel. Yes, that's it! We are lovers. I like that story very much."

Vicky pulled back, feeling the hard roll of the window ledge in her ribs. A crackling noise burst over the intercom, followed by the pilot's voice announcing that they were about to land. She sensed the plane angling downward.

The professor was still talking: something about how he would not have to invent a story after all, how he'd been on the phone with his associates when he'd seen her at DIA, how Father O'Malley had just driven into the mission.

"What are you saying?" Vicky heard the note of panic in her tone.

Emil stared at her, surprise in his eyes. "Why, didn't I tell you? My associates arrived at St. Francis Mission this afternoon. How fortuitous that Father O'Malley happened to drive up, just when they were running out of ideas of where to look for the ledger book. I'm sure they made quite a greeting party for your friend. If for some reason I were not to arrive at the mission thirty minutes after this plane lands, I gave them specific instructions. Need I say that unlike me, my associates are armed. If you want to see your friend alive, I suggest you do exactly as I instruct you."

Vicky stared out the window again: the treetops reaching upward, the shadow of the plane elongating below. And then they were down, bumping and speeding on the landing strip. She could call his bluff, she was thinking. She could start screaming. And then would begin the long wait for a police car to creep toward the waiting plane, the explanations, the stories. And the minutes would tick by—ten, twenty, thirty. And then what? Three people were already dead.

The scream hardened into a lump in her throat. She couldn't take a chance with John O'Malley's life. She couldn't bear the thought that anything might happen to him.

The plane had stopped moving. The door ahead was open, and hot air flowed along the aisle. There was the sound of seat belts clicking loose, of overheads snapping open. The businessmen in front were already moving toward the door. In a series of slow, deliberate motions, Emil Coughlin lifted himself out of the seat, pulled down her carry-on, and stepped back, motioning her into the aisle.

As Vicky slipped out he took her arm and leaned

close, so close she could smell the Scotch-sour breath. "You will walk with me through the airport," he whispered. "We will take your car. You did leave your car in the lot, I hope. It will save us precious time."

Vicky shrugged away from his grip and started along the aisle. She hurried down the steps, aware of the heavy clump of footsteps on metal behind her. The sun flooded the tarmac with a hot, white light. *Now*, she told herself. Run across the tarmac, through the building and out to the front lot where she'd left the Bronco. She could probably outrun him. But to what end? He would simply stop at the first telephone, and John O'Malley would be dead before she reached the mission.

She kept the same pace—one foot in front of the other through the sunshine, into the coolness of the building, and back into the sunshine, the footsteps behind her all the way to the Bronco. Her hand trembled as she found the key in her bag, jammed it into the lock on the driver's side, and pulled open the door. Emil Coughlin was on the other side. The instant she hit the unlock button, he had the door open and was lifting her carry-on into the back. Then he slid in beside her. "Very good," he said. "You deserve an A-plus."

Vicky turned the ignition and waited, muscles tense, as the engine spurted and belched into life. Then she slid the gear into reverse and backed out. In forward now, she careened through the lot, tires squealing into the heat, as she turned into Airport Road and then on to Main Street.

◆ 28 ◆

"You will slow down," Emil Coughlin ordered. Then, in a reasonable tone: "It would never do, my dear, for the police to pull us over. A waste of precious time, wouldn't you agree?"

Vicky let up on the accelerator. *Keep calm*, she told herself. She had at least twenty minutes. Twenty minutes to navigate the empty, Sunday-afternoon streets of Riverton. Twenty minutes in which John O'Malley was still alive, and so was she. Twenty minutes to negotiate with a madman. But she had no illusions as to what would happen once she and Emil Coughlin reached the mission. Three people already dead . . .

She said, "Why would an intelligent man such as yourself believe he could get away with this? You must realize I've already met with Detective Clark. He knows everything. Even if you kill us—"

"Kill you!" The professor let out another loud guffaw. "Oh, my dear, how you disappoint me. I have no intention of killing either you or your priest friend. It is my sincere hope we can reach an understanding. There's already been too much violence. If the others had only been as rational, as logical, as you and Father O'Malley, it might have been avoided. I do hope we won't have any repetition."

The professor was quiet a moment. Marshaling his argument, Vicky thought. She waited. The flat-roofed buildings of Riverton's main streets passed outside her window—garage, motels, supermarkets. A few other cars moved slowly ahead, stopping at lights, turning into side streets. Normal. Normal.

The professor's voice again: "My associates and I are not unreasonable. Surely we can all come to some kind of equitable understanding. No doubt an Indian mission could use some extra cash, as I'm sure you could, my dear. After all, I'm well aware of how much trouble you've gone to, how concerned you are about the ledger book. Let me assure you, the book will not be destroyed. My associates and I have located a wealthy collector interested in the entire book. He is willing to pay a premium for that privilege, but we will all feel better, won't we, knowing the book will not be destroyed? We'll be meeting with him in Tokyo the day after tomorrow. Of course, that means we must have the book. You do understand, don't you?"

"Look, Emil," Vicky began. *Calm, calm*, she told herself. "Neither Father John nor I knows where Todd put the ledger book." True, she was thinking. At least, she didn't know the exact location. She was only sure Todd had left it somewhere at the mission. "The reservation is a large place," she went on. "It could be anywhere. Hidden in a cave, an old building . . ."

He reached over and touched her arm. His palm was wet with perspiration. "Please save your breath. I believe you and the priest know exactly where the poor boy would have hidden a precious treasure. If you don't tell us . . ." He took his hand away. Out of the corner of her eye, she saw him patting back a strand of hair, a tentative gesture, as if he were trying to sort through several possibilities, all distasteful. "I'm afraid my associates will have to take St. Francis Mission apart, board by board. Believe me, they are capable of doing so. As for you and your priest friend, well . . ." He raised both hands toward the windshield. "Let us hope such unpleasantness will not come to pass."

Vicky turned right onto Seventeen-Mile Road. An oncoming pickup loped by. A couple of kids were playing stickball on the bare dirt yard in front of a small house. Another turn, and she was in the mission compound. Her heart raced as she came around the bend of Circle Drive. The red Toyota pickup was parked in front of the administration building.

She wheeled in next to it, switched off the ignition, and turned to the man in the passenger seat. "The police are on the way," she said, struggling to hide the desperation of the lie. She was clutching for a lifeline, like a rock climber dangling over the precipice.

Her statement seemed to give him a moment of thought. He frowned, pulled his lips into a tight line. Then: "A nice try, my dear. But how could that be true? Why would the police be on their way here?"

"I called them." Her voice was steady.

"You called them? When you were running through the airport to catch a plane? When you hadn't even seen me?" He gave her a disparaging smile. "Get out," he ordered.

Vicky lifted herself outside, her legs numb beneath her. He was already around the Bronco, gripping her arm, propelling her up the cement stairs and through the wide front door—the familiar door—and into the entry with slats of sunshine crisscrossing the wood floor. There was a quiet vacancy about the building.

Still pulling her along, Emil Coughlin moved toward the closed door with the sign in the middle: FATHER O'MALLEY. He gave a sharp, quick rap. The door flung open, and in the center stood a man Vicky had seen before—about six feet tall with sandy, shoulder-length hair swept back behind his ears and red-veined eyes behind the thick glasses from too many hours—too much of a lifetime—spent peering at the tiny print on the pages of ancient, mouse-gnawed books. He was holding a small black pistol.

The book dealer Richard Loomis gave a little bow and stepped back, boots crinkling the papers strewn over the floor. Behind him, Vicky glimpsed the books toppled on shelves, piles of folders and papers strewn over the desk, drawers falling out of filing cabinets. She gripped the edge of the doorjamb. *They've already killed him.* Then she heard John O'Malley shouting: "Are you okay, Vicky? Did he hurt you?"

She pulled free of Emil's grasp and darted into the office. Father John was about to get out of the barrel-shaped chair he kept for visitors. Standing over him was another man she'd met—the Lakota student at CU-Denver, the same student who had come to Richard Loomis's bookstore.

"Get back in your chair." The Lakota gave Father John a little shove.

Emil was at Vicky's elbow. "You know my esteemed friend Richard Loomis," he said, pointing toward the man with the gun. "A highly knowledgeable dealer. I depend upon him to fetch the highest prices for my best finds. Of course he understood the ledger book was a once-in-a-lifetime opportunity that would free him from the prison of that dreary bookstore. You can thank him, my dear. Richard made contact with the Japanese collector who has promised to preserve the book. The Japanese have such respect for tradition."

"Shut up, Emil." The book dealer waved the pistol.

"Now, now." The professor shook his head. "There is no need for incivility. In any case, I hardly believe you are the one to caution me. Not when you allowed yourself to be taken in by these two." He waved toward Father John and Vicky. "A mission priest and his attorney shopping for an Arapaho ledger book, and you believed their story! Give me your best bid, you told them, or something to that effect, making it perfectly clear the ledger book was available. Until then, they had no proof it even existed."

The professor exhaled a long breath, as if he had just flunked a student he had once hoped would graduate with honors. "We must put all that behind us," he said. Then, a glance at the Lakota. "Have you met my student Skip Bearing? A very cooperative and farseeing young man, unlike, I'm sorry to say, Todd Harris."

The Lakota waved the pistol between Vicky and another barrel chair across the office. "Over there."

"Please, Skip," Emil Coughlin was saying as she walked over and took the chair. "This entire matter can be settled amicably."

"Skip and I will handle this," Richard Loomis said. "So far your brilliant ideas have resulted in nada, zip. The kid didn't have the book. And the girls turned out to be a lot of useless trouble. We've got a meeting in Tokyo day after tomorrow. I'm out of time and patience."

Emil held out one hand, as if to object, but Richard Loomis had already walked over to Father John. "You, Father, are going to tell us where the book is. No more games. No more of your Irish stories about going off to Boston and not knowing anything about a ledger book. All stories, and now we're going to have the truth."

"May I interject?" Emil Coughlin stepped into the middle of the room. "Vicky claims she has notified the police. I doubt her story, but we may not have much time."

"Relax," Richard Loomis said. "This will not take long. Father O'Malley is about to give us a million-dollar ledger book. His other choice is to watch Skip"—a nod toward the Lakota—"destroy the face of this beautiful woman."

Vicky started off the chair, every muscle in her body coiled for flight, but the Lakota was advancing toward her, a sickening pleasure in his eyes. Even when the fist crashed against her face, she hadn't expected it, hadn't seen it coming. The blow sent her reeling back along the sharp knobs of the chair, spiraling down toward a blackness eclipsing everything except the pain that seared her jaw and coursed through her body.

She grabbed the edge of the chair, fighting to stay conscious, dimly aware of John O'Malley shouting, "No! No!", of the Lakota staggering backward, whirling about as the room erupted in shouts and bellows. Fists thudded into flesh, and bodies crashed into the desk, against the bookcase, and back into the center of the office, rolling across the debris-strewn floor and staggering upward again.

She blinked, trying to focus beyond the pain, and realized that John O'Malley was ramming her assailant against the wall while Emil Coughlin—stumbling and screaming—was grabbing at his shirt, trying to pull him away. Out of the corner of her eye, she saw Richard Loomis edging along the desk, pistol outstretched in both hands, taking careful aim. She swung around, grabbed the phone off the desk, and threw herself against the man, smashing the phone into the side of his head.

The pistol clattered to the floor as he staggered sideways, groaning and holding his head. Vicky dropped to her knees, scrambling for the small black pistol lost in the piles of paper. A sharp crashing noise of doors slamming and boots stomping reverberated through the floorboards beneath her hands. More of them coming, she thought, groping frantically for the pistol, feeling her fingers curl around the cold metal.

She struggled to get upright amid the black boots and dark pant legs swimming around her, the chorus of shouting voices. "Police." Not until she was almost on her feet did she realize that Ted Gianelli, the local FBI agent, was pulling her upright, slipping the pistol out of her hand, telling her that everything was okay, everything was under control.

John O'Malley pushed through the crowd of uniforms, and instinctively she moved toward him, feeling his arms encircle her, his heart pounding. He held her a moment, then stepped back and lifted her face. His fingers ran across her cheek. "You're going to have a beautiful shiner," he said.

There was a cut along his cheekbone, a knot bulging on his forehead. The front of his shirt was ripped, and when she took his hands in hers, she saw that the knuckles were raw and bleeding. "You don't look so hot yourself," she said.

Glancing past him, she saw Richard Loomis and Emil Coughlin facedown on the floor, arms stretched behind. Officers were leaning over them, snapping handcuffs around their wrists. Gianelli had stepped across the room, where Skip slouched against the wall, eyes closed. "This one's gonna need an ambulance," the agent called.

Then he was back beside them. "Jesus Christ, John. Where'd you learn to fight?" He held up one hand. "Don't tell me. You were an Irish kid in Boston." He shook his head. "I feel sorry for the other kids."

"How did you happen to get here in time for all the fun?" Father John asked. He kept one arm around her, and Vicky found herself leaning against him, steadying herself.

The agent kept his eyes on the police officers helping the handcuffed men to their feet, pushing them toward the door. "Thank a homicide detective in Denver by the name of Steve Clark. He called with some story about a ledger book worth a million dollars being stolen from a Denver museum and brought up here to the mission. Said we better check it out, that Vicky was taking the noon flight to Riverton and would probably go right to the mission. He was afraid she could run into trouble.

So I called the police on the reservation. We decided it might be a good idea to stop by here. I'm only sorry we didn't get here sooner. You had quite a free-for-all going when we arrived."

Suddenly there was a commotion: Emil Coughlin twisting his shoulders and pulling away from the hands guiding him toward the door. "I demand to speak to the FBI," he shouted.

Gianelli crossed the room.

"You are making a terrible mistake. I am a nationally known ethnohistorian. I had no idea the ledger book may have been stolen. I came here for a legitimate transaction. These common criminals have duped me."

The agent glanced back at Vicky.

"I'll file charges," she said. "Kidnapping and assault. I can testify as to everything he told me about his involvement in the murder of Todd Harris and two others in Denver."

Turning toward the policemen waiting with the handcuffed professor, Gianelli said, "Get him out of here."

Vicky was curled into the roomy leather chair behind John O'Malley's desk, holding a pack of ice on her cheek. She could feel the lump hardening below her cheekbone, the skin tightening and blackening under her eye. They looked like the walking wounded—she and John O'Malley. They weren't cut out for street fighting. After the ambulance had arrived, the medics had given her the ice pack, then cleaned the cuts on his face and placed a plastic strip over one cheek and another across his forehead. He looked as if he'd walked into a wall, but she knew she didn't look much better.

Slowly the office had emptied out. The medics had carried the Lakota out on a stretcher, although he had come to and was demanding the right to press charges against the priest who had assaulted him. The policemen had gone. Only Gianelli had stayed behind to take their statements.

Vicky had told her story first, explaining about the ledger book, how she'd realized Todd Harris had brought it to the mission, how Emil Coughlin had reached the same conclusion, how he had threatened her on the plane.

"Threatened you?" Gianelli had interrupted.

Vicky stared at him a long moment. Why had she said that? John O'Malley was the one threatened. His life was in danger. Yet on the plane, hemmed in by the professor, crowding her, spitting out the Scotch-laden "instructions" as to what she must do if she wanted her priest friend to stay alive, she had felt her own life threatened. If they killed John O'Malley, she knew that even if she were to escape, a part of her would have died.

She told Gianelli about the instructions Emil had given the others, and as she'd talked she'd felt John O'Malley's eyes on her. *Now he knows*, she'd realized. He knows she had put her own life in danger for him, just as he had jumped her assailant even though his partner held a gun.

Then Father John told how Loomis and Skip were waiting for him when he drove into the mission. Loomis had kept a gun on him while the Lakota had systematically pulled books off the shelves, emptied out desk drawers, tossed folders out of drawers, and generally turned his office into an even bigger mess than was normal. The Lakota had taken a tour through the building and reported that there was one other office and a couple of storerooms and closets on the main floor. Nothing but empty rooms and another storeroom on the second floor.

All the while Father John had kept talking to Richard Loomis, explaining how he'd been in Boston, how he had no way of knowing where Todd Harris might have left the book, how most likely Todd didn't even have the book with him when he came to the reservation, how he'd probably done the most logical thing: placed it in a bank vault in Denver.

But it hadn't worked, Father John said. Richard Loomis had raised the gun and told him to save his breath. Then Emil Coughlin had arrived with Vicky, and everything had switched into fast time. He remembered the Lakota raising his fist and striking Vicky, but after that—a blur. At some point he realized he was pounding the man with his fists, shoving him against the desk, the wall, but the man kept fighting back, landing some blows of his own, including some jabs to the ribs, which he hadn't felt at the moment, but which he was feeling now.

"You're lucky Loomis didn't shoot you," Gianelli said. "If he could've gotten a bead on you without killing one of his buddies, he would have." He glanced around the office; the floor was covered with scraps of paper, as if a large trash basket had been upended. "All this, and the ledger book's not even here."

"It's here," Father John said.

Vicky lifted herself out of the chair and followed the priest and the agent into the corridor. A door opened on the right, and they started down a narrow hallway, past a series of closed doors—the closets and storerooms the Lakota had discovered. She had never been in this section of the administration building. There was so much she didn't know about the man leading the way, so many spaces he occupied about which she had no idea.

He stopped at the far door, pushed it open, and led her and Gianelli inside. "The mission archives," he announced. The room was small, little more than a closet, with a column of sunlight filtering through a narrow window across the table. Cardboard boxes and the spines of old books protruded from the shelves on the walls; a storeroom, the Lakota had called it.

"Todd spent a lot of time working here," Father John explained. "He found several references in the old records to places where the Arapahos had lived in Colorado. He would have left the ledger book with the other records."

Vicky glanced about the small room. She felt both elated and weary. Dozens of cartons, several hundred books. They would have to go through every one.

Father John moved to the shelves on one side. He reached up and brought down a small carton, which he set on the table. Slowly he began pulling out the contents, arranging them next to the carton. "A guess," he said. "Over the years the priests at St. Francis encouraged the elders to write down their stories. Some of them did so. Others were willing to tell their stories, and the priest wrote them down. They're all here. Seems logical Todd would have put No-Ta-Nee's story with the others."

Vicky leaned toward the items spread over the table. An assortment of pads, notebooks, and papers stapled or clipped together. The carton appeared empty. There was no ledger book.

Except that now Father John was bringing out what looked like a tan leather envelope, and she realized it had been placed where Todd had found it in the carton at the museum. On the bottom—quiet and unobtrusive, like the carton itself.

Vicky cleared a space, and Father John set down the package, tied in leather thongs, like the parfleches used to carry small items in the Old Time. Carefully she undid the thongs, pulled back one flap, then another. Inside was a ledger book that looked like a thousand other ledger books manufactured for nineteenth-century merchants and accountants and government

agents: the gray-green color and the black curlicue design on the front cover.

The room was quiet. Gianelli shifted next to her, and
for a moment she thought he might reach out and flip
open the cover. She saw the look Father John gave him,
the nod he gave to her.

She picked up the ledger book and held it toward the
four directions—east, south, west, north. "*Ho'Hou.*'"
She murmured the word four times, thanking the ledger
book for preserving the story, the story for allowing itself to be told, No-Ta-Nee for telling it, Todd for pro-
tecting it. Then she set the book down and slowly
opened the cover. The figures danced across the page,
moving right to left, in muted shades of red, blue, and
yellow. Warriors on horseback, dogs pulling travois
piled with household goods, women and children trail-
ing behind: moving to a new village. Above the head of
one warrior was the glyph of a red bull: No-Ta-Nee.
The details in the pictographs told the story: name
glyphs above the warriors; the colors of the horses; the
types of wagons; the soldiers' uniforms; and the
weapons carried by soldiers and warriors.

She read each page out loud: Chief Niwot leading
the people to Sand Creek. She knew it was the chief by
the figure of a left hand above his head: Niwot meant
Left Hand. The women setting up the village in the
midst of the Cheyenne village, the soldiers appearing on
the bluff, carrying the weapons used at Sand Creek; the
attack at dawn. On she read, her voice quiet and calm,
until she reached the last page. There were six figures:
four children, a woman, with the glyph of a snake
above her head: Mahom, Snake Woman, and No-Ta-
Nee. "The Arapaho survivors of Sand Creek," she said.

She closed the book, but kept her hand on the rough
cloth cover, allowing the power of the story to gather inside her. The sunshine slanting across the table felt
warm on her hand.

Gianelli's voice broke the quiet. "The book belongs to the Denver Museum of the West. And three people were murdered over it. It will be used as evidence. I'm going to have to keep it."

Slowly Vicky slipped the book back inside the leather package and tied the thongs into a gentle, secure knot. Then she picked up the package and handed it to the agent. "Not for long," she said.

❮ 29 ❯

Vicky turned onto Circle Drive, following a flatbed truck with planks of wood hanging out the back. She stopped in front of the administration building, but the truck rumbled on down the drive, its engine growling into the quiet of St. Francis Mission. Slipping out into the sunshine that burst across the graveled parking area, she gave the door a hard slam and studied the facade of the building in front of her. It had the vacant look of three weeks ago, when Emil Coughlin had climbed out of the passenger seat and hurried her up the stone steps.

Now she climbed the stairs alone, her heart sinking. What if Father John had left again? She hadn't heard anything on the moccasin telegraph about his going away, but she hadn't heard he was going to Boston either. Only that one day he was gone. She hadn't talked to him since the day he'd almost gotten himself killed trying to protect her—the day they had found the Sand Creek ledger book. She could still feel the reluctance with which she had handed the book over to the FBI agent, Ted Gianelli, despite the way Father John had slipped an arm around her and said, "You can trust him, Vicky. He won't let anything happen to it."

He had called the next day to see how she was feeling. She was feeling lousy, she told him, with an egg-sized lump on her face and an eye ringed in black. She looked like a one-eyed raccoon. And how was he feeling? Just great, he assured her. But it was a little tough cleaning up the office with a cracked rib.

"A cracked rib?" she had said.

"The Lakota had a punch that came in like a fastball."

She had offered to come over and help him clean up the office, but he assured her Elena and the grandmothers had already run him out of the place, and by this evening he was sure the office would be in better shape—

"Than you are?" she had said.

He laughed and told her he was having a hard time explaining the cuts and bruises to the kids on the Eagles baseball team. It was really *not* the way to settle disputes, but sometimes, well, sometimes, you had to stand up for the people you—he had stopped, drawn in a breath, and said—the people you care about.

He hadn't called her since, which meant he hadn't needed her help. No kids in trouble. No couple bound for divorce court. Nobody in jail. Which was good news, she realized, and just as well. She'd been so busy the last three weeks, negotiating with the museum for the Arapaho artifacts, tying up the loose ends, arranging for the elders to go to Denver to claim the sacred and cultural items. So busy she hadn't called him; she'd had no reason to call. It was an unspoken rule between them—they never called each other without a legitimate reason.

Inside, the building was as quiet as the last time she was here. The door to Father John's office was closed. She rapped twice, waited, and rapped again. Then she pushed the door open. The office looked as if it had undergone a spring cleaning, books neatly stacked in the bookcases, a daisy blooming in a pot on the filing cabinet, and piles of papers arranged on the desk, instead of tumbling across it. Unlike his desk.

Just as she closed the door she heard the soft noise of a chair scuttling across the floor. She made her way down the corridor, past the closed door that led to the archives, and stopped at an opened door. A man with close-cropped sandy hair and light, plastic-rimmed glasses sat at a small table across from a desk, tapping on a typewriter. "Father Geoff?" she said.

He swung around, a startled look in his eyes. "You must be Vicky Holden."

She gave him a smile, but it was not reciprocated.

"He's not here, if you're looking for Father O'Malley." The priest turned back toward the typewriter.

"When will he be back?" Vicky persisted.

The priest leaned back in his chair, his profile to her. "I suppose you won't be satisfied, will you, until you have won him completely over to your side."

Vicky was quiet a moment, trying to comprehend what the man was saying. Then: "I'm afraid you misunderstand."

Father Geoff swiveled toward her. "Do you have any idea how difficult it is when you keep coming around? How hard it was for him after your little trip to Denver?"

Vicky could hear the sound of her own breathing, could feel her heart speeding. "I know what you think," she said, "and you are wrong. You have misjudged Father O'Malley and me."

"Have I?" His eyes were as gray and impenetrable as the surface of a lake.

She turned on her heels and retraced her steps down the corridor, past Father John's office, through the heavy front door, slamming it hard behind her. She was flushed with anger. What right did this priest have to assume anything about her, about her life, about her most private feelings—feelings she did not even want to admit to herself? She flung open the door to the Bronco and slid onto the seat.

Another truck wheeled past as she was about to back onto Circle Drive. She watched it pull in behind several other trucks parked at the far end of the mission in front of the old school. Pushing the gear into drive, she started after it.

Two men were already unloading large sheets of wallboard when she parked beside them. A hot gust of wind caught her skirt as she got out. "Is Father O'Malley here?" she called.

"Inside." One of the men jerked his head backward.

She hurried up the steps. The minute she walked through the door, she spotted Father John partway down the shadowy hallway, talking to three workmen. As if he'd sensed her presence, he turned around and walked toward her. Even in the dim light, she could make out the reddish line on his cheek, the mark on his forehead.

"Welcome to the Arapaho Museum," he said. Then, glancing back at the workmen, he explained, "We have our first visitor."

Vicky still felt shaky with anger. She wished she could have stepped into his arms, felt the comfort of his touch. She started circling the entry, forcing herself to focus on the way the light cascaded down the new staircase, the taped drywall on one side of the hall, the smells of plaster and fresh-sawed wood. "So, it's really happening," she said after a moment, when she felt more in control. "I didn't think it would happen so soon."

"So soon?" Father John said. He moved closer. "What are you saying?"

She let out a long breath. "The provincial—Father Rutherford, I believe his name is—said he'd been considering the museum after meeting with you." She made another circle. "He probably would have approved it even if I hadn't called."

"You called the provincial?" There was a mixture of amusement and incredulity in Father John's voice.

"That's what I came to tell you," Vicky said. "The provincial and I had a long talk last week. I told him I'm the attorney in charge of reclaiming a great many Arapaho artifacts and that we had no place to store and exhibit them. I told him how desperately we needed this museum."

Father John started laughing. "He's too busy to take my calls, but you call him up and have a long chat." He folded his arms and leaned back against the wall, shaking his head. "The provincial's assistant called last week and gave me the go-ahead on the museum. I thought I'd witnessed another miracle."

"Yes," Vicky said, making another little circle, "we lawyers often work miracles." She stopped, catching his eye. "What do you mean, another?"

"I got a call from Doyal last night. The University Press in Colorado is going to publish Todd's thesis."

Vicky closed her eyes a moment, allowing the sun cascading across the entry to warm her. "How wonderful," she said. "A permanent record of all the places in Colorado where the people had once lived. Some of the lands may belong to us again someday, if I have anything to say about it." She gave him a long smile. "The tribe has hired me to negotiate with the bureaucrats in Washington over claims to the lands promised the Sand Creek tribes."

Father John was nodding, smiling at her. "That's good news. The bureaucrats don't have a chance."

"I wouldn't be so sure," Vicky said. "They've stalled for more than a hundred years. They'll probably stall a few more, but eventually—"

"Eventually, you might see justice."

"It would be nice." She glanced around. "I wish Todd could be here to see it. I wish he could see this."

She waved toward the corridor with the new wallboard—the museum taking shape.

Father John was quiet a moment. "It's going to be hard to find the kind of director he would have been."

Vicky made another little circle. "I have a suggestion," she said. "There's a young Arapaho woman, Lindy Meadows, who works in a museum in Florida. Maybe—just maybe—she's ready to come home. You could call her—"

Father John held up one hand. "But you could get through."

"Fair enough." Vicky laughed. "In the next month or so boxes of artifacts will be arriving here. We'll be getting most of the items listed in the inventory."

"Most?"

"Not every item falls under the rules of NAGPRA. But all of the sacred objects will be returned."

"The ledger book?" Father John said.

"The ledger book." Vicky held his eyes a moment. "After Emil and his associates stand trial for murder, kidnapping, theft, and a lot of other charges, the ledger book will finally come home. It belongs to Charlie Redman and No-Ta-Nee's other descendants. They've agreed to place it here in the old school with the rest of the artifacts."

"We'll display it right here," Father John said, sweeping one arm toward the shaft of sunlight in the center of the entry. "In a large Plexiglas display case. It will be the first thing people see when they visit the museum. They will read it. Scholars will study it. Everyone will know the true story of Sand Creek."

Vicky kept her eyes on the entry. In the column of sunshine, she could imagine the display case with No-Ta-Nee's ledger book propped inside, opened and inviting. "It will be beautiful," she said.